THE SENSE OF RECKONING

AN ANN KINNEAR SUSPENSE NOVEL

MATTY DALRYMPLE

WILLIAM KINGSFIELD PUBLISHERS

In memory of my mother, Mary Ellen Dalrymple, who introduced me to Nero and Archie.

"O God of battles! steel my soldiers' hearts;
Possess them not with fear; take from them now
The sense of reckoning, if the opposed numbers
Pluck their hearts from them."

Henry V
William Shakespeare

1

1947

The seven blasts of the fire horn that signaled the evacuation of Bar Harbor rang in Chip Lynam's ears. He turned from the Express Office where he had been headed toward Great Hill, which was framed by the buildings along Cottage Street, and gasped.

Flames licked at the trees at the top of Great Hill, jerking and cracking in the wind that suddenly careened into town. For a moment the sky above the flames was clear, and then black smoke billowed over the crest of the hill. The wind-whipped October leaves were now mixed with black ash, spinning up into funnels where the air rushed around the buildings.

As Chip gaped at the sight, the town, which just moments before had been muffled by a tense quiet, sprang to frantic life. A woman who had stopped on the sidewalk to tie her little boy's shoe snatched up his hand and dragged him in the direction of the athletic field, the town's evacuation rally point, the boy stumbling and tripping over the loose lace. A teenage girl just stepping out of one of the stores raised an arm to her face to ward off the swirl of smoke and grit, not noticing when the wind snatched her straw hat from her head and sent it tumbling down the street. An old man carrying a battered leather suitcase picked up his pace, hobbling to his car where he tossed the case into the backseat, jumped in, and sped down the street to disappear around the corner.

Chip wondered how far the old man would get. If the fire closed the roads, they might be forced to evacuate by water from the town wharf. He didn't envy anyone who had to leave Bar Harbor by boat—the gale-force winds that had blown the flames toward the town had also whipped the water around Mount Desert Island into a white-capped frenzy.

But his mind wasn't on the residents of Bar Harbor—they had town officials and the soldiers from Dow Field to take care of them. His thoughts were with the captive at the grand house on the hill.

Chip scrambled to his truck, slammed it through a three-point turn, and headed back toward the flames, Great Hill, and The Lady.

Ann Kinnear watched her dead dog disappear into the woods outside her cabin, following his dead master.

She used to catch glimpses of them fairly regularly, when she was chopping wood or sipping a glass of wine on the dock on Loon Pond, but it had been several days since she had last seen them. It had been even longer since Beau had come to the cabin, and Ann had never seen the old woman come that close. But Ann could hear her clearly—hear the occasional whistled commands coming from the woods, commands Ann had taught Beau.

Part of Ann was glad that her abilities allowed her to see her dog's spirit, but part of her wished their relationship had ended as such relationships usually do: the dog dies, the person mourns and then moves on. But in this case, it was Beau who was moving on—bonding with the spirit of the ancient woman who had been instrumental in Ann's survival.

She should be happy. Her role in exposing Philadelphia society scion Biden Firth as a murderer had boosted the demand for her particular kind of consulting services. The fact that she had been able to receive messages from Biden's murder victim had marked a leap forward in her ability. And the assurance of her fellow senser, Garrick Masser, that Biden's spirit did not haunt Ann's Adirondack cabin should have enabled her to slip comfortably back into the peaceful existence she had enjoyed before the spirit of Biden's victim had grabbed her hand and dragged her toward the one piece of evidence that would implicate Biden Firth in the crime.

But Ann was not happy. She found excuses to turn down the consulting engagements that her brother Mike, as her business manager, proposed. She avoided places and situations that might call upon her to apply her newly expanded sensing skills. And the cabin she had loved before Biden tried to kill her in the kitchen, gunning down Beau instead, was no longer a refuge. It was a lonely place, becoming more lonely as her dead dog withdrew from her and turned instead toward his new, ghostly master.

With a sigh, Ann turned from the porch where she had been standing. She hitched up her jeans—she had lost weight over the last months, her usually slender frame now running toward gaunt. She pulled her mobile phone out of her pocket, checking for an email or a missed message from Mike, although he had called only the day before. There was nothing. Cradling her mug of coffee against the chill of the October morning, she re-entered the cabin's kitchen.

The floorboards had been replaced where the bloodstains—hers, Beau's, and Firth's—had proven impossible to scrub clean, even for her friend Helen Federman. Now the new boards stood out in raw contrast to the rest of the scuffed floor. The cheerful striped curtains that Helen had hung to replace the burned remnants of their predecessors distracted the casual observer from the charring still visible on the ceiling above the window.

Ann contemplated her options for passing the day: explore the Adirondack Park for flora she could photograph as subjects for the paintings she sold in the local art galleries; go to her studio a few minutes away to work on one of the paintings she lately had a tendency to start but not finish. She could go down the hill to the small dock on the pond ... and do what? She should get a boat. She briefly thought about pouring herself a glass of wine but decided it was a bit early even for her, although she had begun to pay less attention to such social niceties lately.

She resigned herself to the less enjoyable but more necessary option of unloading the dishwasher.

She was removing glasses from the top rack, questioning the wisdom of having gotten a dishwasher—she used so few dishes that it sometimes took her a week to fill it—when she noticed a red smear on the wine glass she held. Putting the glass down, she opened her hands and saw a slice across one of the fingers on her left hand, oozing blood. She had a queasy and disorienting moment while she tried to make sense of blood in the midst of such a banal activity, but then she noticed the crescent of glass missing from the rim of glass she had been holding, the edge so sharp she had not even felt it when it cut her.

"Damn!"

Now the cut was starting to sting. She grabbed a paper towel and wrapped it around her finger then, going to the bathroom, rummaged through a shoebox of first aid supplies. There weren't any Band-Aids, so she cobbled together an awkward bandage from gauze and tape, managing to stain a white hand towel with blood in the process.

"You've got to be kidding me ..."

She ran cold water in the bathroom sink and sloshed the towel around in the water, realizing too late that the result would be to impart a pinkish hue to the entire towel.

"Oh, come on!"

She took the sodden towel out of the sink, dropped it in the small washing machine across the hallway from the bathroom, dumped in some detergent, and clanged the washer door shut on its tiny load. She had to get out of the house, just as soon as she finished unloading the stupid dishwasher. She returned to the kitchen.

She plunged her right hand into the utensil basket and a dagger of the most exquisite pain she had ever experienced shot up her arm.

"Goddamn it!"

She jerked her hand back. Dangling from under her middle fingernail was a stainless steel paring knife. She jerked it out, bringing a strangled cry to her lips and a gout of blood to the floor. She staggered back to the bathroom and, pulling the mate of the delicately stained towel out of the cupboard, wrapped it around her hand where a bloom of blood immediately appeared.

She collapsed onto the toilet seat and bent over, squeezing her newly wounded hand between her torso and her thighs. It hurt so much she wanted to cry, but it hurt too much to cry. Her stomach roiled.

Gradually, the jagged daggers of pain were replaced by a violent throbbing and the red stain on the towel halted its advance. Trembling, she unwrapped her hand to examine the damage, then quickly rewrapped it when she saw. She stumbled into the dining area off the kitchen and, locating an almost-full bottle of Macallan, poured herself two fingers of Scotch, the neck of the bottle chattering on the rim of the glass.

Holding the glass in her less-injured hand and the bottle under her arm, she went back to the bathroom and found a bottle of aspirin which she wrestled open, taking two, then two more. Aspirin seemed laughably inadequate but it was the best she had. Aspirin and Scotch.

She made her way a bit unsteadily to the sitting room and lowered herself onto the scuffed leather couch. She ran a finger along a scratch that Beau had left when he had been awoken from a nap by the sound of Walt Federman's pickup and had rocketed out the door to greet his friend. Her throat tightened and she took a sip of Scotch, surprised when it emptied the glass. She poured herself a refill.

She needed to rest, then she'd feel better. She carefully placed the bottle and glass on the floor next to her and checked to make sure the towel had stanched the bleeding, then lay down. She pulled a mohair blanket from the back of the couch, suddenly cold, and as she drifted off to sleep she thought she heard a ripple of cruelly amused laughter.

3

"Honey?" Ann felt a gentle shake. "Ann, honey?"

Ann opened her eyes to a dusky light and Helen Federman's hand on her shoulder. She tried to sit up but fell back at the pounding in her head. She covered her eyes with a groan, then winced as her hand put up a vague protest. "What time is it?"

Helen looked at her watch. "Almost five."

Ann sat up in alarm, her head clanging. "Five? Are you kidding?"

Helen glanced at her watch again. "Uh, no. What happened?" She gestured toward Ann's towel-wrapped hand.

"I skewered myself on a knife." Ann held her hand out and Helen began carefully unwrapping it.

"What were you trying to do, juggle them?" Helen asked, nodding toward the makeshift bandage on Ann's other hand.

"Unrelated incidents," Ann grumbled.

"Holy cow!" exclaimed Helen as she drew away the towel. "Practically took the nail right off!"

Nausea swept over Ann and she lay down again.

"We should get you to the hospital. Or at least a doctor's office."

"It doesn't really seem like an emergency room situation. And it stopped bleeding."

"True, but you can't function with the nail like that, and I'm sure not going to take it off for you."

"Helen, stop, you're going to make me throw up," said Ann plaintively. "What are you doing here, anyway?"

"Brought you some strawberry jam," said Helen, gesturing toward the kitchen. "Good thing too, I think." She reached down and picked up a half-empty bottle of Macallan.

Ann took the bottle and examined the contents. "Some must have spilled out. It was practically full, and I didn't drink that much."

Helen raised her eyebrows. "If you say so. Let's see if we can't get you to Dr. Phipps's office before he closes."

Helen called Dr. Phipps to tell him they were coming. She must have snuck in a call to her husband Walt as well, because he was standing outside the door to the doctor's office as they pulled up in Helen's car. Walt was a pilot and, with Mike booking Ann into engagements up and down the East Coast and sometimes beyond, Ann often made use of Walt's charter services in his four-seat Piper Arrow. Walt and Helen were also the closest thing Ann had to parents, her own mother and father having been killed in a car accident when she was in college.

"He won't go in," Helen whispered to Ann, even though they were still in the car and Walt couldn't possibly hear them. "Not crazy about doctors."

Walt opened the passenger door to let Ann out, carefully averting his eyes from the bloodstained towel that Helen had rewrapped around Ann's hand.

"I'll just wait here," he said, hurrying ahead of them to open the office door.

Helen shepherded Ann through the empty waiting room and called to Dr. Phipps, who emerged from his office and waved them into an exam room.

Dr. Phipps earned Ann's eternal gratitude by not only giving her a shot of something that numbed her finger but also by rigging up a little screen to keep her from seeing what he was doing.

"I could just look away," said Ann, embarrassed at the trouble he was taking.

"Patients say they'll look away but at some point curiosity always gets the better of them and they take a look," he said, working busily behind the screen. "My nurse left for the day so I can't take a risk of you fainting." He covered the wound with a tidy bandage and replaced the gauze and tape on Ann's other hand with a Band-Aid.

Walt greeted them when they emerged from the building. "That wasn't too bad, was it?"

"Walt, you have no idea whether it was bad or not," Helen scolded.

Walt shrugged good-naturedly. "Want to go get ice cream?"

"She's a grown woman, she doesn't want ice cream for being a good sport for the doctor."

"Actually I'd trade ice cream for a burger, my treat. I'm starving," said Ann.

They compromised by having dinner at the Federmans' where, Helen promised, she could provide a burger that would be much better than anything they could get in a restaurant—and ice cream, too, if Ann liked.

WALT AND HELEN dropped Ann off at the cabin after dinner. The call from her brother came so quickly after their departure that

Helen must have been dialing his number before Walt even had his truck turned around in the gravel driveway.

"Hey, I heard you hurt your hand," said Mike.

"Jeez, can't a person get any privacy around here?" said Ann, getting a bottle of Viognier out of the refrigerator.

"Helen said you were passed out on the couch."

"I wasn't 'passed out,' I lay down because my hand hurt and I fell asleep."

"For the whole day? With a half-empty bottle of Scotch next to you?"

Ann returned the bottle of Viognier, unopened, to the refrigerator. "Mike, I only had two glasses, my hand was killing me. You should take anything Helen says with a grain of salt, she's a worrier."

Mike sighed. "Well, she said the bandage was pretty big—sorry, bandages, I understand you injured both hands—so you should come down to West Chester a little early and let me and Scott take care of you."

"Damn, I forgot that was this weekend." Ann had been working on a painting for Joe Booth, the Philadelphia detective who had investigated the Biden Firth case: a portrait of his niece and nephew based on a photograph he had given her. "I won't be able to finish the painting in time—the big bandage is on my painting hand."

"I thought you were done with it."

"I need to fix some things. There's a reason I've never done people before, they look more creepy than cute at the moment."

"I'm sure he'll understand about the delay, it was a wound suffered in the line of housekeeping duty. You come down here tomorrow and we'll still have dinner with him on Friday like we planned. I'll make him something nice as a consolation prize."

Ann thought back to that morning—that unpleasant feeling

of being at loose ends, the absent dog whose presence would have made being alone enjoyable, the general sense of unease she had felt since returning to her cabin after Biden's attack.

"You know, that does sound good. I'll find out when Walt can bring me down."

4

W alt was free the following day and he and Ann made a midmorning departure from the Adirondack Regional Airport into cloudless blue skies. As they flew, the giant's shoulders of the Adirondacks lowered into the spine-like ridges of the northern Pennsylvania mountains and then the flanks of the rolling hills of Chester County. The foliage in the Adirondacks was in full fall glory but as they flew south the colors settled into the verdant green of the Indian summer that Pennsylvania was enjoying.

Ann had brought a book with her to pass the time but, with the thrum of the engine filtering through her headset and the world slipping by beneath them, she fell into a reverie. Specks of cars glided along the narrow ribbons of road; the anonymous expanses of shopping mall and warehouse roofs clustered around highway intersections; small airports appeared, marked with the tiny white crosses of parked aircraft. It was hard to imagine this as anything other than a meticulously constructed model, free of all the complications and messiness of real life.

Walt's Arrow made the trip from the Adirondack Regional Airport to the Brandywine Airport in about two hours. His radio calls as he flew the pattern into Brandywine roused Ann from her daydream and she spotted Mike's Audi in the small parking lot next to the terminal. While Walt got the plane settled after they had landed, Mike and his partner, Scott Pate, strolled out to meet them, Scott waving enthusiastically. Mike was a shade shorter than medium height, stocky, with dark hair and eyes. Scott was taller and thinner, with clipped blond hair and pale eyes behind chunky Ray Bans. Hugs for Ann and handshakes for Walt were exchanged.

"How about lunch before you head back?" Mike asked Walt. "Your choice."

"Wouldn't say no to a slice or two of pizza," said Walt.

Mike drove them to Caruso's Pizza, Scott ceding the front seat to Walt.

When they finished their slices and Ann excused herself to use the restroom, Mike leaned across the table to Walt.

"So, how do you think she's doing?"

Walt fiddled with the straw in his soda. "I don't know. Helen says she seems unhappy."

"I don't know why she stays in that cabin," said Scott. "Such terrible memories." He shuddered.

"We keep telling her she should move back to West Chester," said Mike. "Or upgrade the studio." Ann had built a studio on a mountaintop a few miles from her cabin to provide her with the light she needed for her painting. "If she did that, she could stay there in the summers, if she still wants a place in the Adirondacks. She should sell the cabin."

"Although it might be hard to sell, considering ..." said Scott.

"Or easy to sell, depending on the buyer," said Mike. "Some people like that kind of thing."

Scott pushed away his plate, empty save for two crusts. "I can see why she would be unhappy. Of course it would be difficult for her to live in the place where Biden Firth attacked her, but I hope it's not more than that."

"What do you mean?" asked Walt.

"I hope she doesn't feel guilty about what happened. She didn't have any choice—if she hadn't shot him, he certainly would have killed her."

Mike shook his head. "I guess there's no logic about a thing like that. I'm sure she never thought of herself as a killer—"

"Hi there!" said Walt in an uncharacteristically hearty greeting. Mike and Scott turned to see Ann approaching the table.

"That was fast," said Mike.

"There was a line, I can wait." She looked at the three of them suspiciously. "What's up?"

"Talking airplanes," said Scott breezily. "Did you know that planes fly because the air pressure sucks the wings up? Speaking of which, shouldn't we be getting back to the airport?"

Back at Brandywine, Mike discreetly slipped Walt his payment for the flight, then Mike, Scott, and Ann lingered in the small terminal watching two- and four-seater planes arrive and depart, listening to the radio calls on the PA system. When the Arrow had taken off and shrunk to a pinprick in the autumn-blue sky, Mike turned to Ann.

"What now? In the mood to do anything special?"

Ann shrugged. "Nothing in particular. Did you guys have anything planned before I showed up?"

Mike wrinkled his nose. "Just stuff around the house. Scott was going to plant some spinach in the pots on the patio."

"The weather has been so warm I thought I might be able to get one more crop in," said Scott. "But I don't think gardening is going to work out so well with a bandage on your hand. You could sunbathe."

"I'd fry, even in October," said Ann.

"We'll put the umbrella up and you can read."

When they got to Mike and Scott's townhouse, Mike went grumblingly upstairs to do battle with a leaking faucet while Scott got the patio umbrella set up for Ann, then collected his gardening equipment. Ann discovered a stack of *Philadelphia Magazine*s in the living room and brought them out onto the patio.

Scott glanced over at what she had. "There's an article about the Firth case in one of those. Just so it doesn't take you by surprise."

"Really?" said Ann, looking at the stack of magazines with distaste. "Which one?"

"It had a sports person on the cover."

"What did it say?" Ann glanced down at the magazine she was holding. The cover was a photo of one of the Flyers and his wife. "Never mind, I'll read it later. I'm not in the mood." She picked up another magazine from the stack—it featured a well-known actress, originally from Ardmore, holding a cheerful-looking pit bull. Ann got herself comfortable in the shade of the umbrella and began paging through the magazine.

Pretty soon Mike showed up looking grumpy. "Plumbing sucks," he said, flopping into one of the other patio chairs. "Is it five o'clock yet? I need a beer."

"You couldn't have been working on it more than about ten minutes," said Ann, looking at her watch.

"You should just call the plumber to begin with. Trying to do it yourself just puts you in a bad mood," said Scott, emptying a bag of potting soil into a ceramic planter.

"Yeah, you're probably right," said Mike, He moved his chair so he could look over Ann's shoulder. "Whatcha got there?"

"Article about pit bulls."

"Dog article, eh?"

"Uh huh," said Ann. "This actress is having a sort of PR campaign for the breed."

Mike and Scott exchanged a glance.

"Pit bulls seem like good dogs," said Mike.

"Yeah, seems like it," said Ann without looking up.

"Do you think you might get another dog?" Mike asked cautiously.

Ann turned a page. "I don't know."

"If you're going to stay in the cabin, I'd feel better if you had a dog."

Ann sighed and flipped a few pages forward to a review of Waterman's restaurant. "I don't need a dog. I'll get some pepper spray."

"A dog wouldn't be good just for protection," Mike pressed on. "He'd be good company, too."

Ann tossed the magazine onto the patio table. "Mike, I don't want a dog right now. Maybe later. I'm going to take a nap." And she went inside, leaving Mike and Scott on the patio.

Scott shook his head. "Poor Annie."

"Yeah," said Mike, "I hope we can snap her out of it."

5

As he had done all their lives, Mike sprang to Ann's defense—this time in response to the cloud of depression that still clung to her. As a distraction, he set a goal for them of sampling the mushroom soup of every southern Chester County restaurant that advertised it as a specialty.

They stopped at one of their favorite destinations, a restaurant in Kennett Square that drew a well-heeled crowd from the surrounding gentleman's farms. Soaring ceilings and polished concrete floors were softened by scuffed wooden tables and white linen napkins. Ann ordered an old fashioned and talked Mike into ordering a cocktail featuring Laphroaig Scotch and a house-made pine liqueur. When it arrived she wrinkled her nose.

"Holy cow, it smells like something you'd clean the kitchen counters with!"

Mike sniffed it suspiciously. "How come you always make me order the weird drinks?"

"Because you're braver than I am," she said, sipping her drink.

Mike's eyes widened slightly.

"Well, not so much braver as more foolhardy," Ann continued, then noticed that Mike was looking over her shoulder. "What?" She started to turn around to see what had attracted his attention.

"Don't turn around," he whispered.

She stopped. "Why not?" she whispered back.

"Dan Kaminsky is at one of the tables behind you."

Ann's fingers actually loosened their grip on her heavy cocktail glass, which went crashing down onto her bread plate. An immediate hush fell over the previously buzzing dining room.

"Smooth," muttered Mike.

"Is he looking?" hissed Ann.

"Of course he's looking. Everyone in the restaurant is looking." Mike glanced over her shoulder and raised his hand in greeting, a somewhat strained smile on his face.

Their server appeared at their table with a stack of napkins and began blotting up the mess. He handed several napkins to Ann. "I think you got some in your lap, ma'am." The murmur of conversation began to rise around them again.

"Sorry about that," said Ann, her face burning. "I'm just going to go clean up." She grabbed the leather knapsack she used as a purse and wended her way through the tables to the back of the restaurant, her eyes on the floor. The door to the women's room was locked, but the men's room was unoccupied so she went in there.

In all the years she had been visiting Mike and Scott in West Chester, she had never run into her former boyfriend. She had originally met Dan when he'd taken over the vet practice to which she took her lab, Kali, and he had won her over with his sweet manner, his obvious devotion, and his meltingly brown eyes. But Dan was a scientist in spirit as well as profession, and he had been skeptical when he finally found out—not from Ann

—about her spirit-sensing abilities. When he had implied she should see a psychiatrist about her belief in her own skill, Ann had been devastated. She had left unreturned the voicemails and emails he'd sent for weeks, until they slowed and finally stopped. And when Dan showed up at the apartment she shared with Mike, she told Mike to tell him that she had no interest in speaking with him—a message that Mike, always her staunchest defender, had no doubt delivered with convincing finality.

She had gotten through those post-breakup months when she expected to see Dan in every store, on every West Chester street corner, at any concert featuring music that she thought he might enjoy, but almost a decade had gone by since then and it had been years since she had thought of him. Much.

And when I finally do see him—hell, I didn't even see him myself —I drop my glass like a ditzy blonde in a bad sitcom. She gave a shaky laugh that was one moment of loosened self-control away from tears.

Her face was flushed and she ran cold water on a paper towel and pressed it to her cheeks. She had a junior high moment of wondering if she could leave the restaurant by a back entrance, even as she realized that anything other than a calm and collected return to the dining room would make the incident even more embarrassing than it already was.

When she had dabbed the remains of old fashioned off her jeans, smoothed back a few tendrils of hair that had escaped from her ponytail, and applied some tinted lip balm, she returned to the dining room. Her stomach lurched when she saw that Mike was standing at Dan's table, and lurched again when she saw that Dan wasn't alone. Of course—why would he be?

She crossed to the table, being extra careful not to sweep any diners' glasses off the tables as she passed with her knapsack. Dan had grown a beard and mustache, and his hair was just beginning to show a few strands of gray at the temples, but otherwise he looked much the same as he had the last time she had seen him. Across from him sat a beautiful woman—Indian or Pakistani—her jet-black hair pulled back in a long braid, her dramatic coloring set off by a cherry-red sweater that looked like cashmere. Next to the woman sat a little girl, the perfect combination of the two adults—dark hair with Dan's curls, dark brown eyes with Dan's sparkle. Their table was in front of the restaurant's large front windows and the light created a halo behind the little girl and shimmered off what must have been metallic threads in her shirt.

Dan stood. "Hi, Ann."

She wiped her palms on her jeans, hoping no one would offer to shake hands. "Hey, Dan."

"Ann, this is Dan's wife, Amita," said Mike.

Ann smiled and nodded. "Pleased to meet you."

Amita nodded back, a bit formal but not unfriendly.

"Mike says you're visiting from the Adirondacks," said Dan.

"Yes."

"Scott and I are always trying to get her to spend more time in West Chester," said Mike. "Especially during the winter—Pennsylvania is practically balmy in comparison. But she's tougher than I am. How's the vet business?"

"Going well," said Dan distractedly. "It's turning into a family business—Amita's my partner now."

"And how about your daughter?" asked Ann. She turned toward the girl. "Are you going to become a vet and join the family business when you grow up?"

Amita's expression froze. Dan followed Ann's gaze and then looked back at her, the blood draining from his face.

"I'm sorry," Ann stammered, "I just thought—"

Mike took her elbow. "Well, Dan, it was nice to see you," he said, extending his hand, which Dan took mechanically. "Nice to meet you, Amita. I recommend you stay away from that Scotch cocktail, unless you want to knock down a few cold germs." He steered Ann back to their table.

Another old fashioned had appeared at her plate. She took a gulp, clunked the glass down on the table, and leaned forward. "What did I say wrong?"

Ann had at first thought Mike was annoyed with her, but now she saw his lips were twitching with what might have been an almost-suppressed smile.

"You didn't say anything wrong," he replied.

"I just thought—" started Ann, turning to glance over her shoulder toward Dan's table.

Dan and Amita were bent together across the table, Dan holding his wife's hands while she whispered low and fast, casting occasional glances toward Ann. It looked to Ann like she was about to cry. And the little girl was not in the chair next to her.

Ann turned back to Mike. "Where did the daughter go?"

"She didn't go anywhere," said Mike. "It was always only Dan and Amita at the table."

MIKE WASN'T BUYING Ann's argument that they should leave.

"I ordered the food while you were gone," he said. "Plus, it would be weird to leave."

"I'm sure they'd be thrilled if I left—I make them think about a little girl who is obviously their dead daughter and now Dan has to try to convince his wife that it's all parlor tricks."

"Well, obviously it's not parlor tricks," said Mike, and leaned forward. "That's extraordinary that you saw a spirit so clearly that you thought it was a living person!"

Ann took another gulp of her drink. "The sun was behind her, I couldn't see her that well."

Mike shook his head. "Now you're being silly—this is a huge leap forward and you know it."

They both sat back as the server delivered their mushroom soups. Mike tried for a while to engage Ann in a discussion of the movie they had seen the night before—*The Blues Brothers*, a personal favorite of Mike's—but she responded in monosyllables and he finally gave up.

When their entrees arrived, Ann pushed her food around on the plate, her stomach clenched by the distraction of wondering what was going on behind her. Mike gave her periodic updates —"They just got their lunches" ... "Looks like they're not getting dessert"—and finally he reported that they had paid and were leaving. He gave them a wave.

Mike got Ann's uneaten entree boxed up and wished the hostess a good day as they left. Ann wished he wasn't so damn cheerful.

They were walking toward Mike's Audi when the driver door of an immaculately clean pickup opened and Dan emerged. He trotted toward them and they stopped to let him catch up.

"Hey," said Dan when he reached them. "Would it be okay if I talked to Ann for a minute?"

Mike glanced at Ann, who nodded. "Sure, no problem," he said and strolled away.

Despite the warm October afternoon sun, Ann pushed her hands deeper into her jacket pockets. They stood in silence for a few seconds, then Dan said, "Wow, that was something."

Ann looked toward where Mike was looking in the window of a women's clothing store. Women's clothing not being Mike's thing, she guessed that he had picked it as a location far enough away that they would have no fear of being overheard but close enough that he could get back to Ann quickly if she looked like she needed help. "Dan, I don't—"

"I'm so sorry that I didn't believe you when you told me what you could do," he blurted.

Ann's eyes snapped back to him. "Really? I mean, you believe I saw something?"

"How could I not? You saw my daughter, right? Little girl with dark curly hair?"

"Yes."

Dan shook his head and ran his fingers through his hair. "That's just unbelievable," he said, then waved his hand as if trying to erase something in the air between them. "No, I don't mean unbelievable—I completely believe you."

Ann glanced toward the pickup. "How about Amita? Does she believe me?"

Dan also looked toward the truck, his face tightening with concern. "Well, at first she thought you were playing a joke on us —a really horrible joke. She thought you must have heard about our daughter from one of our old friends."

"No, I didn't."

"Of course you didn't. I think I convinced her you aren't that kind of person."

Ann hesitated. "What did happen to your daughter? If you want to talk about it."

"Leukemia. It was terrible. Truly terrible. Especially after losing my sister to cancer so soon before. Well, you can imagine." He ran his fingers through his hair again. "When you saw her, was she ... clear?"

"Yes, quite clear. It's not always like that." Ann didn't specify that it had never been like that. Even with Elizabeth Firth, who had been the most lifelike spirit she had seen before Dan's daughter, she would never have mistaken her for a living person.

"What was she doing?" Dan asked eagerly.

Ann thought back to what she had seen. "She was sitting in the chair next to your wife, following the conversation. She looked interested in what was going on—very engaged. She looks like a smart little girl."

Dan smiled. "Oh yes. She wanted to be an astronaut. One time she made a 'Martian rover' out of a coffee can and hitched it to the cat to pull around. You can imagine how successful that was."

Ann smiled with him, and felt a tug at her heart. This was the Dan she had missed so much. She could just imagine the talk he would have had with his daughter after that incident—gentle but firm about her responsibility not to treat the cat like a toy.

"What's her name?"

His smile widened. "I like that you ask that in the present tense. Her name's Sylvia."

"A pretty name for a pretty girl."

Dan nodded, the smile still on his face. "Yes, she was. She was a sweetheart." His voice caught a little on the last word. He glanced back at the pickup. "Listen, I need to get back. Amita was okay with me talking with you but she didn't feel like she could handle it right now herself. We lost Sylvia less than a year ago." He looked back to Ann. "But I really wanted to tell you that I'm sorry for doubting you. I was trying to find a scientific explanation for what you experienced, but now that doesn't seem so important anymore. Maybe I had to have a child to be able to see that there's more to life than science and logic. Do you forgive me?"

Ann felt tears burn and in her mind's eye she saw the scene the way it might have been: her and Dan and their own child—a healthy child—going to a restaurant for lunch for a special occasion. Maybe it would be a little girl with curling, reddish-blond hair and sparkling green eyes telling them about a Martian rover, and speculating about ways of powering it. Maybe that little girl's pet would be Beau, who would be only too happy to tow a rover if it made his person happy. She nodded at Dan. "Yes. Of course."

He stepped forward and extended his arms tentatively, and she walked into a hug that was both awkward and wonderful. It lasted only a moment before he stepped back.

"I'm so glad we ran into each other," said Dan. "I read about you finding that woman's murderer. I must admit that at the time I didn't know quite what to make of it, but knowing what I do now, you have a lot to be proud of."

Not trusting herself to talk, Ann made a dismissive shooing motion.

"But your dog—I was really sorry to hear about that. I remember how much you loved Kali. I know this dog must have meant just as much to you. What was his name—Beau?"

She nodded as tears threatened to spill over.

He gazed at her for a moment. "Are you okay?"

She nodded again.

"Well, I better go. All the best to you, Ann. Give my best to Mike and Scott, too." He stepped forward again and gave her another quick hug, then turned and walked back to the pickup. He walked quickly, like a man with good news that he was excited to share.

Ann watched him go and in a moment Mike was by her side. "Did that go all right?"

Ann nodded and searched in her pockets for a tissue as the tears finally fell. "Yes. He believed me."

Mike put his hand on her shoulder. "Of course he did, Ann. He'd be a fool not to."

THEY CONTINUED ON AS ORIGINALLY PLANNED to Longwood Gardens. Mike went to the conservatory to see the latest display. He enjoyed the symmetry of the building and the plantings, and had confided to Ann and Scott his secret desire to sneak into the conservatory after hours and lie on the luxuriant, and off-limits, lawns around which the displays were arranged.

Ann begged off the conservatory and headed instead to the Meadow Garden, where she knew from experience that she could walk the perimeter of its eighty-six acres and never have to see a soul—living or dead.

6

On Friday, Joe Booth, the Philadelphia detective who had been in charge of the Firth case, drove out from Philadelphia to West Chester for dinner. After Joe had exhausted the more traditional means of investigation, it had been at his invitation that Ann got involved in the case.

Joe arrived on the doorstep with a bouquet of flowers for Ann and a bottle of wine for Mike and Scott, looking uncomfortable in a snug sport coat, which he removed as soon as he saw that everyone else was dressed casually. Joe was a big man, a previously athletic physique softening a bit in middle age. He was in his mid-forties but looked older, due in part to the premature graying of his pale blond hair.

Mike had made rack of lamb, roasted potatoes, and asparagus, and opened a couple of bottles of Palmaz Cabernet Sauvignon. Now, they were all pushed back from the dining room table, too full and comfortable to move into the living room. Even Ann, relaxed by the wine and the company, was eating everything Mike served her.

She was just finishing up her last asparagus spear as Mike

and Joe talked sports when she glanced over Mike's shoulder and said, "Hey, it's Scooter!"

The three men turned to look.

"What?" said Joe.

"Where?" said Scott.

"Our cat, Scooter," said Mike.

"You have a cat?" asked Joe. "I'm usually allergic—"

"Scooter's deceased," said Scott. "Where did he go?" he asked Ann.

"He just crossed the hall, but he was very clear. I could even see the white tuft on his chest."

"He was always just a gray fuzzy spot before," said Scott to Joe.

"First Sylvia, now Scooter," said Mike.

"Who's Sylvia?" asked Joe, trying to catch up.

Mike looked to Ann. "Can I tell?" After a nod from Ann, he recounted the story of Dan and Amita's dead daughter.

Joe looked at Ann. "That's pretty impressive."

She shrugged, embarrassed. "Now if I can just find a way to do something more productive than upsetting grieving mothers and locating dead household pets ..."

"A.—" Mike began.

Ann stood up. "I made chocolate chip cookies for dessert."

"I can get them," said Scott, popping up, but Ann returned him to his chair with a push on the shoulder.

"You guys have been spoiling me all week—I need to start acting like a grown up sometime," she said, and disappeared into the kitchen.

"So, it sounds like her skills are developing," said Joe to Mike.

Mike glanced toward the door to the kitchen. "Yes. I was hoping she'd be excited about it, but it doesn't seem like it's making her any less conflicted about her abilities. I'll admit that the little girl's mother was initially upset, but Ann doesn't mention that the father was pretty happy she'd sensed his daughter's spirit."

"And I'm always happy to get an update on Scooter," added Scott.

"If she's really starting to be able to see dead people in detail, there's a lot of good she could do," said Joe. "And not just in criminal investigations. There was a plane crash in Lancaster a couple of weeks ago—no one knows what happened, the pilot and passengers died. If Ann could go to the site, maybe check things out—"

Joe's sentence was cut short by a muffled cry from the kitchen, a crash, and an unmuffled, "Damn it!"

The three men rushed to the kitchen to find Ann standing at the sink running water on her hand. On the floor lay an upended tray, a scattering of broken ceramic, and a pile of sodden cookies in a large puddle of steaming coffee.

"What happened?" asked Mike.

"I got one of those damn pains in my hand right when I picked up the tray, and when I dropped it, the coffee spilled on my hand!"

"Let's see," said Scott.

Ann held her hand out to Scott.

He took it gently and turned it back and forth, examining the damage. "Ouch. And on the same hand you stabbed," he tutted. "You keep running cool water on it." He put his finger under the stream of water. "Good heavens, not that cold, you don't want frostbite." He adjusted the temperature and moved her hand back under the water. Meanwhile, Mike was swabbing mug shards, cookie fragments, and coffee into a dustpan and dumping the mess into the trash can.

"Sorry about that, you guys," said Ann bleakly.

"It's okay," said Mike. "You've been having pains in your hands?"

Ann shut off the water, grabbed a dish towel, and flopped down on a kitchen chair. "Yeah, for the last couple of weeks. It's like getting a charley horse in my hand, and it always seems to hit at the worst time and I end up hurting myself."

"Is that what happened there?" asked Joe, nodding to her still-bandaged finger.

"No, that didn't hurt until I impaled myself on a knife when I was unloading the dishwasher. That happened right after I cut my hand on a broken glass. But a couple of days before that, I got one of those hand cramps when I was splitting logs and I almost chopped my foot off." She thought for a moment. "And before that, I tripped on the porch steps and tried to grab the railing but my hand cramped up and I missed it and fell."

"Is this unusual, hurting yourself this much?" asked Joe.

"Yes, of course it's unusual," said Ann irritably, "otherwise I would have put myself in the hospital by now."

Joe looked thoughtful.

"Why do you ask?"

"Because I knew someone who hurt his hands a lot, although in his case it was intentional—self-inflicted injuries."

"Sounds screwed up," said Ann. "Who was that?"

"Biden Firth."

THEY RETIRED to the living room with a plate of store-bought cookies and a fresh pot of coffee.

Joe said, "I remember when I was interviewing him and asked him about the conditions of his wife's will, he got upset and did something to his hand with a pen or pencil. And at the autopsy, they found evidence of injuries to his hands and nails, likely self-inflicted."

Ann said suddenly, "You know, I remember something like that. When I was alone with him in the shore house, I remember him playing with a letter opener, pushing the point into his hand ..."

"So what are you thinking—that Ann somehow picked up this habit from Firth?" Mike asked Joe. "I don't think Ann would be intentionally hurting herself," he added, a little defensive.

Joe took a drink of his coffee. "I'm not sure what I'm thinking. It just struck me as odd when Ann mentioned all the times she's hurt her hands since Firth died, especially if it wasn't happening before." Joe looked questioningly toward Ann, who shook her head. "Maybe he sort of, I don't know, hexed your hand?" he ended feebly.

"Hexed it?" said Mike, his eyebrows raised. "Now what do we have to do—kill a chicken to cure it?"

"I think the chicken-killing thing is voodoo," said Scott.

Ann ran the fingers of her unburned hand through her hair. "I could buy that Biden Firth might be behind the injuries I got at the cabin—after all, that's where he died—but they're happening here too. Plus, Garrick checked the cabin when I was in the hospital and he said Biden's spirit wasn't there."

"Let's keep our minds open to the possibility that the great Garrick Masser might not always be right," said Mike.

Ann ignored his tone. "But Garrick was there so soon after Biden died, I think he would have picked up something if there had been anything to pick up."

Joe shrugged. "It was just a passing thought. You guys are the experts."

After some more speculation about possible causes of Ann's recent run of manual misfortune, and her assurance that she would finish the painting for Joe as soon as her hands were healed, Joe excused himself for the evening. After seeing Joe out, the three of them returned to the kitchen. Mike and Scott cleaned up while Ann sat at the table, her burned hand agitating for attention, in a state of forced inactivity she found increasingly irritating.

"I think it's worth considering that Firth may have caught up with you at your cabin," said Mike. "It's certainly the kind of situation that could lead to a spirit staying at a location—a violent death, motive for revenge ..."

Scott shuddered. "You need to get out of there, sweetie, and not just for a long weekend. You should stay here with us for a while."

Mike nodded his agreement.

"You're both sweethearts," said Ann, smiling wanly. "I'll think it over."

"Except you have to stop taking Mike out to eat every day, or he'll get fat," Scott said, and poked Mike in the stomach.

Ann levered herself out of the chair, feeling old and creaky. "Do you guys have some aspirin in the downstairs bathroom?" she asked, starting down the hall to the powder room.

"Want a shot of Scotch to knock that back with?" called Mike after her.

"Ha ha, very funny," replied Ann as she sorted through the contents of the medicine cabinet.

She came back to the kitchen with a bottle of aspirin, which Scott opened for her. Swallowing them with a gulp of wine, she said, "You know, there is a common thread among all these times my hand has hurt."

"What's that, sweetie?" asked Scott, drying a platter.

"I had just sensed something."

"Did you sense Firth at your cabin?" asked Mike.

"No, I had just seen Beau."

"You've seen Beau?" asked Scott, putting down the platter. "That's wonderful! So you have company at the cabin after all!"

"Well, no ... He's taken up with someone else."

"Who's that?" asked Mike.

"An old woman. Very old. And from very long ago, I think."

"Well, that's ..." Scott said as he tried and failed to think of a positive spin to put on this.

Ann continued, "I had seen Beau—and sometimes Beau and the old woman—right around the time I had the pains in my hand. And tonight I had just seen Scooter. Maybe this is my new reaction to sensing—it used to be nausea, now it's hand cramps."

"That seems a little ..." Mike began, then stopped.

"A little what?" asked Ann sharply.

Mike considered. "Seeing past pets doesn't seem like it would trigger such a dramatic reaction. Plus," he said, perking up, "you didn't have any pain when you saw Dan and Amita's daughter, did you?"

"No," retorted Ann, "but when I saw her, I didn't realize she was dead."

Scott put his hands up. "Kids, kids. It seems like there are lots of possible explanations for what's happening, including just a straightforward, old-fashioned physical explanation. Maybe we should ask a hand specialist to check it out."

"But you said that sometimes when you hurt yourself it wasn't because you got a pain in your hand—like when you stabbed yourself when you were unloading the dishwasher. Maybe you're just being klutzy," said Mike.

"Gee, thanks," said Ann. She sighed and finished up the last of her wine, then gave herself a small top-off from the almost-empty bottle of Cab. "I'm turning in."

Ann retired to the bedroom that was reserved for her visits, made snug with quilts, a set of first-edition N. C. Wyeth-illustrated children's books, and an antique rocker Scott had recently found in Adamstown. She paged through *Treasure Island* for a few minutes, then tossed it aside, got out her phone, and dialed Garrick Masser.

After a few rings, Ann heard the mechanical click of a landline phone being picked up. "Yes," came the sepulchral greeting.

"Garrick, it's Ann."

"The celebrated Miss Kinnear," said Garrick testily. Ann guessed he was a little put off by the publicity she had gotten as a result of the Firth case. "How may I help you?"

"Just checking in," she said brightly.

"Hmph," said Garrick, then was silent.

After a few moments, Ann sighed—she should know better than to try to make small talk with Garrick Masser. "I've been hurting myself lately."

"Intentionally?"

"No, not intentionally," replied Ann.

"Seriously?"

"Yes, seriously, I haven't been hurting myself intentionally."

"Have you been hurting yourself seriously?"

"Oh. No, not very seriously. It all has to do with my hands. I'm getting these sudden pains in my hand." She recounted the theories—Joe's that it was Biden Firth's influence, Scott's that it could have some perfectly normal physical explanation, Mike's that she was having a sudden attack of chronic clumsiness, and her own that it was a reaction to sensings.

"So the detective and your brother think you are being haunted by the spirit of the man you killed?"

Ann winced. Everyone else referred to Biden as the man she had brought to justice or the man who had tried to kill her. "Well, they floated it as a possibility, but I think it's farfetched. Don't you think it's more likely that it's a physical reaction to the sensing?"

She was warming to this theory. Ever since she had gotten out of the hospital, she had had looming over her shoulder the specter, so to speak, of the resumption of the spirit-sensing consulting engagements. If she was now actually suffering pain and injuries as a result of exercising her skill, there could be no question about her continuing it as a business, could there?

Then she thought of another attraction of this explanation. "That might explain why Beau won't come to me even when I go out into the woods. Maybe he senses that he's causing me distress."

"Possibly."

"Why else wouldn't he come to me?" she asked, defensive.

"Because he's ..." Garrick stopped, at an uncharacteristic loss for words.

"He's what?"

"Dead," Garrick finished flatly. "He's not of the same world you are anymore."

Ann felt her throat tighten.

After a pause, Garrick added, "The fact that he presents himself to you at all is quite unusual."

Ann waited, hoping there was more, but Garrick was silent.

Finally she gave up. "In any case," she said, "you told me Biden wasn't at the cabin."

"He was not," he said, clearly relieved that the delicate topic of her dog's waning devotion had been dealt with. "But then, you weren't there either."

A chill ran down Ann's spine. She asked her next question even though she suddenly knew what the answer would be. "Why would that make a difference?"

"Because, my dear, it's possible Biden Firth is haunting not your house, but you."

She felt a thud in her gut. She didn't want what Garrick was suggesting to be true. Not only did it challenge her current favorite theory—a physical reaction to the sensing experience—but it represented a complication she had never considered in her own experience with spirits.

"I've never encountered a spirit that haunted a person and not a place," she said, but then realized that that was exactly what she had seen with Dan and Amita's daughter. Sylvia would hardly be haunting a Chester County restaurant; it was her parents she was tied to.

"It is surprisingly uncommon," Garrick was saying. "Or perhaps merely underreported, since those who are being haunted might be hesitant to admit to the act that triggered the haunting."

"Couldn't a spirit want to stay with a person for good reasons?" asked Ann. Sylvia had looked happy to be sitting in a nice restaurant with her parents.

"One would think so, but it's not often the case."

"Why not?"

"Who can say?" said Garrick, sounding unaccustomedly uncomfortable. "It's not a strict rule, only a general observation. Perhaps spirits who have positive feelings for someone who is still alive are more willing to let nature take its course to reunite them."

"Do you believe they are reunited?"

"It doesn't matter what I believe," said Garrick, back to his usual irritable self. "It only matters what they believe."

Ann was silent for a moment, her thoughts a jumble. Garrick evidently felt no compunction to fill the silence. "But why can't I see him?" she eventually asked.

"From what you have told me about Biden Firth, it seems as if he was a man who regularly caused people pain but was ineffectual—not good at making himself 'seen,' even in life."

"But if he is haunting me, what can I do about it? If he were

at the cabin, I could just move somewhere else, but if it's me ...
Can you fix it?"

"I'm not an exorcist, my dear—plus, we're not even sure
that's the case. I only mention it as a possibility."

"But I need to find out. Could you come to West Chester and
see me?"

"Not possible, I'm in the middle of a tedious but potentially
lucrative engagement conducting a series of interviews with a
spirit here in Maine."

"I could come there."

"Highly unusual."

Since this didn't seem like an outright refusal, Ann decided
to wait it out.

Just as she was about to give up, Garrick said, "But not
impossible."

"I'd be curious to hear about your engagement," said Ann to
be polite.

"Impossible. The client insists on strict confidentiality."

Ann sighed. "Fine. But can I come up there?"

"I must say the case does hold some interest," said Garrick.
"Very well, you may come to Maine."

"That's great, Garrick, I really appreciate it," said Ann,
feeling better now that there was a concrete action she could
take to try to address her situation. "I need to get back to the
Adirondacks to get my car, then I'll drive up there. Hopefully I
can get there in the next couple of days. How long should I plan
on staying?"

"It will be difficult to say until you are here and I can assess
the situation. Are you under time constraints?"

"No." She had rarely felt as unconstrained by demands on
her time as she had lately.

Garrick gave Ann the necessary logistical details. When the
call ended, Ann was tempted to call Walt to arrange her flight

home, but it was late and she resigned herself to waiting until morning. She climbed into bed, but her hand hesitated as she reached to turn off the light. She scanned the room, senses alert for even the faintest sign that usually signaled the presence of a spirit—the lights or scents she had been able to perceive all her life, or the more lifelike manifestations that were a more recent development. There was nothing. But what if Biden Firth was haunting her? What else could he do to take revenge on her for ruining—and ending—his life?

ANN FOUGHT HER EXHAUSTION, knowing what awaited her, but eventually the relentless hand of sleep seized her and dragged her down.

She was on her dock on Loon Pond. Dark clouds boiled, distant on the horizon but so close she could feel the breeze from their movement. An oily black ice covered the pond, heaving slightly with the movement of waves trapped underneath. She heard a scratching sound coming from under the end of the dock and, taking a step, almost fell on the slippery boards. She dropped to her hands and knees and crawled to the end of the dock, lowered herself onto her stomach, and peered over.

In an ice-free space under the dock was Beau. He was trying to climb the piling. He would wrap his front legs around the piling and pull himself up, then, claws scrabbling on the ice-slick wood, would slip down under the icy water, then burst to the surface with an almost human gasp and try again. Each time, his surfacing took longer, his movements slowed by a cocoon of ice accreting on his fur like wax on a candle wick.

The dream-Ann watched him dispassionately, calculating the length of his next submersion. Then she heard a whistle in the wind and, looking up, saw the old woman shuffling across the ice toward her, her gait accommodating the movement of the ice the way a sailor's walk accommodates the rolling of a ship. Mesmerized, Ann watched her come. When the old woman neared the dock, Ann looked down and realized that Beau hadn't resurfaced.

The old woman reached the hole in the ice into which Beau had sunk and, kneeling down, pulled the sleeve of her garment back and lowered her arm into the water. She moved her arm back and forth, seeking. Then a look of satisfaction slightly smoothed her wrinkled brow and she drew out of the water a puppy Beau, dangling by his scruff, a look of placid contentment on his face.

The old woman tucked the pup under the robe draped around her shoulders and turned from Ann.

"Wait, he's mine," said Ann, a sudden panic gripping her, but the sodden air absorbed the sound. The old woman shuffled away and disappeared into the clouds, which had now lowered to form an impenetrable fog over the surface of the ice-covered pond.

The cabin. Her Beau would be there. She turned and began to crawl back along the dock, feeling cold rain stabbing her back, which was now bare. She hooked her fingers into the spaces between the boards and dragged herself forward. Then the ground became somewhat softer, covered with tendrils she was able to grasp for purchase.

The ground was slippery but now warm. She had crawled under some sort of overhang that sheltered her from the rain. At the back of the cave created by the overhang, she began to dig, burrowing into the warm wetness, tearing at a network of roots that bent her fingers and broke her nails. The wetness swallowed her up—soaking her arms, then her shoulders, then her whole body. Her hair stuck to her neck, slimy and grasping.

Then, like a movie camera zooming out, she was both in the

cave and far away looking at herself toiling away. Only then did she realize where she was.

The tendrils were chest hairs, the overhang a chin, the roots the bones and sinews of Biden Firth's neck, into which she was burrowing like a rat.

She shot upright in bed, her neck damp with sweat, the covers bunched in her fists, and choked back a sob. Biden Firth was haunting her indeed.

7

"You're going to Maine?"

"I don't know what else to do." Ann, haggard from her restless night, poured herself another cup of coffee.

"Well ..." Mike began, then took a hefty drink from his own mug as he cast about for alternatives.

"I think it's a good idea," said Scott. "Mr. Masser will be able to see what's up, and maybe he'll have an idea of how to get rid of whatever is causing Annie to hurt herself."

"But he's such a ..." Mike began irritably, then trailed off again.

"It would be discreet," said Ann. "I know Garrick won't tell anyone about this unless we want word to get out."

"Oh, he acts like he's all publicity-averse, but he makes sure all his stunts get in the news. Plus he charges a fortune. How much is this going to cost?"

Ann hadn't thought to ask that. "Don't worry about it, I'll take care of it."

"So the plan is to have Walt fly you back home and then

you'll drive to Maine? I'll bet you could drive to Maine from here in about the same time," said Mike, determined to be difficult.

"Sure, if you'll loan me your car," Ann shot back.

"I have an idea," said Scott. "Why don't I drive you to Maine?"

Ann and Mike turned to him.

"Well, if Ann needs to be driven to Maine, I can certainly do that," said Mike sheepishly.

"Don't be silly," said Scott, "you can't stand Garrick Masser, it would be a disaster."

"I can drive myself to Maine if that seems to be the most efficient plan," said Ann. "I could rent a car here—"

"Sweetie, if he can make you stab yourself with a knife, let's not give him a chance to see what he can do with a car."

Ann and Mike looked at each other, their eyes wide.

Scott patted Ann on the arm. "I'm probably being an alarmist, but just to be on the safe side ..."

Scott called his supervisor at Bryn Mawr Rehab, where he worked as a physical therapist, and explained that he was going to take some personal time to take a relative out of state to consult with a specialist of an unspecified type. If it had been up to Scott they would have left that morning, but less impetuous heads prevailed.

Ann called Garrick to let him know they would be arriving the next day. She tapped away on her iPad as they talked.

"Hey, Garrick, you have a website!"

"Of course I have a website."

Ann scanned the page for tabs or links. "It's only one page."

"Of course it's only one page. Why would I need more than one page?"

"It gives a business address in Somesville. We can get a place to stay near there. Do you have any recommendations?"

"How should I know? I live here," Garrick responded in what Ann suspected he thought of as his patient voice.

"I'll see if we can find somewhere in town."

"There is nowhere in town. That I know of," he amended.

Ann pulled up a map. "You're right, I don't see much in Somesville. Looks like it's not that far from Bar Harbor."

"Good heavens."

"What?"

"Tourists."

"Well, where then?"

"Perhaps Southwest Harbor. Fewer tourists. Or at least fewer cruise-ship tourists."

After a brief internet search, Ann located an appealing-looking inn and called to make a reservation.

"Is the inn haunted?" she asked, as she always did when making lodging reservations.

"No, I'm afraid not," said the innkeeper despondently, anticipating a lost booking from someone obviously interested in ghosts.

"Perfect," said Ann. "We'll likely be staying two nights, maybe longer if the rooms are available."

ONE OF THE standing agenda items when Ann came to West Chester was for her and Mike to review her financial position. Ann counted herself lucky to have a brother who was a professional financial planner, and she was happy to let Mike take care of her bank account as well as her consulting engagements. Since Ann and Scott wouldn't leave for Maine until the following morning, she and Mike decided to take advantage of the free morning for the review.

They walked from Mike and Scott's townhouse to Mike's

West Chester office, located over an art gallery on High Street, on their way passing near the house where they had grown up. Once at Mike's office, they settled behind his desk, sharing a 3 Musketeers bar from which Ann cut bite-sized slices with her Swiss Army knife while Mike tried to interest her in a series of graphs and charts he brought up on his monitor.

Their parents had left them with a considerable inheritance, the income from which Mike referred to as the "paying-the-rent" money while the income from Ann's spirit-sensing engagements and his financial-planning business was the "having fun" money.

"The fun will have to be curtailed somewhat if we don't start accepting some engagements," said Mike, clicking through reports. "Considering how your abilities are expanding—especially you seeing Dan and Amita's daughter like you did—we could raise our rates considerably."

"I don't think it will be that way for all of them."

"Still, no way to know for sure unless you give it a try. I can keep charging the old rates for now if you want. Maybe that woman in Virginia who wants her horse barn checked out ...?"

Ann pushed her chair back from the desk. "I could just stop, right? I mean, maybe I'd have to cut back on some expenses, but we don't really need the money."

"You'll need a chunk of money if you're asking Garrick Masser for advice."

She waved her hand dismissively. "I said I'd take care of that."

Mike swiveled his chair to face her. "No, we don't need it. But why do you want to stop?"

"Why would I want to keep doing it?"

"A., you stopped a murderer—how many people can say that?"

"I didn't stop him, I just gave him a new potential victim—

me. If I hadn't gotten involved, he probably would have spent the rest of his life harmlessly frittering away his family's money."

"You saved his daughter from growing up alongside the man who killed her mother."

"She would never have known that, so what difference would it have made? Besides, her grandparents would have ended up raising her anyway." Ann sat back, arms crossed, staring morosely at the monitor.

Mike reached over and snapped it off. "I feel so bad when you talk like this. You have an extraordinary gift, you can do so much good—"

"I'm doing no good!" Ann burst out. "I got Beau killed, I got myself shot, I got myself in a position where I had to kill someone, for God's sake. I can find people once they're dead, but can I find them when there's still a possibility of helping them? No! If you hadn't decided it would be a good idea to butt into the Firth business—"

"God, I know, I'm so sorry about that, I don't know what I can do to—"

"—and now you want me to keep doing it? To keep putting myself through this? To keep having these pains in my hands? Maybe you're the one who needs the extra money."

She stopped, realizing she had gone a step too far.

Mike clamped his lips shut against his retort, his face flushing. A few moments ticked by, then he said tightly, "That wasn't fair."

"I know, I'm sorry—"

"If you feel like that, you should find someone else to manage the business."

"No, I'm sorry, I don't know why I said that—"

Mike stood and strode to the window overlooking High Street. Ann sat miserably at the desk, drilling a hole in the candy bar with the knife. After a moment, Mike turned, his color subsiding.

"I mean it. I never want you to think I'm in it for the money. I just wish you appreciated your skill as much as the people around you do—me, Scott, your clients, the spirits of the people you find. And I have no objection—none—to guaranteeing that I don't benefit from your work financially if you decide to keep doing it. You need to do what's right for you and I will do my best to butt out of it." He gave her a slight smile. "Even if it means curtailing the fun."

Ann felt her throat get tight. He might be her baby brother, but even as children it was usually Mike who had defended her and rarely vice versa. She sliced a chunk off the candy bar, speared it with the knife, and held it out to Mike.

"Let's see how it goes. But don't be a pest about it, okay?"

"Me? A pest?" said Mike with mock effrontery.

"Yes, hard as that is to imagine," replied Ann. "Can we do something else? This is boring."

They decided on pork sandwiches at the Mexican restaurant.

8

Early the next morning, Ann found Scott humming away in the kitchen, filling a cooler bag.

"I'll bet we can find someone to sell us food along the way," she said, getting a banana out of a basket on the counter.

"Rest-stop food—yuck," said Scott.

"Humor him," said Mike, seated at the kitchen table with a cup of coffee, reading the BBC news on his iPad. He and Ann were accustomed to avoiding news about events that might turn into consulting engagements, so on the theory that the UK was farther than they were likely to go for business, they generally used the BBC to keep current on world events. "He's so excited. It almost—*almost*—makes me want to go along, even if it meant putting up with The Count."

"You're missing out on a road trip because you can't contain your snarkiness around Mr. Masser," said Scott happily.

Scott and Ann were about to start loading up Scott's Prius when Mike appeared with his keychain.

"Why don't you take Audrey, it'll be more comfortable," he said, handing the keys to Scott.

"You're letting us take Audrey? Are you sure?" Audrey was an older model Audi, but so meticulously maintained by the car detailer, to whom Mike sent a bottle of good vodka every Christmas, that it could pass as new.

"Sure, why not. You're a better driver than I am anyway." Mike patted the hood of the car. "Take good care of my girl."

Ann and Scott headed out at eight o'clock. The day was sunny and the weather continued to be unusually warm. Ann threw her down parka in the trunk only at Scott's insistence.

Scott had a five-miles-over-the-speed-limit, both-hands-on-the-wheel, cruise-control-is-cheating driving style that Ann found preferable to Mike's somewhat competitive approach. Scott chatted as they drove, commenting on the scenery or other drivers or whatever song was on the radio; Ann found it soothing because he seemed equally content whether or not she responded. As they navigated the area around New York City, she teased him about his tendency to make excuses for irresponsible driving: "Goodness, he must be late for an appointment," or, "He probably couldn't see me—he's missing his side-view mirrors."

At various stops throughout the trip, Scott produced from the cooler a mid-morning snack, lunch, and afternoon tea, complete with a thermos of Earl Grey. They consumed each picnic meal in as scenic a spot as Scott could find without venturing too far from the route.

It was dark when they passed through Trenton, Maine, and crossed the short bridge over Mount Desert Narrows that brought them onto Mount Desert Island. In the dark, only the lack of lights distinguished the water from the land. They passed through Somesville and continued on to Southwest Harbor.

The inn where they were staying was located on a residential side street. Theirs was the only car in the small parking lot, but the house was cheerfully lit. Scott got his small leather satchel from the trunk. Ann had a wheeled carry-on that Mike had loaned her—since she kept clothes at Mike and Scott's house, she never had to bring luggage when she visited them. The temperature had dropped as they drove north, and Ann was glad to have the parka.

Scott held the door for her and they stepped into the lobby of the inn. It was charmingly furnished in a style that suggested Victorian without being cloying. The walls were hung with quite nice paintings of Maine coastal scenes, each with a discreet tag with the artist's name and the painting's price. Classical music played softly. A bowl of Hershey's Kisses sat on the reception desk next to a small brass bell, which Scott rang.

The person who appeared could hardly have been less in tune with the surroundings: black hair so short it was almost a crew cut, pale skin made more pale-looking by the dark liner around the eyes, a row of rings along the edge of each ear, a nose ring, and a lip ring. A frayed denim jacket, fully buttoned up, hung loose on a thin frame.

"Welcome to the Clarks Point Inn," said their greeter, whose light voice revealed it to be a girl. She managed to sound like a recording, except for the slight lisp caused by the post in her tongue.

"Good evening!" said Scott. "I'm Scott Pate and this is Ann Kinnear, and we have a reservation for the next several nights."

"My mom had to go out so she asked me to show you to your rooms when you got here," she said, striking a balance between following the script her mother had obviously given her while injecting a barely discernible level of sullenness to indicate that this was not how she would have preferred to spend her evening.

"Well, we certainly appreciate that. What's your name?"

"Mace."

"Mace?" asked Ann. "Like ... what you spray on muggers?"

"Uh huh," said Mace.

"Pleased to meet you, Mace," said Scott.

Mace nodded an acknowledgement. "Do you need help with your bags?"

"Oh no, I think we can manage—can't we, Annie?"

Ann would have like to have asked the girl to carry the bags just to see how that would have gone—Ann guessed that, as light as they were traveling, their bags would have represented a good portion of the girl's own weight. "Yup, we can manage," she said.

"Right this way," said Mace woodenly.

She led them to the second floor and showed them into adjoining rooms, both just as tastefully decorated as the first floor. Ann guessed Mace hated the decor. "Is there anything I can get you?" It was clear that the desired answer was "no."

"Do you have any recommendations for where we could get dinner without driving too far?" asked Scott.

"I think Bloom's Cafe is still open," said Mace. "It's right down the street."

"Within walking distance?"

"Yeah."

"Perfect!" said Scott. "We may be here for a few days—is there anything you especially like to do on the island that you would recommend?"

"Uh ... hiking and stuff?"

"Where do you like to go hiking?"

"Well, not me, but tourists, you know ..." she mumbled. Mace was clearly not comfortable when the interaction with the guests went off script.

"But what do *you* like to do? It's always much more interesting to try out things that people who live in a place enjoy doing."

"Well," said Mace, warming to the topic despite herself. "Bar Harbor is just a tourist trap during the day, but there's stuff to do there at night."

"Oh yes? And what do you do there?"

"Well ... they have live music." Mace was working hard not to let her enthusiasm show.

"No kidding, what kind?"

"All kinds. Jazz sometimes."

"I love jazz!" exclaimed Scott.

"Yeah, they get some pretty good people coming through." Mace smiled shyly, and Ann could see that underneath all that metal and the black hair—that, based on the girl's fair complexion, was probably naturally blond—was a non-truculent person struggling to get out.

"Well, I'd very much like to see that," said Scott. "Could you let me know how I can get more information?"

"Sure, I'll print some stuff out for you." Mace sidled past Ann and banged down the stairs, her heavy boots thudding on the treads.

Since it was late, Ann and Scott didn't bother unpacking before walking the short distance into town for a late dinner. Bloom's Cafe had a coffee bar near the door, a bar decorated with strings of white lights along the back wall, and fewer than a dozen tables with mismatched wooden chairs crowded into the remaining space. There was a small but boisterous group at the bar, but Ann and Scott were the only diners. They both ordered risotto, which Ann deemed to be too rich but Scott enjoyed, and Bar Harbor Real Ales.

After their plates were cleared away, Scott glanced at his watch. "Want to go back to the inn?"

"Not yet, it's nice here. We could have an after-dinner drink."

"Okay. What do you want?"

"Hmmm ... How about a glass of port?"

"Okay." Scott went to the bar to place their order and struck up a conversation with the group there. In a few minutes he returned to the table with Ann's port and another beer for himself.

"Guess what I found out!"

"What?"

"It's not Mount 'DEH-zert,' it's Mount 'De-ZERT.'"

"That's weird."

"It's French for 'barren'—I guess because it looked barren to the first Europeans who came here. Who must have been French."

"Huh."

"Plus I learned that we're 'from away'!"

"What?"

"'From away' means we aren't locals. Evidently your family has to have been here forever or you're considered 'from away.' I guess Mr. Masser must still be considered 'from away,' even though you said he's lived here for quite a while." He took a sip of his beer. "Mike would think that was interesting." He pulled out his mobile phone and speed dialed Mike.

9

Garrick gripped the steering wheel and hunched forward, peering out the windshield, although he would have been able to see equally well had he sat back. One of his greatest annoyances with his current engagement was that he was not able to hire someone to drive him to it, especially since it meant driving at night, which he particularly disliked.

Garrick dreamed of a vintage Rolls Royce and a chauffeur, but even his excellent reputation and delivered results were not quite enough to fund that dream. He had compromised on a black Cadillac Fleetwood with a comfortable amount of room for his long legs, and usually hired a neighbor to drive him. But the client's insistence on secrecy extended to not having anyone know the location of the engagement, so he was forced to drive himself.

He saw the sign for Lynam's Point Road and slowly turned off, much to the relief of the motorist who had followed him from Somesville. Lynam's Point Road ran perpendicular to Indian Point Road for a short distance, then turned left, to the south, before looping north to run along the shore of the peninsula. Most of the peninsula was part of Acadia National Park and thus undeveloped, but as he approached the northern tip of the peninsula, he passed between two stone pillars that marked the entrance to the Lynam's Point Hotel property. Shortly after that, he passed on his left the Lynam family cemetery, utilitarian granite headstones surrounded by an unpicturesque chain-link fence. Finally, a circular drive came into view. It was lined with dim lights, the uneven spacing of which showed where some of the bulbs had burned out. Beyond the glow of the lights, one could sense the mass of the old hotel blocking the stars beyond. Other than the lights at the drive, which the client had turned on—somewhat reluctantly—at Garrick's request, the only illumination was the dim glow of a lamp burning in the hotel's lobby.

Garrick eased the Cadillac behind a rust-pocked Jeep Cherokee and, getting a flashlight out of the glove compartment, unfolded himself from the car. The crunch of his boots on the gravel drive was loud over the murmur of the water surrounding the hotel on its point of land. The client must have been watching for him because as soon as he stepped onto the veranda, the lights along the drive were extinguished.

Ellen Lynam pushed open the door of the hotel and stood aside to let Garrick in, then closed and locked the door behind him. She was a large woman, not fat but physically formidable. Weathered skin and thick hair pulled back in a messy bun made her look older than her forty years. She wore worn corduroy pants and a hand-knit sweater, stretched unnaturally long by the weight of whatever she carried in its pockets. Thick tortoise-shell glasses magnified her hazel eyes. A delicate jade pendant hung from a black ribbon around her neck.

Garrick turned off the flashlight and dropped it into a coat pocket, then drew the collar of his coat up. "It's colder in here than it is outside."

"Good evening to you too, Garrick," she replied, leading the way through the lobby. "I can't heat the whole building for just the two of us. I have a space heater running in the lounge."

They entered what had, in more prosperous times, served as the hotel's restaurant and now, in these leaner times, as an overly large and under-furnished sitting room. Along the wall to the left was an elaborate bar, its shelves now bare. On the right was a wall of windows, cold mirrors against the darkness outside. Three dining room chairs stood in the center of the room, grouped around a small heater that clicked softly.

Garrick took off his gloves, rubbed his hands together, then pulled out a pocket watch and glanced at it. "It's early, we could put the kettle on."

Ellen glanced at her wristwatch. "All right, but let's do it quickly."

Garrick followed Ellen to the far end of the lounge and through a pair of swinging doors that led to the hotel kitchen. The kitchen was a strange amalgam of large and small scale. The wide metal counters held a microwave, a toaster oven, a four-cup coffeemaker, and a considerable amount of clutter for one person—a scattering of unopened mail, cans of fruit and boxes of cereal, some unwashed plates near the sink. On the large central worktable, a meat mallet held open a food-spotted book. A stack of *Hotel Management* magazines threatened to spill onto the floor. A small refrigerator, more appropriate for a college dorm room, hummed in the corner next to the large commercial refrigerator, the door of which was propped open, the interior dark. Ellen took a tea kettle from the stove to the cavernous sink.

"Tea?" she asked.

"No, just water."

She filled the kettle and set it to heat on one of the burners of the industrial gas range.

Garrick passed back through the swinging doors and walked through the lounge to the lobby. A painting hung in shadows over the fireplace. Even in the dark, Garrick could picture its somewhat primitive depiction of the hotel in its heyday. Except for a couple of chairs upholstered in faded chintz, most of the furniture had been covered with sheets, and rolled-up rugs had been pushed against the wall. Garrick remembered when those chairs held lounging visitors and the rugs muffled the steps of Topsiders-clad feet.

Soon he heard the whistle of the kettle and a minute later Ellen appeared with steaming mugs—one of which had the string of a tea bag draped over its rim. She handed the other to Garrick. They stood looking out at the lobby for a minute, sipping their hot drinks.

"We've had lots of sensings here, haven't we, Garrick?" said Ellen as she glanced around the lobby.

"Yes."

"Remember Mr. Holl, the one who died of a heart attack in his room, who kept coming to the front desk asking for his money back?"

"Yes."

"And that Indian you saw by the boathouse?"

"Yes."

"They're still with us, aren't they?"

"Not Mr. Holl."

"Well, no, you did a good job of explaining to him that there wasn't anything we could do for him." Ellen sipped her tea. "It's too bad the 'Evening with Spirits' idea didn't work out. Tourists usually like that sort of thing."

"Tourists usually like seeing the spirits for themselves, not just being told about them."

"Yes, you warned me, but you were a good sport to give it a try anyway."

"Yes, well ..." Garrick took a sip of his hot water.

"I wonder why we never saw Daddy."

"He might have been content to pass on."

"Yes, maybe." She swirled her tea contemplatively with the tea bag. "But no one really completely leaves, don't you think? Dying isn't really about disappearing, it's about experiencing existence in a different way." She waited for a moment for a reply and, not receiving one, prompted, "Don't you think?"

Garrick sighed. "We've had this conversation before, Ellen. I can only tell you that some people continue to exist as a spirit that I can perceive and some don't."

"Well, I think when a person dies they don't leave us, they just ... change. Maybe change for the better."

"It's a theory."

"Although certainly Loring hasn't changed for the better. He's just as difficult dead as alive."

"Loring had a difficult life—inheriting the hotel so young when your father died, taking care of you."

"Yes," said Ellen grudgingly, then burst out, "But he never loved it! He never loved the hotel like Daddy and I did!"

"It was foisted on him when he was seventeen. I think he had other plans for his life than running a hotel. Plus, he had a seven-year-old sister to care for. And your father didn't leave him in the best position financially."

Ellen took a distracted sip of tea. "Daddy had a lot of problems to deal with. MDI wasn't as popular in the seventies."

"Hmmm," said Garrick noncommittally.

"Plus," she said reluctantly, "I think Mother had more of a head for business from what Daddy and Loring told me. They met when they both worked at one of the grand houses in Bar Harbor, did you know that?"

Garrick did, in fact, know that. He nodded.

"If she hadn't died when I was born, I might have learned a lot from her. I've seen pictures of her, she was very pretty."

Ellen put her mug down on the registration desk, crossed the room, and straightened the painting over the fireplace. She turned and surveyed the lobby and ran her fingers along the frayed piping of one of the chintz chairs. "Garrick," she said anxiously, "if we don't find the lady, some rich bigwig is going to tear down the hotel and put up some modern monstrosity. Probably with a pool, for God's sake. Surrounded by water and they always want to put in a pool." Ellen glanced at her watch. "It's almost time, bring your water along," she said.

Garrick followed Ellen back to the lounge and settled himself into one of the chairs. Ellen sat in another that had a notepad and a pencil lying underneath it.

They sat in silence for some time, Ellen glancing impatiently at her watch. Finally she said, "Is he here yet?"

"No, Ellen, he's not here yet. I'll tell you when he arrives."

"He's usually here by now," said Ellen fretfully.

"He's not going to be any more considerate dead than alive."

They sat in silence again—Ellen fidgeting, Garrick with his hands clasped loosely in his lap.

Finally Garrick said, "He's here." His gaze was fixed on the doorway to the lobby, then tracked to the third chair.

Ellen glanced toward the chair, then switched her gaze back to Garrick. "Ask him where the lady is."

Garrick sighed. "Loring, Ellen would like to know where the lady is."

"Tell him about the deadline—"

Garrick waved a hand to silence her, his gaze fixed on the invisible presence in the third chair. He shook his head once, then a few moments later said, "No, that's not what she—" and then, "I don't think it's necessary to provide the entire—" and finally sighed resignedly. "He's ready to talk about the lady."

"It's about time!" said Ellen with relief.

"But he says you need to hear the whole story."

"Uh, okay ..." said Ellen suspiciously.

"It may take some time, he says."

"No! Tell him we're running out of time! We only have five more days!" She looked at her watch. "It's after midnight—we only have four more days!"

Garrick turned back to the chair. "Loring, your sister needs to find this lady she is looking for soon. She believes the lady can help her save the hotel. She's running out of time." He sat looking attentively toward the third chair, then turned back to Ellen. "He thinks it's important for you to understand some things about the lady first."

"Garrick, doesn't he want to save the hotel?" wailed Ellen.

"Evidently not tonight."

Ellen jumped to her feet. "Can't you make him tell us where she is?"

"What inducement could I provide that would make him tell us something he obviously doesn't want to tell us tonight?"

Ellen flopped back into her chair. "Does he know he's making me crazy?"

"Yes, I believe he does," said Garrick.

Loring Lynam sat back in his chair. He was a lean man in his late forties, with short, uncombed brown hair, skin darkened by a lifetime spent in the Maine elements, and light gray eyes, now narrowed speculatively at Garrick.

"So we're getting down to the wire, eh, Garrick?"

"Yes, Loring."

"And she thinks the lady's going to help her out of this jam?"

"That's her hope."

"Well, to understand the lady, you have to understand Dad."

"Very well."

"And to understand Dad, you have to understand about his mother."

Garrick raised an eyebrow. "The connection is becoming somewhat tenuous."

"Humor me, Garrick."

"Do I have a choice?"

"None at all. One of the benefits of being dead." Loring settled in his chair, getting comfortable—if getting comfortable was a concept one could apply to a spirit.

10

1936

Six-year-old Chip Lynam was examining the equipment that would smooth the ground where the hotel's new croquet court was to be built when he saw Uncle Edward's truck trundle up the drive, his mother in the passenger seat. He ran to the veranda, snapping a flower off one of the potted geraniums as he passed. He slipped in the side door to the lobby, skirted the registration desk where Amy, one of the new hires, was chatting with a guest, and snuck down the hall to the kitchen. He was relieved not to have run into his father, who didn't like seeing Chip in the public areas of the hotel. He scrambled up on a stool at the end of the counter, the flower hidden behind his back.

His mother came through the back door followed by Uncle Edward, who was carrying a box of produce. Uncle Edward was the new cook, one of several new hires who were filling up the staff rooms on the top floor of the hotel. He was the most fun of any of them—he let Chip sit in the kitchen with him and told him stories about growing up in Canada. Sometimes he played catch with Chip on the gravel drive outside the kitchen entrance. Chip didn't have a lot of experience with catch and wasn't very good, but Uncle Edward, who had not only lived in another country but also seemed pretty smart about sports, had given him some tips and he was getting better.

His mother unpinned her straw hat and put it on a shelf next to the back door, then joined Uncle Edward at the big worktable in the center of the kitchen to sort through the produce. Uncle Edward said something—Chip didn't catch what it was—and his mother laughed. Chip loved to watch his mother when she was happy. She had been happier now that there were more guests and they had been able to hire some help.

Her dark hair was pulled back and caught in a small clip at her neck. Her dark eyes danced with a smile as she chatted with Uncle Edward. Her arms were rounded where they extended from the sleeves of her flowered dress, but her waist was small. Best of all was her skin—pinkish and smooth, like the inside of a rose petal.

She turned from the worktable to the sink, a small smile still flickering on her lips, while Uncle Edward continued to sort through the produce. She washed her hands then dried them, her smile gradually fading. She turned the towel in her hands much longer than Chip thought was needed to get them dry, her movements rote, her expression distracted. She gazed out the window where the afternoon sun brightened the trees and set off a sparkle on the water beyond.

She absently folded the hand towel and laid it on the counter next to the sink. She patted her hair and, discovering a strand that had come loose from the clip, unfastened the clip and began smoothing her hair back to reattach it.

Just at that moment, Uncle Edward glanced up from the pile of vegetables and noticed Chip. "Hey, sport, whatcha up to?"

His mother turned, framed in the window. Wisps of hair

caught the backlight. There was a moment before her eyes focused on him. Where a minute before she had been lively and laughing, she now looked weary and distracted.

Then her eyes found him. She swept her hair back and caught it in the clip, then crossed the kitchen to where he sat and tousled his hair.

"What are you doing inside on such a pretty day, my little man?" Her voice had a hint of a French lilt, inherited from parents who had never bothered to learn English after they moved to Mount Desert from Quebec after the Great War.

"I brought you a flower!" He produced the flower from behind his back.

His mother smiled at him. "That's nice of you to think of bringing me a flower, but perhaps you shouldn't pick your gifts from the flowerpots on the veranda."

Chip flushed.

"But it's very pretty, Chip. Thank you." She kissed him on top of the head. She took one of the small bud vases that, with a rosebud from the garden, had decorated the tables at breakfast, added Chip's flower to it, and set it on the window ledge over the sink.

Uncle Edward disappeared into the pantry just as Chip heard the clack of heels coming down the hallway that led from the lobby to the kitchen. Amy appeared at the door.

"Mrs. VanValin would like tea on the veranda."

"Milk or sugar?"

"Just sugar."

"All right. Thank you, Amy, it will be out in a minute."

Amy nodded and disappeared back through the door.

His mother put the kettle on and prepared a tray with a china cup and saucer, teaspoon, tea strainer, sugar bowl, and sugar tongs. She folded a cloth napkin on the corner of the tray and, glancing around the kitchen, added one of the other bud vases to the tray—not, Chip was happy to see, the one with his flower in it. When the kettle whistled, she used the boiling water to warm a small teapot, then added the tea leaves and filled the pot. She went to the door to the hall, pushed it open, and glanced out. Through the open door, Chip could hear Amy's voice in conversation with a guest. His mother started to remove her apron and then glanced at Chip. He sat up straighter. She examined him appraisingly and then a small smile tugged at her mouth.

"Do you want to bring Mrs. VanValin her tea?"

Chip could scarcely believe what he was hearing. He scrambled down from his stool and crossed to the counter where the tray was. His mother hefted it experimentally, then removed the flower vase.

"It's going to be heavy," she said.

"I can do it," said Chip, reaching out his arms.

"All right then." She lifted the tray by its handles and bent down to hand it to him. "Now don't try to hold it out from your body, rest the back of the tray on your belly." She got the tray positioned. "Now hold onto the handles." He gripped the handles. "Have you got it?" He nodded vigorously. "I'm going to let go now, you let me know if it's too heavy." He nodded again, his eyes glued to the tray. Gradually his mother released the weight onto his hands then, letting go, stepped back. "Okay?" He nodded again, too nervous to speak. "Let me get the door for you. Walk very slowly, and watch the sill." Chip inched toward the door. "That's it. Still okay?" Chip was too focused on keeping the tray level to nod. His mother opened the door. "You go ahead, I'll get the doors for you."

Chip inched gingerly across the kitchen and stepped over the sill, the cup rattling ominously on its saucer. The hallway to the lobby, which he normally skipped through in an instant, suddenly looked as long as a bowling alley. He switched from a walk to a shuffle, which seemed to keep the china quieter. He could hear his mother following him down the hallway, but he didn't dare turn around to look at her.

"Very good, Chip," she said when he got to the end of the hall. A group of young women was chatting near the fireplace. One of them saw him and nudged her neighbor and gestured with her chin and her friend turned to watch Chip carry the tray through the lobby. Behind the registration desk, Amy glanced up.

"Oh, Mrs. Lynam, I can get that," she said, starting around the desk.

"No need, Amy, Chip's got it."

His mother passed him to open the screen door to the veranda. "Mind the step down," she murmured.

Chip's arms were starting to shake, the cup and saucer rattling.

"Where's Mrs. VanValin sitting?" she asked Amy.

"Right around the corner," Amy said, sounding anxious.

His mother came up behind him and put her hand on his shoulder. "Right around the corner, Chip," she said.

Chip felt as if his arms were going to crack off, like a too-small tree branch he had once tried to swing from. He shuffled down the veranda and around the corner of the building and almost ran the tray into Mrs. VanValin's wooden rocker. Mrs. VanValin was turned in her chair, having been alerted to Chip's approach by the rattling, which was reaching machine-gun proportions.

"Well, if it isn't young Master Lynam," she said. She pulled out a wicker table from next to her chair and reached for the tray. "May I take that from you?"

"I can do it," squeaked Chip tautly. With his last bit of strength, he hoisted the tray up and crashed it down onto the table.

Mrs. VanValin jumped. "Heavens!" she said, putting her hand to her wattled throat.

Chip stepped back and looked in consternation toward his mother. She stepped forward to survey the tray. "All in order," she said. "Will there be anything else, Mrs. VanValin?"

"No thank you, Mrs. Lynam. Thank you, Chip." She pulled a coin purse out of a bag of knitting next to her chair, removed a quarter, and held it out to Chip. Chip looked at his mother again.

"Oh, no need, Mrs. VanValin, Chip's just practicing for when he'll be running the hotel." She rested her hand on his shoulder for a moment, then said, "Come along, Chip."

He followed her back inside, his fingers cramped, his aching arms hanging at his sides, his legs trembly.

Maybe things had turned around. Maybe he would always be this happy.

11

A nn and Scott ate a breakfast at the inn featuring blueberries in many forms. They were the only guests and the innkeeper, Nan, who had returned from her errand of the previous night to resume her duties, hovered about with offers of additional pancakes or coffee top-offs. She seemed especially intent on fattening up Ann.

"I hope Maisie took good care of you when you checked in," she said.

"Ah, Maisie," said Ann.

"Yes. How did she introduce herself?" asked Nan nervously.

"Oh, definitely 'Maisie,'" said Scott.

After breakfast they headed out for Ann's appointment with Garrick. The morning sun hadn't done much to dispel the chill of the previous night, and Ann pulled her parka more snugly around her—she had lost her resistance to cold along with her weight.

They took Main Street north out of Southwest Harbor, past the prosperous-looking storefronts and the tiny shingled library set back from the street behind a tiny square of lawn. The businesses spaced out as they left town, giving way to

white clapboard houses sitting close to the road, some adver-
tising services such as landscaping or small-engine repair, a
number with For Sale signs posted. Soon, the deciduous trees
near town gave way to pines, beyond which rose the gray-green
mounds of low mountains. Blocky granite outcroppings pushed
out of the pebbly soil. They passed a body of water on their left,
the October sun glinting on its surface. Ann glanced down at a
map Nan had given them on which she was following their
progress.

"That's Echo Lake. Look," she said to Scott, pointing at the
map. "All the bodies of water run north to south."

"Glaciers. They scraped out the valleys."

"How do you know this stuff?"

"Didn't you have one of those books about the island in your
room?" asked Scott. "It has lots of interesting stuff in it."

"If you were left at the kitchen table with a cereal box, you'd
find something interesting on it," said Ann with a smile.

"Never underestimate the educational value of a cereal box,"
said Scott.

Soon after they left Echo Lake behind, another body of
water appeared on their right—Somes Sound, which cut
through the middle of Mount Desert Island and, according to
Ann's internet research, separated the quiet western side from
the more touristy eastern side. Pine woods gave way to leafy
trees and the ubiquitous white clapboard houses as they
approached Somesville, where Garrick lived and conducted his
consulting business. They passed a ridiculously picturesque
church—more white clapboard—whose steeple balcony was
encircled by a white picket fence.

"Here we are," said Scott, pulling up across the street from a
nineteenth-century Federal-style house whose light gray clap-
boards looked renegade among the uniform white of the other
buildings. The fact that Garrick ran his business from the house

was indicated only by a small brass sign that read "Garrick Masser, Consulting."

"I don't know how long I'll be," said Ann. "Do you want to go do something and I'll call you when I'm done?"

"Sure," said Scott. "There's supposed to be a cute building down the road, I think I'll go take some pictures of that. Also there's a library, maybe I'll check that out."

"Another one? There's one right down the road in Southwest Harbor."

"There are loads of libraries on this island," he said enthusiastically.

"How do you know that?"

Scott raised his eyebrows.

"Book in the inn?"

"I told you it had interesting stuff in it."

Ann patted Scott's knee. "I'll call you when I'm done." Scott waited until she had crossed the road before pulling away.

She took a flagstone walk across the small, minimally landscaped yard, crossed the bare, freshly swept porch, and tapped the door with the heavy brass knocker.

In a moment, the door swept open and Garrick Masser stood in the doorway. Even with his perennially stooped posture he stood over six feet tall, and with his hooked nose, longish hair—black shot with gray—and gaunt frame he brought to mind an emaciated vulture.

"Ann, my dear," he said in a gloomy monotone.

"Hi, Garrick," said Ann. She took a step forward, then pulled up short when Garrick didn't stand aside to let her in. Instead, he peered around and behind her—as if, Ann thought, he was looking for another visitor. Then she realized that was exactly what he was doing. She stood still under this scrutiny until Garrick uttered a muffled "hmph" and beckoned her inside.

The symmetry of the exterior of the house was continued in

the interior, which, to Ann's eye, appeared to have been well cared for and largely unmodernized. The center hall was dark, the only light coming from the open front door and from a wrought-iron chandelier. The stairs to the second floor were on the left side of the hall, with a bench of the same era as the house on the right wall. The wall above the bench held a series of framed, handwritten, antique-looking documents. Near the door was a row of pegs, on one of which hung a long black coat. The door to the left was closed. Garrick waved her through to the room on the right.

On the wall opposite the door was a brick fireplace flanked by two narrow windows. Two windows on the right-hand wall overlooked the front yard. Wall space not occupied by windows, fireplace, or doors was lined with floor-to-ceiling bookcases, the higher shelves of which were accessible via a wheeled ladder attached to a brass rail at the top of the bookcase. Ann had always coveted such a setup but had never lived in a house with ceilings high enough to justify it.

To the right, facing toward the center of the room, was a large desk, with two well-worn leather wing chairs facing it. Garrick waved her toward the chairs and took a seat behind the desk. Ann shrugged out of her parka and deposited it on one of the chairs and sat in the other.

Garrick rested his elbows on the arms of his chair, steepled his fingers, and peered at her over them, his eyes continuing to flicker around her. Ann sighed and settled in for the examination.

After a minute or so, Garrick said, "Well."

Ann raised her eyebrows expectantly.

Garrick rose from behind the desk and circled behind her chair, then sat down again. "There might be something."

"What is it?" she asked, startled. She somehow hadn't expected Garrick to perform his assessment so quickly.

"It's hard to tell. Whatever it is, it's very faint."

"A spirit?"

"Perhaps. It came in with you."

Ann glanced around nervously. "Where is it?"

"Behind you. It's a bit amorphous."

Ann felt the hair on her neck stir. She had never been on this side of a sensing before. She turned in her chair and looked behind her, but saw nothing.

"Is it Biden Firth?"

"I have no idea, I can't even tell if it's human." Garrick resumed his examination of Ann and her immediate surroundings. When it became clear he was going to do this without any accompanying conversation, Ann passed the time trying to read the titles of the books on the shelves, none of which looked familiar and many of which appeared to be in foreign languages. Ann, a book lover herself, had the library of an inveterate reader, but Garrick Masser had the library of a scholar.

Finally Garrick sat back in his chair. "So, tell me about what you're experiencing."

Ann recapped the series of injuries to her hands and described the connection Joe had made to Biden Firth's intentionally inflicted injuries.

"Have you had any incidents since you left Pennsylvania?"

Ann thought back over her uneventful trip up to Maine. "No, nothing."

"Have you sensed anything?"

Ann shook her head.

"Not at all? How about when you were in the hospital?"

"There were spirits at the hospital, but I didn't have a sense that any of them were especially interested in me. And I don't recall hurting my hands while I was there."

Garrick nodded thoughtfully. "It's possible, if it is Biden Firth, that it took him some time to rally his forces, or that he drew some strength from being in the location where he died once you returned home."

"But is it him?"

"I told you, it's not clear. For me, a spirit usually appears either much as he or she was in life or not at all. But this whatever-it-is surrounding you could be a weak spirit having difficulty manifesting itself or a strong spirit largely but not completely hiding itself from me. You met Mr. Firth—which would be your guess?"

Ann considered. "Weak, I suppose. He seemed indecisive. Ineffectual. I understand from the detective who investigated the murder that it seems likely he killed his wife after his father chewed him out about an unsuccessful investment, and it may be that his wife also made some insulting comment that made him snap."

"Well, weak isn't necessarily less dangerous than strong. A child playing with matches can burn down a house as quickly as a professional arsonist."

Ann shifted nervously in her chair, resisting the urge to glance over her shoulder. "What can I do about it?"

"I don't know. It's a bit difficult to formulate a plan of attack if one is not even sure who the enemy is. Or what." He gazed thoughtfully at her. "You could go back to the scene of his wife's murder. See if you could leave him there. Like removing muck from one's shoes on a boot scraper," he said, clearly enjoying this rhetorical flourish.

"Do you think that would work?"

After a moment Garrick said, "No. How long are you staying in Maine?"

"As long as I need to."

"I can't imagine an extended stay will be required—within another day or two I should be able to tell you whether it's possible to assist in this matter. However, it might be informative to see you at various times of the day. You killed him in the evening, correct?"

"Jeez, Garrick."

"He died in the evening, correct?" he amended.

"Yes."

"And I believe that he also killed his wife in the evening, yes?"

"Yes, that seemed most likely."

"Very inconvenient, in view of my other engagement."

"Ah, the mysterious 'other engagement.'"

"It's highly confidential."

"So you said."

Garrick raised an eyebrow at her crossly, then took a sip from a mug on his desk. "I can tell you that it involves a woman seeking information from her deceased brother. He appears for only a brief period around midnight and insists on discussing other topics, so it is taking some time to obtain the desired information. There is some urgency to obtaining the information, however, which is why I can't reschedule the engagement."

"What is the information she's looking for?" asked Ann.

Garrick examined her speculatively for some time, then said, "I'm afraid I'm not at liberty—"

"Of course."

Garrick tapped his fingers together. "This evening is not possible. Why don't you come back tomorrow at, say, ten o'clock in the morning and we will see if this whatever-it-is around you has become more clear. If not, and depending on how my engagement goes tonight, perhaps tomorrow evening would be a possibility."

Ann, recognizing her dismissal, stood and retrieved her parka. Garrick followed her to the front door, opened it for her, and shut it behind her without a word.

Ann pulled her cellphone from her knapsack and pushed the speed dial for Scott.

"That was fast," he answered.

"Yes. He saw something but he can't tell what. I'm supposed to come back tomorrow."

"Well, that sounds promising—at least he can see something."

"Yeah." Ann felt unaccountably discouraged, although she realized she shouldn't have expected instant results. "What are you up to?"

"I'm just down the road at that cute building, want to meet me here? Then we could go for a walk, there are lots of hiking trails. I hope you're wearing comfortable shoes."

"When have you known me to wear anything other than comfortable shoes?" said Ann. "I'll see you in a minute." She slipped the phone back in the knapsack, slung the knapsack onto her back, and descended the steps to the walk. She didn't notice Garrick watching her from the window, his hands clasped behind his back, a worried look on his gaunt face.

12

M ount Desert Island reminded her of home.

The hulking masses of the mountains were gentler here on the Maine coast, and the hundreds of jewel-like ponds and lakes of the Adirondacks were replaced with quiet coves and the magnificent stretch of bays and ocean beyond, but the pine trees and boulders lining the well-worn roads, the mix of almost-hidden opulence and tourist kitsch and hard-scrabble living, that sense that the place had not changed much in a hundred years, gave her a pleasant feeling of familiarity with the surroundings.

The warm weather in Pennsylvania had lulled her into a false sense of complacency about her travel wardrobe, and other than the parka that Scott had insisted she bring, she had no other cold-weather accessories. She and Scott drove into Bar Harbor to remedy the situation.

They parked near the village green and strolled down Main Street. The season was winding down, with a few shops already closed. In one that was still doing a brisk business, Ann bought a knit cap and gloves, while Scott found a pair of red flannel pajamas decorated with a pattern of small black moose for Mike.

"From a distance you can't even tell it's moose," said Scott. "I think it's pretty classy, as moose-themed clothing goes." He also insisted on getting Ann a moose-decorated nightshirt, and Ann retaliated by getting him moose-decorated boxer shorts.

After their clothing needs were met, they continued down Main Street toward the water. The old wooden buildings, their second stories painted a jaunty mixture of creams and blues and raspberries, stepped down toward the channel that separated Bar Harbor from Bar Island. Couples and families wandered the sidewalks, gazing in store windows or huddling on the sidewalk benches licking ice cream cones. Cars waited with varying degrees of patience for pedestrians in the crosswalks. At the end of the street, another small park—Agamont Park, according to Scott's map—offered a view of the pleasingly named Sheep Porcupine Island. On the point stood the Bar Harbor Inn, its glass-enclosed dining room jutting prow-like toward the water, its white trim sparkling against the silver of the shingle siding. They stopped at the seawall to take in the view, watching a cruise ship make its way through the narrows assisted by a barge boat, dwarfing the sailboats and lobster boats that dotted the water.

"I wonder if cruise ships are ever haunted," said Ann.

"Not if no one died on it, right?" said Scott.

"Right. I wonder what a cruise line would think if I called up and asked them if anyone had died on a particular ship."

Scott became aware that a couple standing next to them at the seawall had glanced over. He smiled at them and wiggled his fingers at the little boy with them. He turned back to Ann. "Are you thinking of going on a cruise?"

Ann shrugged. "Maybe. Not on one of those giant ships, but maybe one of the small ones."

"Mike and I took that cruise to Bermuda in a smallish one. It was nice. Good food."

"With my luck I'd book a cruise on a clean ship and then someone would die during the cruise."

The couple turned and moved away, herding the little boy ahead of them. Scott sighed and turned back to Ann. "Well, a cruise sounds nice. If you wanted company, maybe Mike could go along."

"What about you?"

"I think I've used up my vacation time for this year."

Ann looked back out at the ship, which was now disappearing behind one of the islands. "Because you're babysitting me."

"Don't be silly, this is fun. What next? Look, there's a place that does whale-watching tours." And Scott and Ann headed down to the pier to see what Bar Harbor had to offer two people with a free afternoon.

13

That evening at the hotel, Loring arrived later than usual. He appeared to be slightly inebriated, although Garrick couldn't recall ever encountering a drunk spirit before. Garrick thought back to the young man he had first met at Lynam's Point so many years ago—doggedly working to keep the hotel afloat, old beyond his years with responsibility. But during the off-seasons when the hotel was closed and his only responsibility was to keep it from falling down over the winter, Loring Lynam had had a reputation as a hard drinker. And in the last few years of his life, it wasn't only during off-season that he had overindulged. When they had found his body, there had been an empty bottle of bourbon in the room.

It appeared that Loring was once again in a storytelling mood.

"So now you know how much Dad loved his mother."

"Yes," said Garrick cautiously.

"What did he say?" asked Ellen.

"Ellen, please don't be a distraction," Garrick said to her and turned back to Loring.

"It's probably helpful for you to know how Dad felt about his father."

"Helpful to whom?" glowered Garrick.

"Oh, I'm sure you'll be able to pick up some gems of wisdom from the story," said Loring. He stood, with that slight over-carefulness of the drunk, and walked to the window overlooking the lawn. "I never had the pleasure of meeting my grandfather—he had a heart attack on a dock in Bernard where he had gone to buy lobsters back when the dining room was open. Forty-nine years old. Forty-nine's a bad age for the Lynam men. Or maybe I should say fifty's a bad age for the Lynam men, since we never get to see it. Anyhow, from some of the stories Dad told—and Dad did love to tell stories—it sounds like Granddad was no treat to live with ..."

14

_1936_

Chip lay in bed, thinking over the day, savoring his triumph with the tea tray. That the hotel would be his someday—he had never thought about that before. It had always been his playground, the hotel itself with its odd nooks and crannies to hide in, the grounds with the pine woods to explore, Lynam Narrows with its trove of interesting pebbles. But if he had to take care of it himself—it might be possible, with his mother's help.

He tossed restlessly as a new thought struck him. If the hotel was his, that would mean it would no longer be his father's. Chip turned that thought over in his mind.

He could just barely remember a time—before all his parents' talk was about where they would find the money to pay for this or that—when his father would laugh and smile. He could remember days when his father would take him—Chip had been just a baby then—down to the water to watch the boats, or throw him in the air so that he would shriek with delight.

Then things had gotten bad—Chip knew from listening to his parents talk when they thought he wasn't around. They talked about the Crash of '29—it was after that that the rooms started to go empty, even in high season. (Chip wondered what could have crashed that would have kept people away from his parents' hotel—maybe a train crash that frightened people traveling from faraway places like New York City and Philadelphia? He figured if it had involved a boat, it would have been called the Wreck of '29.) At first, a few locals had occasionally stopped by to eat in the practically empty dining room, but then his parents had had to close the dining room when they couldn't afford to pay the cook. One season they hadn't opened at all—Chip had been too little to remember it himself, but he had once or twice heard his father refer to it in the same strained tones he used to discuss "bank balance" or "room occupancy."

Just the year before, Chip had more than once woken up in the middle of the night in his bedroom on the top floor of the hotel and, unable to go back to sleep, had gone to his parents' room across the hall to find it empty. He knew that if he went looking for them he would find them, as he had one night, huddled over the ledger books at the big worktable in the hotel's kitchen. The first time he had gone looking for them and peeked through the swinging kitchen door, his father had had his head in his hands and his mother had been distractedly smoking a cigarette, something she never did during the day. He had snuck back to his room hoping they hadn't known he was there—there was something embarrassing about having observed his parents so unguarded and demoralized. A few days later, a truck had come and his father had helped a man load the piano from the now-empty dining room into the back; a few days after that the same happened with the old grandfather clock that his father had taken such pride in winding each Sunday.

But this year business was better. The people his parents

referred to as "the regulars"—some from so long ago he hadn't even been born yet—were back. His father's shoulders weren't quite so stooped these days, and he moved with more purpose, although with an underlying wariness that reminded Chip of a squirrel eating at the bird feeder while keeping an eye out for the neighborhood cat. Even now, with his mother saying things were looking up, it was as if his father believed that only frantic activity would keep bad luck at bay. His only leisure was working in the wood shop in a shed behind the hotel, but even then his projects were almost always for the hotel: repairing a dining room chair or mending balusters broken by guests as they hauled their luggage up the steps to the guest rooms on the second and third floors.

In fact, the only event that had elicited some enthusiasm from his father was the installation of the new elevator—he liked to brag that not even some of the fancy hotels in Portland had elevators yet. Chip longed to operate the sliding door and metal grate, to move the handle that sent the elevator up or down, but his father had made it very clear that the elevator was not a toy and implied that there would be dire consequences if he found Chip using it as such.

His father had said "toy" with such disdain that Chip had begun to fear for his actual toys, and he had fashioned a hiding place for them—a wooden box he kept under his bed. It was possible to see under his bed from the hallway, so he had gotten a board from the workshop of the same color as the floorboards and had propped it up in front of the box. It wouldn't withstand close scrutiny, but it provided effective camouflage from a casual glance.

He would feel better if he had his bear, Timothy—he could put him away before his father came to wake him up in the morning. He climbed out of bed, slid aside the board, pulled out the toy box, and removed Timothy.

But even holding Timothy didn't soothe him. His brain flickered from thought to thought, he couldn't get his legs in a comfortable position, a seam of his pajama bottoms was digging into his hip. He looked at the clock on his bedside table—the big hand was on the two. He squeezed his eyes shut and counted to one hundred several times then opened them again—the big hand was still on the two.

He decided to go downstairs and get a glass of milk. His mother sometimes warmed milk for him when he couldn't sleep, but she wouldn't be up anymore and, since he couldn't use the stove, he hoped cold milk would work just as well as warm.

Even though it was highly unlikely that he would encounter any guests, he pulled on his robe and slipped his feet into his slippers as his father had instructed him to do if he had to leave the top floor at night. He made his way as quietly as he could down the stairs to the first floor and through the hallway that led to the kitchen.

He was just about to push the door open when he heard voices inside, low but strained. It was his mother, his father, and ... Uncle Edward? It sounded like they were arguing and Chip, who avoided arguments whenever possible, had turned to go when he heard his father's angry whisper.

"You whore!"

Chip froze. He heard a murmur from his mother and then the third person—he was pretty sure it was Uncle Edward—and then his father cutting through both their voices.

"Don't you defend her. I can't believe you're even still standing in my kitchen. You traitor." His father's voice was getting louder, violating his own rule that any personal conversations must be whispered so as not to disturb the guests.

Now he could hear Uncle Edward's words as well. "Listen here, Lorry—"

"Don't you call me by my first name—you are the help, you will call me Mr. Lynam," his father hissed.

Then he heard his mother: "Stay out of this, Edward, this is between me and him."

"Ha!" spat his father. "That's rich—if it was between you and me, and he had stayed out of it, we wouldn't be having this conversation, would we?"

"Perhaps not this exact conversation," said his mother, her voice cold. "But it's high time we had some kind of conversation, although I wish it wasn't in these circumstances." There was a pause, and when she spoke again Chip could tell she had moved closer to his father. "Perhaps I should call you Mr. Lynam as well? Am I the help too? Because that's how I feel sometimes. Like the hired girl."

"You're being ridiculous."

"Am I? I remember the look in your eyes when you courted me, like I was something special and precious. You won me with that look. But once we were married, you know what I realized? That I was only as special and precious as your elevator or your ridiculous croquet court."

"I did not ... I ..." his father spluttered. After a pause he said, "You, get out."

"I'm not leaving," said Uncle Edward.

"I need to speak to her."

"You can speak to her with me in the room."

There was a long pause. Chip inched forward and pressed his ear to the door.

Finally he heard his father speak, a strangled sound. "I never thought of you like an elevator or a croquet court, for God's sake. You were ... you are ..."

There was another long pause, and then his mother. "I am what?"

Then Chip heard the scrape of wood on wood. What was

happening in there? Before he had a chance to think, he pushed open the door and stepped into the kitchen.

His mother and Uncle Edward stood next to each other, dressed in their day clothes but looking rumpled, like they had slept in them. His mother's hair was down—he thought of how she had looked earlier that day, when she had stood in front of the window and undone her hair from the clip that held it, but only to fasten it more neatly into its restraint. She never kept her hair down except when she was in their quarters on the top floor, when she would sometimes let Chip brush it. Chip was suddenly jealous that Uncle Edward was getting to see her in this private state.

They faced his father, who was wearing his pajamas and a robe and slippers—an adult version of Chip's own clothes. The scraping sound he had heard was his father pulling out a chair, the back of which he was leaning on, his knuckles white, his face a frightening shade of gray. The three of them turned to Chip.

Uncle Edward said, "Damn," and looked down at his feet.

"Darling—" said his mother. She started toward Chip, but his father stopped her with his words.

"Don't even think about it. You're no mother to him. Stay away from him."

"But—"

"No. Go. Now."

His mother looked from Chip to her husband, and then to Uncle Edward, whose eyes were still on the floor. "But I can't just—"

"I mean it. Go now. When you and"—his father gestured to Uncle Edward with his chin—"get wherever you're going, you let me know and I'll send your things. I want you out of here."

His mother looked back at Chip. Her eyes were weary and disillusioned—as if she expected life to be difficult and people to be cruel, and life and people had lived down to her expectations.

Chip's heart was thudding in his throat. "I can ..." he began, then realized he couldn't, whatever it was. He was too young. He was too small.

"Oh, sweetheart," said his mother. His father began to speak again, but she silenced him with a gesture, without even glancing in his direction. "Chip, I need to leave for a while, but when things settle down we'll work things out. You'll be a good boy for your father, yes?"

Chip tried to say "Yes," but the word caught in his throat.

His mother got her hat from the shelf by the back door and her purse and a sweater from the closet and, with a quick backward glance at Chip, stepped out the door, followed by Uncle Edward.

"And don't you take my truck!" his father called after them in a choked voice.

Chip stared wide-eyed after them, and then turned to his father, who still held onto the back of the chair. His father's face was pasty and his breath whistled in his throat.

"Go upstairs. Go to bed," he said thickly.

Chip backed out of the kitchen, through the swinging door, then turned and ran to the lobby and stood at the window until he saw Uncle Edward's truck go by, his mother a dark silhouette in the passenger seat. As the taillights receded down the drive, he heard his father's steps behind him and he turned, tears of confusion and fear in his eyes.

But his father looked less furious than defeated, and his voice was weak. "Go to bed. We'll talk in the morning." He turned back to the kitchen and in a minute Chip heard the faint sounds that meant he was making coffee.

Chip crept up the three flights of steps to the top floor, glancing into his parents' room as he passed. He noticed that only one side of the bedclothes was rumpled. He went to his own room and closed the door, then huddled under the covers with Timothy, wondering miserably how his life had become so bad so quickly.

In the morning, Chip's father didn't talk about what had happened. The days went by, and still he didn't talk about it. Chip heard some of the guests asking his father where his mother was, and his father telling them that she had had to leave unexpectedly to take care of a sick relative.

A week or so later, a policeman showed up at the hotel carrying an envelope. He and Chip's father went into the office behind the registration desk and stayed in there with the door closed for some time. Chip positioned himself in a corner of the lobby where he could watch the door, and when they emerged his father held the envelope. Even from across the lobby, Chip could see his hands trembling. His face was ashen. The policemen touched the brim of his hat to his father and his father turned back into the office and shut the door again.

Late that night, when Chip heard his father go to bed, he went downstairs and searched the office but found no envelope. He eventually discovered it, several days later, in the Bible in his parents' room. It contained a clipping from the Portland newspaper of a traffic fatality—a car had hit a tree when, according to witnesses, the driver swerved to avoid a wounded moose that had staggered into the road from behind a granite outcropping. The truck was owned by Edward Blaine; the driver was Evangeline Lynam. According to Mr. Blaine, Mrs. Lynam was headed to Mount Desert Island at the time of the accident.

After that, Chip's father hired a woman from Bar Harbor to manage the staff. Chip came in from playing one day to find his bed had been moved to his father's room to make room for the new manager. His box of toys, with Timothy in it, was gone. Chip's father never talked about that, either.

15

L oring finished his story and sat back, looking at Garrick expectantly. Ellen had reached such a fever pitch of agitation that Garrick had sent her into the lobby.

Garrick gazed tiredly back at Loring. "That is your story."

"Yup."

"And that in some way bears on your sister's request for you to identify the location of the lady?"

"Well, not that story particularly," said Loring, examining his nails. "I'm just giving you some useful background information."

"What's going on in there?" called Ellen from the lobby.

"We're finishing up our conversation. Stay there. I'll be out shortly."

He heard a faint huff from Ellen. He turned back to Loring.

"Loring, if you don't intend to give your sister the information she is seeking, perhaps it would be kinder for you to simply state that and let her pursue some other option for saving the hotel."

"And miss the opportunity to spend this quality time with you?"

Garrick glared at Loring for a few moments then, after a glance toward the lobby, said in a lowered voice, "Might you be willing to reveal the location of the lady to someone other than me?"

Loring snorted out a laugh. "And who else do you suggest I give that information to? My pool of conversational partners has gotten a little limited, what with me being dead and all. Hell, not only can't I make myself heard to anyone, I can barely hear them myself anymore. I could hear my sister for a while, but even she's fading out now."

"I'm suggesting the possibility of involving another senser. I'm not the only person who has this ability. Even though others' abilities may be less than mine, they might be able to perceive your answer should you be willing to give it to them."

Loring shook his head. "Garrick Masser, admitting he is not up to the challenge. Thought I'd never see the day."

"Obviously I'm 'up to the challenge,' as you put it, but if you refuse to put our previous differences behind us and give me the information, I'm willing to bring in someone whom you might find more congenial."

A slow smile spread across Loring's face. "Is she pretty?"

"Yes. Very attractive," said Garrick briskly.

"Garrick, are you pimping out a lady senser?"

Garrick stood up. "You have the emotional maturity of an adolescent. I will tell your sister you will not cooperate." With a whirl of his long coat he strode toward the door to the lobby.

"I'm looking forward to meeting your girlfriend, Garrick," Loring called after him.

Ellen, who had been sitting in one of the chintz chairs, shot to her feet when Garrick entered the lobby. "What did he say?"

"Nothing useful," Garrick growled.

Ellen flopped back into the chair. "What am I going to do, Garrick?"

Garrick drew his gloves from his pocket and pulled them on. "Ellen, are you sure you don't want to engage another senser? Loring's animosity toward me might prove to be an insurmountable challenge."

Ellen popped back up out of the chair. "No, Garrick. If it's just you, it will be okay, but if someone else knows ... no, no one else. You promised."

"Yes, I did," he said gloomily. "Very well. I will do my best."

They walked to the front door.

"Tomorrow night, same time?" asked Ellen, pushing her glasses up on her nose.

"Yes. Tomorrow." Ellen opened the door and Garrick stepped outside. "Ellen, the lights," he said irritably.

"It's only a short distance. Don't you have a flashlight?"

"You are going to be the death of me," said Garrick, and drew the flashlight out of his pocket. He clicked it on and followed its oval of light to the Cadillac, folded himself in, started up the car, and glided slowly around the circular drive and down the road.

GARRICK MADE it a practice to concentrate only on driving when operating a motor vehicle, but tonight he could hardly avoid having his thoughts veer back to Ellen Lynam and the impending deadline.

He remembered a day many years ago when a less worn, less harried, teenaged Ellen had started engaging him for sensings at the hotel. There was an especially thorny financial situation to be dealt with and Ellen had asked him to come to the hotel to attempt to contact her father—efforts that had always in the past proven unfruitful. He advised against the continued attempts, but Ellen had insisted and Garrick himself had bills to pay and so he had agreed.

It had been a dreary late afternoon in March and there was an unpleasant slush of old snow on the ground. The front door of the hotel was unlocked and Garrick stepped in and heard voices coming from the office behind the reception desk. Drat. He had dared to hope that Loring might have business elsewhere—his presence would merely make the entire undertaking even more awkward than it already was. He stepped around the desk to the door of the office.

Loring, then in his late twenties, was seated at the desk, papers strewn across its surface, a bottle of beer beside him. Ellen was standing, her arms crossed.

"It's my money, Lore."

"I'm not arguing that it's your money, Ellen. I'm just saying that there are better things to spend it on than—" Loring glanced over and saw Garrick in the doorway. "Well, speak of the devil."

Ellen turned. "Garrick, I didn't know you were there."

"Always a sneaky one," said Loring, taking a drink from the bottle.

"Should I return later?" asked Garrick stiffly.

Loring picked up a pencil and bent over the sheets on the desk. "Don't let me interfere with your little get-together."

"Lore, don't you want to ask Daddy—?" began Ellen, and Loring cut her off.

"No, I don't want to 'ask Daddy.' He couldn't take care of the place when he was alive, I sure as hell am not going to rely on him to give us advice on how to take care of it now that he's dead."

Ellen's lower lip began to quiver.

Loring glared at Garrick, then stood and crossed to Ellen and put his hand on her arm. "Ellen, it's been ten years. Dad's gone now. Let it go. If you're going to waste your money on this stuff, at least pick some other dead person to try to have a conversation with."

"You're a jerk!" Ellen burst out. She flung Loring's hand off her arm and ran from the room, squeezing past Garrick, who still stood in the doorway. They heard the thump of Ellen's feet on the stair to the second floor and then, more faintly, on to the third.

Loring pointed his pencil at Garrick. "I hold you responsible for the fact that she gets herself all worked up over this kind of craziness." Loring threw himself back into the chair behind his desk and took another swallow from his bottle. "Feel free to show yourself out. I think your work here is done."

Garrick turned from the office and went into the lobby. He started for the front door then hesitated, glanced toward the office, and then crossed the lobby to the stairs.

He found Ellen sitting on a bed in one of the stripped-down guest rooms on the third floor, facing the window looking out over Lynam Narrows, her back to the door. He cleared his throat from the doorway.

"Everything's all screwed up," she said with a sniffle, and then blew her nose loudly into the sodden tissue she was kneading in her hands. Garrick removed a clean handkerchief from his pocket, crossed to her, and held it out.

Ellen gave him a little smile. "Thanks, Garrick." She put the used tissue in her pocket and blew her nose again on his handkerchief. "I'm just trying to help Loring out with this mess we're in. I think Daddy could help."

"Ellen, I don't think your father could help even if I were able to contact him. I think it would be best if you tried some other way to assist your brother."

Ellen shrugged. "He says I'm still like a little girl. Even though I'm almost eighteen."

Garrick was silent.

Ellen glanced up at him from under her bangs. "Tomorrow."

"Tomorrow?"

"I'm eighteen tomorrow."

"Ah." Garrick speculated about what the appropriate response would be. He finally settled on, "Congratulations."

She laughed a watery little laugh. "A girl's eighteenth birthday is supposed to be special. But I think tomorrow is going to be like pretty much every other day around here."

"Are you ... having a celebration?" asked Garrick.

She gave a snort. "Hardly. Loring has to go to Portland to talk to some guy at the bank."

"Perhaps you'll have a celebration when he returns," said Garrick.

"Perhaps," replied Ellen, mimicking Garrick's serious tone. She shook herself. "It doesn't matter. I don't want a celebration." She sighed, then looked up at him. "What do you want to do about the sensing?"

"Ellen, I don't believe your father wishes to be contacted. I believe we should stop pursuing that avenue."

She sighed. "Okay. I guess I knew that, but I couldn't think of what else to do."

After a moment, Garrick said, "I'll take my leave now."

"Yeah, okay, thanks for coming by." She looked at the crumpled handkerchief in her hand. "I'll wash this and get it back to you."

Garrick made a little bow and left Ellen gazing out the window. He gave the office a wide berth on his way to the front door.

Garrick had another sensing engagement that evening, but his thoughts kept turning to Ellen Lynam. What might a girl desire for her eighteenth birthday? Something frivolous, no doubt. It had been almost two decades since he himself turned eighteen—he barely remembered the event.

He briefly thought of giving her a book from his library, but all his books concerned sensing and it seemed inappropriate to encourage her in that direction. The next day, he found himself in a gift shop in Bar Harbor, but fled when the sales girl approached him. He returned home and had almost convinced himself that it was not his responsibility to provide a birthday celebration for Ellen Lynam when a thought struck him.

He went to his sparsely furnished bedroom and drew from the back of the top drawer of his dresser a small cardboard box. He opened it and examined the contents for some time, then closed it and went to his office. He found a sheet of heavy stationery, cut it to the appropriate size, folded it carefully around the small box, and fastened it with a tiny strip of tape. Then he went to his car and drove to Lynam's Point.

He found Ellen in the lobby, scrubbing angrily at a stain on the wooden floor.

"This ... is ... never ... going ... to ... come ... out," she puffed, each word punctuated by a stroke of the brush.

"You shouldn't be scrubbing the floor today," said Garrick.

She puffed a strand of hair out of her face. "Why not?" she asked challengingly.

"Because it's your birthday." He extended the box toward her.

Ellen jumped to her feet. "You got me a present? That's so nice of you, Garrick!" She turned it in her hand, examining the wrapping. "Can I open it now?"

"Of course."

She sat down on one of the chairs and gestured him to another one. Once they were seated, she slipped her finger under the tape and loosened the paper. She removed it and set it aside, then examined the box. "What could it be?" she said, playing out the event.

"It's a—" Garrick began.

"No, don't tell me!" exclaimed Ellen. "Guessing is part of the fun!" She shook the box, producing a slight rattle. "Something's moving in there." Evidently having drawn out the suspense as much as she could stand, she pulled the lid off the box.

"Oh, Garrick," she breathed, "it's beautiful!" She lifted out a jade pendant, teardrop-shaped, with a tiny dragon intricately carved into its surface, the dragon's tail swirling above its head. "Wherever did you get it?"

"It belonged to my mother," said Garrick.

"I just love it—thank you!" Ellen jumped to her feet, ran to Garrick, and gave him a kiss on the cheek.

Garrick stood abruptly. "I must be leaving. I wish you a happy birthday."

Ellen was admiring the pendant. "I'm going to put it on a piece of black ribbon. Don't you think that will look nice? And it's so special that it belonged to your mother!"

Garrick made his way to the front door trailed by Ellen, who continued to wax enthusiastic about the gift.

"I've never gotten such a nice present," she said when she caught up with him at the door.

"Jade is believed to promote wisdom, balance, and peace."

Ellen laughed cheerfully. "Well, we'll see what it can do for me."

"Indeed." He gave a little bow and let himself out. He was pleased that she had seemed to enjoy the gift. He was pleased with himself for having thought of it.

He shook himself back to the present. Ellen obviously badly wanted to know the location of this lady whom she believed could help save the hotel. Perhaps, like getting her the present despite her protestations that she didn't want a birthday celebration, it was time he deviated slightly from Ellen's professed reluctance to involve another senser. Perhaps it was time to take matters into his own hands.

16

S cott drove Ann back to Garrick's at ten the next morning. The temperature had dipped again—when they left the inn, Ann could see her breath.

When they got to Garrick's house, Scott said, "I'll just wait here, it seems like he doesn't take very long."

"Well, don't wait in the car, at least wait inside. It's freezing," said Ann.

"Do you think that would be okay?" asked Scott enthusiastically.

"Sure," said Ann, hoping Garrick wouldn't be unpleasant about it.

Ann and Scott climbed the stairs to the front door. Ann knocked and in a moment Garrick opened it. He glowered at Scott. "And who might this be?"

Scott stuck his hand out. "Scott Pate, Miss Kinnear's chauffeur."

Garrick raised his eyebrows at Ann, who smiled gamely and shrugged.

"Very well, come in," said Garrick and stood aside. Scott put his hand down and he and Ann stepped into the hallway.

Scott gestured toward the bench in the hallway. "I'll just wait here."

Garrick closed the front door. "You may wait in the sitting room," he said magnanimously. He opened the door on the left side of the hallway to a room that was the mirror image of his office, including the floor-to-ceiling bookshelves. This room was much more sparsely furnished, with two Windsor armchairs pulled up in front of the fireplace where a fire had been laid but not lit. Garrick stepped aside to let Scott enter.

"Ah, much nicer, thank you!" said Scott.

"You may light the fire if you wish," said Garrick.

"Oh, I don't believe that will be necessary," said Scott, although the room was quite cold. He settled himself into one of the chairs.

"As you wish," said Garrick, and closed the door.

Ann and Garrick crossed the hall to Garrick's office, where a fire popped cheerfully in the fireplace, and took their accustomed seats. Garrick looked speculatively at Ann. "So."

"Yes?" She awaited his assessment.

"You have a chauffeur?"

"Well, not normally. But we thought that under the circumstances it would be better for me not to be driving."

"Ah, a temporary arrangement." Garrick seemed somewhat mollified.

"Yes." She thought that, considering the instant dislike Garrick and Mike had taken to each other, the less said about Scott's identity the better. "So? The spirit?"

Garrick stood and did a quick circuit of her chair and then resumed his seat behind the desk. "It's not there anymore."

"The ... whatever-it-was?"

"Yes, the 'whatever-it-was' is gone."

"But ... where?"

"I don't know where. I don't even know what it was," he said peevishly.

"Well ... what now?"

Garrick swiveled his chair toward the fireplace and regarded it owlishly. After a minute, he turned his chair back toward Ann. "This may take longer than I had anticipated. I thought the challenge would be determining how to rid yourself of Biden Firth's spirit, not determining whose spirit it is—if in fact it's a spirit at all. I may need to do some research. And I need you close at hand in case 'whatever-it-is' manifests itself again."

Ann nodded, unsure where Garrick was heading.

"We didn't discuss the fee," said Garrick.

Ann nodded again, steeling herself.

"I would consider performing this engagement pro bono publico," said Garrick.

"Really?" asked Ann. "Why?"

Garrick drew his eyebrows together. "Well, perhaps less pro bono and more as an exchange of services. I believe you may be of assistance to me with my other engagement."

"Really?" asked Ann. She had not anticipated this.

Garrick took a sip from a steaming mug on his desk and looked, if possible, even more irritated. "I should not, strictly speaking, be sharing information about my engagement with you. My client has asked for complete confidentiality. However, I trust you to be discreet." He raised a questioning eyebrow.

"Of course," said Ann, curious.

"This discretion extends not only to not revealing your involvement to others. Such as your brother." Garrick scowled at Ann and she nodded. "Or your chauffeur." Ann nodded again. "But also not to the client herself. I am making this highly unusual exception because the client is anxious to obtain an answer to a question she is posing to her dead brother. The answer to this question will evidently avert an undesirable outcome and must be obtained before the arrival of an externally imposed deadline—in fact, within the next three days. And I have reason to believe that her brother may be more willing to share this information with someone other than me. Also," he added, "the fee is significant if I can provide the information she is looking for."

Ann suppressed a smile.

"For you, assisting me not only provides what I believe to be a valuable exchange for my services, but also offers the opportunity to expand your skills. An apprenticeship, you might say."

"Gee, thanks," said Ann, a little miffed.

"Don't mention it," Garrick replied and raised his eyebrows questioningly.

Ann shifted in her seat. "I'm thinking of giving up the sensing business."

"Why?" he asked sharply.

"Because it's not helping anyone, and it's getting me in trouble."

"Ah. Well, you should have no concerns in this case. Should this engagement be brought to a successful conclusion, it will prove beneficial to my client. And no one will know you're involved, so it would hardly get you in trouble."

"What if the sensings are what's giving me the pain in my hands?"

"It seems highly unlikely."

"Why's that?" asked Ann, bristling.

"It would be indicative of a psychological fragility that doesn't seem in keeping with your overall demeanor."

"Uh ... thanks. I think. Still ..."

Garrick waited for several moments, then prompted impatiently, "'Still' what?"

Despite what seemed to Ann like her perfectly legitimate concerns, Garrick's proposal did hold some attractions. For one,

Garrick had traveled to the Adirondacks to ensure her cabin was clean of spirits and although, as far as she knew, Mike had paid Garrick for that engagement, it felt like a favor nonetheless. Here was a simple way to repay that debt. For another, spending the additional time needed with Garrick for this other engagement might hasten his assessment of her situation—would enable her to find out more quickly whether she was really being stalked by Biden Firth, was suffering from some sort of physical condition, or was merely succumbing to "psychological fragility" characterized by some psychosomatic reaction to sensings. Finally, assisting Garrick with his engagement seemed like less of a commitment than taking on one of her own—it could be a trial run for the possibility of continuing her own consulting business.

She sighed. "Nothing. Go on. What is the engagement?"

Garrick settled back in his chair. "The client, Ellen Lynam, is a member of one of the established families of the area. Originally, the family owned an entire peninsula off the west coast of the island and built the Lynam's Point Hotel in the 1880s, at the northern tip of the peninsula. Unfortunately, the family faced some difficulties in their business ventures—the difficulties were sometimes brought on by ineptitude and sometimes by circumstances beyond their control, but it appears they faced financial difficulties from the beginning. As you might imagine, the circumstances were especially challenging during the Depression, and in the early 1930s they sold most of the peninsula to a philanthropist who donated it to the National Park Service as part of Acadia. The family retained only the property around the hotel.

"The hotel did enjoy periods of relative prosperity during the last century, but the difficulties worsened again in recent years and the Lynams have now fallen so far behind in their taxes that the IRS is in the process of seizing the property. It is

going up for auction and the two leading bidders are Ms.
Lynam, who is the last living member of the Lynam family, and
a gentleman of some means who has let it be known that he
intends to tear down the hotel so that he can build a private
home on the site. I understand the hotel has some structural
issues which make it unappealing to maintain as an historical
site. In order to save the hotel, Ms. Lynam must raise a considerable amount of cash within the next three days.

"In support of that goal, she has hired me to discover from
the spirit of her brother, Loring Lynam, the location of 'the lady.'
The question is quite straightforward—'Where is the lady?'—
but the brother's spirit is obfuscating. He has a great deal of
information he wishes to share, but none of it is what the sister
wants. It's all very tedious."

"Who's the lady she's asking about?"

"I have no idea. I assume it is someone—perhaps a distant
relative—who might be in a position to assist financially."

"Why does my involvement have to be a secret?"

Garrick scowled at her.

Ann shrugged. "Just curious."

Garrick sighed. "It's completely illogical. I have asked her
about involving another senser. Her brother and I are not on
cordial terms, and he might be more likely to give this information to someone else. But she is adamant that no one else be
involved."

"So why are you involving someone else?"

The scowl turned into a glare.

"I think I have a right to know if I'm going to be involved,"
said Ann.

Garrick drummed his fingers on the desk. Finally he said, "I
believe that in the end, her desire to save the hotel will outweigh
her desire to keep the involvement of this lady secret. And what
if the lady herself chooses not to keep her involvement a secret?

Ms. Lynam is not always completely levelheaded about matters concerning the hotel."

"It sounds like you know her pretty well." Ann said.

"Hardly," said Garrick sternly.

"Is she a friend of yours?"

"She is a longstanding acquaintance."

Ann sighed. "So what do you want me to do?"

"You merely need to accompany me, secretly, to the engagement, position yourself where it is likely you will encounter the brother, pose the question to him, and listen for his answer."

"What makes you think he'll tell me?"

"Because you're not me. Plus your gender may be to your advantage."

"I feel like you're setting me up on a blind date."

"Don't be ridiculous. Your interaction with him should be very brief. I can't imagine you would want to spend any more time with him than is absolutely necessary. He's quite—" Garrick stopped himself, took a drink from his mug, and tapped his fingers together. "Can you drive yourself?"

"Well, I suppose I could but I would prefer not to ..."

"Understandable," said Garrick briskly. "Not an insurmountable issue. We will meet here at eleven o'clock tonight and I will drop you off before we reach the hotel. You can follow me on foot. The moon is nearly full, so you should have sufficient light."

"Okay. I'll bring a flashlight just in case."

"No flashlight."

"Garrick, how am I supposed to find my way around?"

"I will draw you a diagram." He removed a sheet of paper and a fountain pen from the top drawer. "The sensings are in the family's hotel. When the spirit appears, he always comes to the lounge, where we wait for him, from the direction of the lobby. I suspect that since he is traveling in a somewhat lifelike fashion, you could intercept him outside near the entrance to the lobby."

"I've never actually had any kind of extended conversation with a spirit, you know."

"Yes, I realize the chances are slim that you will be able to provide the information. But as I said, it may be that it won't require an extended interaction. It might be enough for you to ask, 'Where is the lady?' and for you to be able to perceive his response to that specific question." Garrick turned back to his pen and paper, but rather than sketching a stylized aerial view— rectangles for buildings and squiggly lines for roads—he began rendering a quite detailed depiction of an unadorned rectangular building with three main stories, a cramped fourth story suggested by dormer windows in the roof, and a wide veranda extending across the front and around the right-hand side of the building. Light horizontal lines suggested clapboard siding, quick strokes indicated a background of trees and water. Garrick added a circular drive bordered by tiny lights in front.

"These lights will likely not be illuminated. I can't imagine that the few cents she saves on electricity is worth the danger of a fall in the dark," he muttered. He drew an X on the veranda. "I recommend waiting for him here." He handed the drawing to Ann.

"This is very good, Garrick," she said, admiring it with an artist's eye. "I didn't know you drew."

"I don't draw. I'm providing you with directions."

"Well, it certainly shows where you want me to meet up with the spirit when I get to the hotel, but I don't know if it's going to help me get there in the dark after you drop me off."

"You just need to follow the road."

"I know, but I would feel better if I could see it in the daylight first. Could I drive out there and take a look?"

"I thought you weren't driving yourself."

"Damn," muttered Ann. "You could drop me off at the beginning of the road and I could walk the rest of the way."

"No. She might see me."

"Scott could drop me off, I could tell him I wanted to take a hike there."

"That seems like a flimsy excuse."

"Well, he might know something was up, but he wouldn't know what it was."

Garrick drew his eyebrows together and glared at her.

"If I see her, I'll just tell her I'm a lost tourist. She won't have any way of knowing who I am."

"Your picture was in the news after the Firth incident."

"I doubt very much that it showed up in Maine," she said. Then, after a pause, she added, "Did it?"

"I wouldn't know about that," said Garrick brusquely. He considered for a moment, his eyebrows unknitting a bit. "I suppose it would be acceptable." He sighed. "Very well. Do you have a map?"

She went to her knapsack and removed a map of Mount Desert Island she had picked up in Bar Harbor, and took it to Garrick's desk.

"The hotel is here," he said, making a neat X on the map on a finger of land on the west coast of the island. He traced a careful line on the map from Somesville, following Oak Hill Road and Indian Point Road to where one would leave the main road to follow the smaller road to the X. "You should have your driver drop you off here." He drew a small arrow at the intersection. "You should leave soon, it gets dark early at this time of year."

Garrick stood. Ann gathered up her parka and knapsack and they crossed the hall to the waiting room. When Garrick opened the door, Scott turned, his hands clasped behind his back, from where he was peering at a small book on a book stand. Its pages were held open with a weighted strip of leather.

"You have very interesting reading material in your waiting room, Mr. Masser. Much better than old copies of National Geographic."

"Quite." Garrick crossed to the book stand.

"And very appropriate for your business," said Scott, gesturing to the page to which the book was open.

"'I think a person who is terrified with the imagination of ghosts and spectres,'" quoted Garrick, looking out the window, "'much more reasonable than one, who, contrary to the reports of all historians, sacred and profane, ancient and modern, and to the traditions of all nations, thinks the appearance of ghosts fabulous and groundless.'"

"Wow," said Scott, raising his eyebrows. "Very impressive."

Ann joined them. "You want me to help out with a sensing, tell me there's no reason for me not to, and then you have a book in your waiting room talking about someone who is terrified by ghosts?"

"Steel your heart, Ms. Kinnear," said Garrick tartly. He removed the strip of leather and flipped the book closed, revealing a gaudily marbled cover. "The author—a physician named John Alderson—is quoting Joseph Addison, but the purpose of the book is to refute that position. Alderson argued that the belief in apparitions arose from secondary physical causes."

"Ah HA!" said Ann.

Garrick raised his eyebrows at her. "Ah ha?"

"Sounds like an explanation for a physical reaction to sensings."

"You misunderstand the author's intent, my dear. He believed the perception of apparitions to be the result of physical causes—injuries to the head, excessive alcohol consumption, chronic medical conditions—whereas you are arguing that the physical condition is the result of the appearance of the apparition." He waved to the other books. "For any position you may care to take on the subject, I can provide a carefully researched position defending or debunking it." He closed the book and placed it on the book stand. "You may borrow it if you wish to read further."

Ann started to respond, but then realized that Garrick was talking to Scott.

"Really?" He picked it up from the book stand. "It looks quite old. Is it valuable? I'd be nervous borrowing it if it's very valuable."

Garrick waved his hand. "Not terribly old. 1823."

"Why thank you, that's very generous of you."

At the front door, Ann turned to Garrick. "So how did Alderson solve the problems of the people who were seeing spirits?"

"Bleeding, leeches, and purgatives," said Garrick briskly.

"Great," said Ann, turning to leave.

Scott followed Ann to the car, then stepped ahead of her to open the door. When he had gotten in she said, "My, aren't the two of you chummy. What would Mike think?"

"I won't tell if you won't," said Scott with a grin. "Where to now?"

"I need you to drop me off somewhere, I'll give you directions."

"What are we going to do?" said Scott, starting the car.

"You are going to drop me off and I'm going to go for a walk."

"Not with me?"

"Nope."

"Hmm, very mysterious," said Scott agreeably.

17

A short while later, Scott dropped Ann off at the beginning of Lynam's Point Road.

"Where are you going?" he asked, peering around. There were no buildings visible—just stands of pines all around before the road curved out of sight in front of and behind them. A small sign for Lynam's Point Hotel was so faded that it blended into its wooded background.

"Top secret. If I told you I'd have to kill you," said Ann.

"You're no fun. When and where do you want me to pick you up?"

"Let's say back here in an hour."

"Right-o. Here, take a bottle of water." Ann got out of the car. Scott, after consulting his map, drove off to the south.

The air, especially under the shade of the trees, was chilly, and Ann got her new hat from her knapsack and pulled it on. She followed Lynam's Point Road for a short distance before it crossed the tiny spit of land that made the peninsula not quite an island. On her map, she saw that the peninsula ran north to south, paralleling the main island of Mount Desert and separated from it by a narrow inlet on the east. To her right, at the north end of the peninsula and only a few hundred yards away, Ann could see the roof of what she assumed was the hotel. Perhaps she needn't have told Scott to stay away so long; it appeared she would reach the hotel in only a few minutes.

Once across the spit of land, however, the road turned left onto the short extension of the peninsula that lay to the south. Following the road, she soon left the pine woods and came out next to the water and saw that the road followed the shore of Lynam Narrows. The builder of the hotel, and the road, must have found the picturesque view to the west across the Narrows and on to the open water of the Western Bay to be a more appealing route than one following the inlet to the east. She considered backtracking and taking a shortcut along the eastern shore of the peninsula, but it would have meant scrambling across the rocks that lined the shore. In addition, although the area looked deserted, if she encountered anyone, her presence there would be harder to explain than if she stuck to the road. She put on her sunglasses. They not only provided protection from the glare of the sun on the water but also gave her a sense of traveling incognito—although she still doubted that anyone on Mount Desert Island would have followed the coverage of the Firth case closely enough to recognize her.

She walked briskly. The sun, when it was not hidden by the building clouds, sparkled on the water. Small waves stirred by the chilly breeze slapped onto the narrow, stony beach that bordered the road. Yellow seaweed lay like hair across the rocks. Across the Narrows she could see a few small, widely spaced buildings dotting the opposite shore, their wooden sides polished to that silver-gray of oceanside structures. A black bird bobbed on the water, only its head and neck protruding like a periscope. It periodically disappeared under the waves and once emerged with a fish in its beak, which it juggled about until it could gulp it down head-first.

Eventually, the road turned away from the shore and back into the pine woods. Here evenly spaced, mature trees were surrounded by bright green, knee-high seedlings, crowded at their bases like chicks around a hen. Shortly after she entered the woods, she passed between a pair of stone pillars with a sign reading "Lynam's Point Hotel" affixed to one. A chain between the pillars blocked the entrance. The chain wasn't locked, just looped over a hook on the back of the pillar—more a discouragement than a deterrent. She stepped over it.

A short distance beyond the pillars, Ann passed a cemetery on her left. She picked up her pace as she usually did when passing cemeteries, not wanting to be distracted by a spirit. Then the road left the pine woods again and opened out into a cleared area at the tip of the peninsula. In front of Ann was the hotel that Garrick had drawn. He had captured it quite accurately, although he had obviously had its in-season incarnation in mind. Now, in October, the shutters on the second- and third-story windows were closed, and the small parking area was empty. Ann could also see evidence of the financial difficulties Garrick had described—the paint was peeling, the landscaping was threadbare, and one of the posts on the veranda had been knocked loose and leaned outward, a slight dip noticeable in the roof above it. She was glad she was seeing it in the daylight since there were a number of obstacles that could have tripped her up —literally and figuratively—if she had arrived at night under the no-flashlight rule.

There was no sign of life, so Ann decided to make a circuit of the hotel. She followed the drive to the right, bringing into view a glorious vista across what her map told her was the Western Bay. Behind the hotel was a boathouse, as buttoned up as the hotel. Between the hotel and the boathouse, the lawn was oddly terraced—when she got to the back of the hotel, she saw that the ground had been leveled to accommodate a playing area of some kind. She guessed it had been a croquet court.

All the while, she kept her senses open to any spirit. What if she was able to return to Garrick from her scouting trip and tell him how to get in touch with the lady? It would be a satisfying rejoinder to his "apprenticeship" comment. However, she couldn't perceive anything beyond what would be apparent to any visitor: a hotel in need of some TLC and a vista that would likely be hard to top anywhere on Mount Desert Island.

The west side of the hotel was obviously the service area, with a small loading dock and utilitarian doors that she guessed led to the hotel's kitchen. An old Jeep was parked near the back entrance—so Ellen Lynam was likely inside after all.

Completing her circuit, she wondered how close she could safely get to the hotel's veranda, where Garrick thought she might meet Loring Lynam, without attracting the attention of whoever was inside. Just then, the front door opened and a woman emerged, rummaging through a large purse. Ann glanced around quickly, searching for cover, but the woman was going to look up any moment and would certainly be suspicious if she saw someone scuttling away.

"Hello!" Ann called and, when the woman looked up, waved.

"Hello," the woman called back as Ann crossed the lawn to where she stood on the veranda. "Can I help you? The hotel is closed for the season."

"Yes, I know, I hope you don't mind me coming out here—so pretty!" She sounded unnaturally perky to her own ears, and toned it down a bit. "Beautiful view," she said, nodding toward the water.

The woman stepped off the veranda and turned in the direction Ann was looking. "Yes, it is," she said, sounding wistful. "That's one of the most lovely views on MDI. You should come back when we're open, you could sit on the veranda and enjoy it when it's a bit warmer."

"When do you open for the season?"

After a pause, the woman said, "May."

"I'm sure it's lovely. My brother would love hosting a summer party on a veranda like that." A thought popped into her head. "Actually, my fiancé and I are looking for a place for our reception. Do you do receptions?"

"Oh yes, we've done lots of receptions. When are you getting married?"

"Uh ... July."

"It's a busy time around here, best book early. I don't quite know what our schedule is for July, but I can take your name and number and give you a call when we're a little more settled on plans for next year."

Ann was beginning to regret what had seemed like a clever cover story.

"I don't want to put you to any trouble ..."

"No trouble." The woman stuck out her hand. "Ellen Lynam. I own the hotel."

Ann shook her hand. "Kay Near." It was the name she used for the paintings she sold in the Adirondacks and in West Chester.

"Nice to meet you, Miss Near. Let's go inside and I can get your information."

Ann followed Ellen into the lobby, where Ellen went behind the antique registration desk and began shuffling through some drawers. "Everything gets all out of kilter in off-season ..."

Ann took the opportunity to glance around the lobby, opening her senses to what might be there, but the room seemed clean of spirits. However, her vision was somewhat impaired by the sunglasses she had kept on—incognito seemed like an especially good idea now that she was actually speaking with Garrick's client.

"Ah, here we are," said Ellen, producing the stub of a pencil and a pad of paper with the hotel's name on it in an old-fashioned script. She removed her glasses and hooked them into the neck of her shirt. With the glasses off, her face took on the innocent prettiness of a younger woman. "K-a-y?"

"Yes."

"And the last name?"

"N-e-a-r."

"And your fiancé's name?"

"Scott Pate."

"P-a-t-e?"

"Yes."

"And your phone number?"

Damn. Ann gave Ellen her cellphone number.

Ellen tore the paper off the pad and thumbtacked it to a bulletin board behind the desk that contained a jumble of other slips and scraps of paper. "I should know pretty soon what our plans are for July and I can give you a call then. Big reception?"

"Oh no, probably quite small."

"Oh," said Ellen, sounding disappointed, then perked up. "You could have the guests stay at the hotel. If you book early enough, of course. I could show you some of the places where we could host a reception. Or even the ceremony."

"Oh no, I don't want to put you out. Plus I'd like for Scott to be here to see it."

"Are you local?"

"No, but we get up here pretty frequently."

"How long have you been coming to MDI?"

"Oh, for years." Ann was busily trying to keep all the details of her story straight.

Ellen looked like she was going to pursue it further, but then evidently decided to give up trying to pry details out of her reticent visitor. She rejoined Ann in the lobby. "Well, I need to run some errands and I'll have to lock up the hotel, but feel free to look around the grounds if you'd like. It looks much nicer in season, of course."

"Thank you, I will look around a little bit."

Ann followed Ellen out onto the veranda. Ellen pulled a large wallet out of her purse and extracted a somewhat frayed business card. "Just give me a call if you have any questions." Ann took the card. They shook hands and Ellen disappeared around the corner of the hotel and in a minute the Jeep trundled by, Ellen giving a wave as she passed. Ann heard the vehicle grumble down the road, with pauses as Ellen removed the chain, drove through, and replaced it. Then the engine noise receded into silence.

Ann glanced at her watch. She still had some time before she had to meet Scott at the main road. She hoped he hadn't gotten back early, otherwise Ellen's suspicions might be aroused by the sight of a man sitting patiently in a car on an otherwise-deserted road.

Garrick had said the spirit might come into the hotel from the lobby entrance; no harm in spending a few minutes seeing what there was to be seen—or sensed.

Ann sat down on the top step and leaned back on her elbows. The day was chilly, and the warmth generated by her walk was wearing off. The entrance of the hotel faced south, away from the Narrows, and the veranda caught the watery October sun. She had a brief hope of catching some warmth from it, but it was low in the sky and weak. She sat forward and tucked her hands into the opposite sleeves of her parka. Then turned to look at the door.

Had Ellen actually locked it?

FROM ACROSS THE HOTEL LAWN, the spirit watched the two women on the veranda. One of them, Ellen, he had known in life, but the other was new to him. Those still alive were usually faint, flitting forms, but this one was clear. It seemed obvious that this woman was not a spirit herself, but rather a living person with an unusual connection to the spirit world. Not as strong a connection as the man in black, but still strong. And she was pretty—slender, with reddish-blond hair and delicate features.

Ellen left, but the other woman stayed. The woman watched Ellen's Willys disappear down the road, then moved to the edge of the veranda.

Behind where she had stood was a man—tall, dark-haired, pale-skinned.

The spirit pushed himself away from the tree, a buzz of concern starting in the back of his neck. There hadn't been anyone on the veranda a moment ago, he was sure of it.

The woman sat down on the top step and leaned back on her elbows, gazing around the hotel grounds. The man stepped up behind her. She seemed unaware of his presence. Then the man squatted down behind her in a catcher's stance. From where the spirit watched, he almost expected the man to put his hands over the woman's eyes and say, "Guess who!"

But the man made no attempt to alert the woman to his presence, and the way he watched her—like a snake in the grass watching a mouse unconcernedly nibbling a seed—escalated the buzz to a burr of worry.

The woman's hands dangled over the edge of the veranda, near her hips, and the man began reaching his hand toward hers. But before he reached his target, the woman sat forward and tucked her hands into the opposite sleeves of her parka. The man leaned back, annoyed. He was beginning to move toward her again when she turned and looked behind her. The man slid slightly to one side, out of her line of sight, but it appeared in any case that she was looking not at him but at the door. After a moment, she stood and crossed the veranda. The man moved to stay behind her, following her.

She reached for the doorknob and the man's arm shot out. He clamped his hand over hers.

She let out a cry and snatched her hand back. She turned away, cradling her hand, and stumbled away from the door.

The man smirked with satisfaction and took a step toward her.

"Hey—*hey*! Leave her alone!"

The man's head jerked toward the spirit's voice. The spirit broke into a run as the man's face hardened into anger while at the same time his body began to take on a wavering translucence. The spirit reached the veranda and stepped between the man and the woman.

"What are you doing? Get away from her!"

"Who are you—the hotel handyman?" the man asked impatiently. "Get away from here, this doesn't concern you."

He stepped forward. "It certainly does concern me—this is my hotel, and I won't have a thug like you bothering this lady. I want you out of here!"

The dark-haired man raised an eyebrow, although the eyebrow, and in fact his entire form, was becoming increasingly amorphous. "I'm guessing it's not really *your* hotel anymore," he sneered, but his voice, along with his form, was beginning to fade.

"It was mine—it's my family's—and you're not welcome here."

He took another step forward, but the last remnants of the man's form were gone and all that was left was a yellowish light which then swirled off into nothingness on a puff of wind coming off the water.

THE PAIN SHOT from Ann's hand up her arm and curled her fingers into claws. As she pulled back with a cry, she thought she caught a glimpse of a tendril of yellow light retreating from her stricken hand, accompanied by an acrid tang like the smell of an electrical short circuit. She stumbled away from the door, swearing under her breath, tears of pain and fear springing to her eyes.

When she had put some distance between herself and the door, she turned to face her tormentor, but there was nothing discernible there except an area of grayish haze in the middle of the veranda, rimmed by a flicker of yellow. The haze disappeared as she blinked the tears out of her eyes, then reappeared briefly in a weak ray of sunlight breaking through the clouds. The yellow and gray vied with each other for a moment, and then the yellow was gone and she could see for just a moment the gray, solidified into a human form.

It was a man of some indeterminate middle age, with a lean, muscular build. He had tousled brown hair and thin lips touched with the hint of a smile, but most striking were his gray eyes lined with crow's feet—light eyes that were more striking in the dark tan of his sun- and wind-weathered face. He was saying something, but the words faded away as she lost sight of his form, although she sensed that he was still there.

Was this the manifestation of the light she had seen near her hand when the pain struck? She thought not—this spirit, emerging out of the gray light, seemed unthreatening, even concerned. Maybe there had only ever been this one spirit, and the yellowish light she thought she had seen was just a trick of the sun. Maybe this was the man Garrick had hoped she would find.

"Loring?"

She caught a brief glimpse of him again, his smile widening, but then it was gone.

"Loring? Are you there?"

Now she had lost all sense of a presence. She was torn between two impulses. On one hand, she wanted to get away from the hotel—the general sense of creepiness that resulted from being alone in a usually public place was heightened by the shock of the pain in her hand. On the other hand, she wanted to continue trying to engage the spirit she had seen, especially if it meant she might be able to save herself a return trip to the hotel that night. For a little while, the second impulse won out.

She crossed the veranda to the door of the hotel and, with some foreboding and with frequent glances behind her, tried the knob. It turned, and she opened the door and stepped inside. The room—in fact, the whole building—felt empty of any presence, living or dead. Garrick had mentioned that the spirit appeared in the lounge. Was this the lounge? There certainly wasn't a spirit here. She crossed the room to a doorway leading to another room, which looked and felt even more empty than the first. Still nothing.

She didn't fancy searching the hotel any further—the idea of Ellen returning from her errand early kept nagging at her nerves. She hurried back to the front door and gave a little sigh of relief as she closed it behind her.

She spent some time, first on the veranda and then on the

drive and lawn, walking back and forth like a retriever searching for a ball in tall grass, hoping for an angle or perspective that would reveal the man she had glimpsed. But the lights—both yellow and gray—were gone, although when she walked through the space in which the man had stood, she could pick up a faint scent of sun-warmed skin and fresh sweat.

18

E ventually, a glance at her watch told Ann that she had used up the time she had allotted to her reconnais-sance run—she had to hurry if she wasn't going to keep Scott waiting at their meeting place. She again considered taking the route along the inlet, but clouds were building and she had no wish to get caught on slippery rocks in the rain. She headed back through the pine woods to the shore road.

Entering the dimness of the woods was oddly comforting because she thought she'd be better able to see the yellow light if it was in fact a spirit pursuing her. She glanced behind her periodically, looking for any sign of the light that had preceded the pain in her hand. Was it Biden Firth? She hadn't seen anything remotely identifiable, but the noxious presence she had sensed certainly matched up with her brief but tragic acquaintance with Firth. But the more she thought about it, the more likely it seemed that the explanation for the pain was the sensing experience itself. Even if the man who she had eventually glimpsed hadn't intentionally caused the pain, perhaps his very presence had been enough. And it obviously wasn't some malignant intent of the spirit that was causing the reaction—she had experienced it after seeing Scooter, for heaven's sake. And after seeing Beau and the old woman, both of whom she knew from experience were intent on protecting her.

At the small family cemetery, her now-attentive senses picked up two faint lights hovering over two small headstones behind the chain-link fence, accompanied by a barely perceptible and tuneless humming. Probably young children and definitely not the spirit she had encountered at the hotel. She tucked her hands deeper into her pockets, ready for the pain to strike, but she passed the cemetery unaffected. Perhaps it was only when she was caught unawares that the sensing had this effect.

By the time the road left the pine woods and began its run along the shore, the waves on the Narrows had become choppier, small whitecaps forming at their tips. A few minutes later, the clouds closed across the sky like curtains across a stage and she felt the first drops of cold rain on her face. She pulled her cap more firmly down on her head, zipped up her parka, and made fast time back to Indian Point Road.

When she reached the main road, she was chilled to the bone and was happy to see the Audi parked on the shoulder, Scott in the driver's seat with a map spread open across the steering wheel. He saw her coming and leaned across the seat to open the passenger door for her. She fell into the seat, throwing her soggy hat into the back.

"So how did the secret mission go?" Scott asked.

"Okay." She considered how much she could tell him and decided that it wouldn't be violating the oath of secrecy to let him know it involved a sensing; what other reason would Garrick have to send her off on an assignment? "I saw a spirit. And I got that pain in my hand again."

"Really? Are you okay?"

"Yeah, I'm fine." She turned to look out the foggy window at the dreary scene outside. "It certainly is tedious, though."

"Was it Biden? Did he follow you?" Scott glanced around the car.

Ann also glanced around the car, then pulled her sunglasses down to the end of her nose so she could look over them and scanned the car again. "I don't think so." She flopped back in her seat. "I'm starting to think I don't need Garrick, I need a shrink."

"Don't be silly," said Scott. "Whatever it is, it's a real thing, not something you're making up."

"How can you know that?"

He patted her knee. "Because I know you. Why are you wearing sunglasses?"

"I'm traveling incognito," she said. "What were you looking up on the map?"

"The map was my cover story, since I'm masquerading as the chauffeur of someone who's traveling incognito. Just in case someone stopped and asked why I was parked there, I was going to tell them I was looking for Thurston's Lobster Pound."

"I'd tell you more about what I'm doing if I could," she said apologetically. "Garrick says it has to stay a secret."

"Well, I'm sure Mr. Masser knows best," said Scott equably, starting the car. "Where to next?"

Ann shivered. "Somewhere warm—I'm freezing."

"I know just the place!"

"Why am I not surprised?"

THEY DROVE BACK to the eastern side of the island, where they entered Acadia and wended their way along the park roads, then turned off at a sign for Jordan Pond House.

"What's this?"

"The perfect place to warm up—they have tea. And popovers!"

Despite the fact that the tourist season was winding down, the parking lot was packed, with a spillover of cars parked on the sides of the road leading to the parking lot. However, they happened upon a car—a beat-up Honda with a pair of bicycles on the roof—just as it was pulling out and Scott slipped into the space.

Visitors milled about in the restaurant lobby, but Scott had called in a reservation before they left Indian Point Road so they waited only a few minutes before being seated at a table near the floor-to-ceiling windows.

After they had settled in, Scott consulted his guidebook.

"That's Jordan Pond," he said, indicating the body of water at the bottom of the lawn that extended down from the restaurant. "And those," he said, gesturing with his guidebook at a pair of mountains on the other side of the pond, "are 'The Bubbles.'" He looked up and raised his eyebrows. "Sure enough." He set the guidebook aside. "Does your hand still hurt?"

"No. It never lasts very long."

"Do you think it was Biden Firth?"

Ann considered, turning her spoon over and over on her napkin. "I don't know. Wouldn't you think that if it were Biden Firth, I would see him?"

"I have no idea, sweetie. Maybe he has a way of hiding himself."

"I suppose." After a moment, she continued impatiently. "What if it's not something that's trying to hurt me? What if this is some physical reaction to sensing, like with the nausea I used to get? Some completely innocuous spirit shows up, and maybe I have this physical reaction as an aversion to experiencing it?"

"What innocuous spirit?"

Damn, she hadn't intended to mention seeing Loring Lynam

—if that's who it had been—to Scott. "Just theoretically," she said. She hurried on. "Or maybe I just have something completely normal wrong with my hand, like you suggested. What if it turns out I just have carpal tunnel syndrome or something and I'm just making all this up about being haunted?"

"I've had clients with carpal tunnel and never heard about them having symptoms like you're having, but we can always get it checked out when we get back to West Chester. I'll just be glad when you see Mr. Masser again and find out if he sees anything." He picked up his menu. "We have to get the popovers —that's what they're known for."

They ordered those along with salads and bowls of lobster stew. Scott got tea and Ann got a Chardonnay.

When the popovers arrived, it was clear why they were a draw—a magnificent tower of roll which, when its caramel-brown crown was breached, emitted a fragrant puff of steam from its hollow center. Scott took a photo of the popovers and sent it to Mike. He tried to take a photo of Ann, but she shooed him away. Ann took a photo of Scott and they sent that to Mike as well.

"This is nice," said Ann, sipping her wine. "Let's stay here forever."

"Here on Mount Desert? It is nice."

"I was thinking of here in the restaurant, but the island is nice too."

"You could get a summer place here. Spend your winters in West Chester."

"How would I get to engagements? I can't very well ask Walt to fly out to Maine every time I need to go somewhere."

"I'm sure there are charter pilots in Maine. We could look into that while we're here."

Ann laughed. "I just said I liked the restaurant and now you want me to move to Maine?"

Scott shrugged. "I just think a change would do you good. Plus," he added, "maybe you could go into business with Mr. Masser."

"I think Garrick's a one-man show."

Their salads arrived and Scott tucked in while Ann moved the greens around on her plate.

Finally, she pushed back from the table. "I should really call Garrick and give him an update. Is it okay if I abandon you for a few minutes?"

"Sure, I'll ask them to hold the soup until you get back," said Scott, waving to their server.

Ann returned to the restaurant lobby to call Garrick.

"Yes?" answered Garrick.

Ann described her encounter with Ellen Lynam.

"You spoke to her?" Garrick asked, his disapproval clear over the phone.

"Yes," said Ann. "I don't know what difference it makes. She doesn't know who I am and she doesn't have any way of knowing I know you. I told her I was looking for wedding reception sites."

"And she believed that?"

"Sure, why not? It was a good excuse because it gave me a chance to check out the area. She had to leave to run errands and I thought she had left the door to the hotel unlocked, so I was starting to go in and check out the lounge where you said you meet with the spirit, but then I got another one of those pains in my hand. Right before it happened, I thought I saw a yellowish light, but then the light was gray and it partially resolved into a human form. I asked him if he was Loring and I got the sense he was." Ann described the man she had seen.

"Yes, that's Loring," said Garrick. "Very promising."

"Do you think this Loring guy would try to hurt me?"

"I wouldn't think so. His unpleasantness seems more geared to verbal abuse than physical. Plus, based on my studies, a person who is limited to sensing spirits as lights almost always senses a particular spirit as a particular color of light—I hardly think he would have manifested as a yellow light to harm you and then a gray light to interact with you. Your past experience might be instructive in this case."

Ann thought back over her sensing experiences. "I agree that spirits usually appear as the same color over time. In any case, I think he was trying to say something to me, but I couldn't understand what it was. He seemed happy to see me, though."

"Ah, good. Perhaps with more exposure you will become more attuned to his communications. Where did you see him?"

"Right where you showed on the map—near the front door."

"Excellent." Garrick sounded almost cheerful.

"Garrick, when I told Ellen I was looking for a place for a wedding reception in July, she acted like the hotel might be available for that. But doesn't that seem strange if she knows she might lose the bidding war, especially if she can't get in touch with this lady she's looking for?"

"As I said, she is rarely logical when it comes to matters concerning the hotel."

"That seems more than illogical, it seems sort of delusional."

"I hardly believe it would meet the textbook definition of delusional behavior," said Garrick irritably.

"Well, she's your client, I guess you know best."

"Quite. We'll go back to the hotel this evening and see if his presence is more substantial for you then. Have your driver drop you off in Somesville at eleven o'clock."

19

W hen she got back to the table after her call to Garrick, Scott gestured to the server, who brought over their soups. The rain had stopped and weak sunlight struggled to break through the low clouds. When they were done with the soup, they ordered another pot of tea for Scott and another glass of wine for Ann and scooched their chairs together so they could both look at Scott's guidebook.

"We should definitely do a hike while we're here," he said. "Do any of these look interesting to you?" He slid the book over to Ann, who paged through it.

"Here's one right nearby—Jordan Cliffs. How about that one?" She slid the book back to Scott, who read through the description.

"I don't think that would be a good one, sweetie—it has metal ladders to get up the steep parts."

"That could be fun."

Scott raised his eyebrows at her.

"Oh. Right." She tossed her napkin onto the table. "I'm getting really tired of this. What if I have to spend the rest of my life avoiding things that could turn out badly if I get one of these stupid hand cramps?"

"That won't happen. You and Mr. Masser will figure it out. And if that doesn't pan out, we'll take you to a hand specialist in Philly." He pointed to another page in the guidebook. "This one looks nice—right around Jordan Pond."

They finished up their beverages and set out, congratulating themselves on having the path largely to themselves once they passed the small number of walkers near the restaurant. However, they soon found that the normally easy trail had been made challenging by the rain—the rocks they needed to scramble over here and there were slick and branches weighted down with water hung over the path. But they were rewarded with lovely vistas across the water to the surrounding mountains, and Ann was again transported back to the Adirondacks.

She felt the tension of the incident at the hotel begin to loosen its hold on her as she focused on the physical effort—relatively minor though it was—of the walk. Whether the woods surrounding Jordan Pond were actually "clean" of spirits or whether the moisture-laden air and dim sunlight were merely masking their presence, the effect was the same—she was able to relax as she could only when she felt herself unlikely to encounter a spirit.

The rain started up again on the last leg of the walk. They jogged up the hill to the small complex that housed the restaurant, taking shelter in a breezeway between the restaurant and gift shop with the other tourists, whose gabblings bounced off the walls like clucking in a chicken coop. Ann's chest felt tight, whether from the run or from the first twinges of claustrophobia she wasn't sure.

She pulled off her cap and patted her hair, which was soaked below hat-level and squashed flat above. "I think I better make some repairs."

Standing at the edge of the crowd, Scott flapped the excess moisture out of his coat and wiped the raindrops off his glasses with a clean handkerchief. "Okey doke," he said, replacing his glasses. He glanced around. "I'm going to check out the gift shop."

The women's room was quiet after the hubbub outside. When she had dried her hair as best she could, Ann started combing it out to put back in its usual ponytail when she caught a glimpse in the mirror of a yellowish light hovering behind her.

Her comb clattered to the floor as she whirled to face the light. There was no human form she could discern, just a transparent yellow oval about six feet high. She scooped her knapsack up from the floor and moved to skirt the light and reach the exit, but the light moved to block her. She stepped to the other side. Again the light blocked her.

"Loring?" she said hopefully, but she didn't really expect the spirit from Lynam's Point Hotel to have followed her to Jordan Pond, and certainly not to have been lurking behind her in a restroom. "Biden?" she said, her voice catching. She cleared her throat and said with what she hoped was more authority, "Biden Firth?"

There was no response, and no visible change to the floating yellow light.

Ann squared her shoulders. "If you're Biden Firth, you should let me know. This isn't accomplishing anything."

No response, no change.

"Couldn't you have just stayed dead?" she asked angrily.

There was a noise from the stalls and one of the doors opened, a woman peeking out around the door. She scanned the restroom, then her worried look came back to Ann.

"Is there a man out here?"

Ann was silent, her gaze flitting between the woman and the yellowish light.

The stall door opened a bit more and the woman's look changed from worried to suspicious. "Are you talking to someone?"

"There was a man in here a minute ago," said Ann, her voice taut with strain while also flutey with an overenthusiastic attempt at normalcy. "Just went in the wrong restroom, I guess."

The woman emerged from the stall, her attitude shifting now from suspicion to annoyance. "You had an awful lot to say to him."

Ann laughed weakly. "I guess he had had one too many beers in the restaurant—he wasn't paying any attention to me ..."

The woman crossed the room, heading right for the yellow light.

"Wait, don't do that—" said Ann, right before the woman walked through the light.

The woman turned back, pulling her Acadia sweatshirt a little more closely around her but otherwise appearing unaffected by the light. She took a step backward, away from Ann and toward the door. "Don't do what?"

Ann shrugged in what she hoped was a conciliatory way.

The woman turned quickly and left the restroom.

"Damn," muttered Ann, her attention returning to the yellowish light. It was hovering right over where her comb had fallen, and she decided she could sacrifice the comb in the interest of getting out of there as quickly as possible. She tucked her hands under her opposite arms, feinted left, and then dashed to the right, past the light and out the door.

With frequent glances behind her, she caught up with Scott in the gift shop where he was holding two baseball caps decorated with Acadia National Park logos.

"I thought that if it kept raining, it would be useful to have something to keep the rain off our faces. I have one for you, too."

"Thanks, Scott," she said, her fisted hands pushed into the pockets of her parka, her head pulled down into the collar.

Scott gave her a second look. "Are you okay, sweetie? You look pale."

"Yup, just cold from the walk, I guess," she said. Her thoughts were a jumble and she wasn't in the mood to have Scott haul her back to Somesville for Garrick to check her out. Then she caught a glimpse of the woman from the restroom standing by the door to the gift shop, pointing at her. A park ranger was at her side.

"Damn," Ann muttered.

Scott followed her gaze. "What's that all about?"

The park ranger, who looked to be in her twenties, crossed the gift shop to Ann and Scott.

"Ma'am," she said, nodding to Ann. "Sir," she said with a nod to Scott.

"Ranger," said Ann, not knowing quite how one was supposed to address a national park ranger.

"Sir," said the ranger to Scott, "might I speak with this lady alone for a moment?"

Scott turned to Ann, his eyebrows raised.

"It's okay," she said to him.

He retired to a position that Ann suspected was just within earshot.

The ranger turned to Ann. "I understand that a man followed you into the restroom?"

Ann shrugged. "It was just some guy who had gone in there by mistake."

"I understand you were calling him by name."

"Me? No, I didn't know him," said Ann.

"I understand you were calling him Biden Firth."

Ann smiled cheerfully. "No, she must have misheard me."

"Isn't Biden Firth the man who killed his wife in Phil-adelphia?"

Ann's eyebrows rose. "You heard about that up here?"

"Sure, it was big news."

"Well, I guess it wasn't Biden Firth because he's dead," said Ann with somewhat manic levity.

The ranger sidled a bit closer to her, speaking low so as not to be heard by the other browsers, who were now aware of the conversation and drifting into their vicinity, trying to keep up an appearance of disinterested nonchalance.

"Are you Ann Kinnear?"

Ann experienced a confusing mixture of alarm and pride; so they knew about her in Maine after all. She smiled weakly. "That's me."

The ranger lowered her voice further. "I followed that story on the Yahoo group. Is his ghost following you? Do you think you're in danger?"

"There's a Yahoo group about the Firth murder?" Ann asked, louder than she intended.

"There's a Yahoo group about you. It's about all your cases. But I followed the Firth case especially closely because I'm origi-nally from near Philadelphia. And because, you know, of what happened to you ..."

Still digesting the fact that there was a Yahoo group dedi-cated to her, Ann shook her head. "I thought I saw him, but I was wrong," she said, sounding as businesslike as possible. "I'm sorry to have caused trouble."

The ranger straightened up. "No problem, ma'am. Just please let us know if anyone is bothering you in the park." She began to turn away.

Ann said, "Excuse me ..."

The ranger turned back. "Yes ma'am?"

"I'd prefer it if she doesn't know who I am or who I was talking to."

The ranger smiled conspiratorially. "Yes ma'am, I understand. We don't want her to think that both of us are crazy." And with a tip of her hat, she turned away.

20

Of course, Ann had to explain to Scott the ranger's interest in her, but managed to avoid having him immediately whisk her off to Garrick by making the argument that she would be seeing him later that evening.

Then, after Scott dropped her off in Somesville that night, she had to put up with a lecture from Garrick. "Good heavens, are you hoping it will just pop up in my consulting room? It would greatly facilitate my assessment if you would come to me when it makes an appearance."

Now, an hour before midnight, Ann was traveling down Indian Point Road in Garrick's Cadillac, her body tensed in anticipation of a slow-driver-precipitated road-rage event.

They turned off Indian Point Road onto Lynam's Point Road and made their circuitous way around the peninsula. Just as they were entering the woods at the northern end of the penin- sula, a small, dark form shot across the road in front of them.

"Jesus!" exclaimed Ann. "What was that?"

They were going so slowly that Garrick barely had to brake to stop. The creature stopped in the safety of the pine seedlings by the side of the road and turned toward them.

"That was a raccoon."

"Well, it looks like a little demon with those glowing eyes." The raccoon turned away and trundled out of the range of the headlights.

"Scared of ghosts?" Ann could tell by a slight tightening of Garrick's mouth that he thought he was being amusing.

"No, I'm not scared of ghosts, but this whole thing is giving me the willies. It's all very cloak and dagger."

"You don't find the surreptitious nature of the assignment intriguing?"

"No," said Ann, crossing her arms. "It's creepy."

"Well, the sooner begun, the sooner complete." He looked down the road. "I'll let you out here, it's only about a hundred yards to the hotel."

"Maybe I could hide in the backseat and you could take me all the way to the hotel. It's black as pitch, Garrick."

"Don't be silly, you just need to let your eyes adjust." Garrick made a shooing motion. "Out you go."

Ann opened the door and stepped into the cold October night. Garrick had turned off the dome light before they had left Somesville. He leaned over to peer out at her in the faint light of the moon.

"Come back here when you're done at the hotel and I'll pick you up on my way out."

"How much time will I need?"

"I have no idea. How much time do you think you will need?"

Ann considered. "He appeared pretty quickly before. But it might take me a while to understand what he's saying."

"Very well, I'll plan to be here again in approximately two hours."

"What will you be doing in the meantime?"

"I'll conduct my usual engagement with the client. If he

appears to me, I will continue to attempt to make progress on the assignment on my own. If he doesn't appear to me, I'll assume you are engaging him and will ensure the client stays away from the entrance to the lobby." Garrick gestured impatiently. "We're taking too long. Shut the door."

Ann swung the big car's door shut and winced at the loud thunk it made. She could imagine Garrick glowering. The car glided away down the road.

She watched as the taillights disappeared around a curve, although she could continue to track the car's progress as the headlights cast a ghostly illumination into the woods. She saw a line of lights flick on—the lights along the drive, she guessed. Her ears now more attuned to the night's sounds, she heard the car engine shut off and a few moments later the line of lights flicked off.

She started off toward the hotel.

For a time, she kept to the path by adjusting her direction when the crunch of the gravel gave way to the muffled thud of her feet on the grassy verge of the road, but gradually the mass of undifferentiated blackness resolved itself into suggestions of tree trunks, the darker shadows of understory growth, and the silvery glow of the roadway curving off into the pines. The woods around her were quiet, but then she heard a howl somewhere ahead of her that was answered by one nearby and then passed on to another in the darkness behind her.

Eventually, she passed the cemetery on her left, the headstones vague, hunched forms in the darkness. As the pine woods thinned out, the sky opened over her, the lack of artificial light making the stars brilliant despite the almost-full moon. Across the lawn loomed the darker mass of the hotel.

She followed the road to the circular drive and then kept to the drive to avoid tangling with the row of now-extinguished lights, placing her feet carefully to minimize the crunching of the gravel. When she reached the veranda, she squatted behind the branches of a rhododendron near the stairs to screen herself from the lobby windows.

She listened for voices coming from inside the hotel, but she could only hear the slap of water on the point and, far off, the almost-inaudible hum of the engine of a boat on a midnight run. She waited a minute and then two, becoming increasingly nervous about the possibility of Ellen Lynam emerging unexpectedly from the hotel. How would Loring know she was there? She was wondering if she would have to reveal herself more obviously—to Loring and to whoever might be looking out the lobby windows—when she became aware of a presence near her. A second later, she had to stifle a squawk when she heard a voice right by her ear.

... come to see me?

It was like listening to a very old recording—a wax cylinder engraved by Edison. Only once before had a spirit actually spoken to Ann, and in that case it had been a largely one-sided conversation—the spirit of Biden Firth's wife attempting to give her instructions, but not expecting any response from Ann beyond compliance. But to have a spirit ask her a question, to invite an interaction, was a new experience.

"Are you Loring Lynam?" she asked.

Suddenly she could see his face, illuminated by a bright smile.

Why yes! And you—?

The rest of the sentence faded and she lost it.

"I'm Ann Kinnear. Could we go somewhere else to talk?"

Of course. Follow—

He turned toward the stairs to the veranda, his face disappearing, his form indicated only by a slight opacity that blurred her view of the objects behind him. Ann made a *psst*-ing noise and he turned, his face once again visible.

"Can we talk somewhere outside?"

He made some noise of agreement, then ...

... *boathouse?*

"Yes, that would be good."

His form descended the steps and passed Ann and then completely disappeared into the darkness. Ann followed in the direction he had taken, recalling from her earlier visit the general location of the boathouse. She stayed on the grass bordering the drive to avoid the crunching of gravel this close to the hotel, relieved when she turned the corner of the building and was out of sight of anyone who might be looking out the lobby windows.

On the point behind the hotel, the moon provided more illumination and she was able to make faster progress. She crossed the lawn quickly, uncomfortably aware of the large windows—designed to take full advantage of the view—overseeing her progress. She stepped onto the porch of the boathouse, searching the darkness for some sign of Loring, when a light—evidently motion-activated—snapped on. Blinded, she stumbled along the porch to where it turned the corner, putting the boathouse between herself and the hotel. She waited there, pressed to the wall, listening for the sound of a door opening and closing, someone coming to investigate, but heard nothing. In a minute, the boathouse light clicked off.

"Loring? Are you there?" she whispered.

Yes, right here.

The voice once again was right beside her and again she jumped.

... *go inside? ... not much warmer ... sit down.*

The voice faded in and out, like a sloppily tuned radio.

"I'd rather not have the light go on again," said Ann. "I don't mind standing." She burrowed her gloved hands deeper into her pockets—she hoped the conversation wouldn't be a long one. "I have a question for you from Ellen. Where is the lady?"

21

1947

Chip stood at a workbench in the shed just inside the stand of pines that surrounded the hotel lawn, fiddling with a cage trap he had devised to catch a rabbit that was wreaking havoc in the hotel's vegetable garden. If he caught it, he would drive it to the mainland and let it go.

"Chip!" He heard his name and looked up from his work. His father stood in the doorway and, based on his expression, Chip guessed it was not the first time he had called his name. His father gripped the frame of the door—these days, he always seemed to be holding onto something to steady himself.

For a moment, before returning completely from his reverie, he saw his father as others must see him. Never a large man, the lean, muscular build Chip could remember from his childhood had given way over the years to a frailty that made him look much older that his forty-four years. His formerly wavy brown hair had thinned, his cheekbones jutted, his face was cut with deep lines. He looked, Chip thought, like a scrawny fox that might eat the rabbit that was grazing in their garden.

His father cleared his throat, as if the effort of getting Chip's attention had taxed his voice. "Pritchard called. They're putting on a party and need some extra hands. Seems a little late in the season for a party. Aren't they usually gone by now?"

Chip put the trap on the workbench. "Yes. I guess with the weather being so hot and dry, there's no reason for them to go to Florida just yet."

His father tried to peer around him. "What kind of trap is that?"

"Nothing. I'm just experimenting."

"Well, if you want to experiment, you could try experimenting on those lawn chairs when you get back—they'll need sanding before we paint them. Don't be too long, I need you here."

Don't be too long, I need you here was a refrain so familiar that Chip barely registered it except as a kind of ache in his jaw. Now that Chip was seventeen, his father seemed torn between the competing desires to send him out on errands in the hotel pickup truck or to set him to work on hotel projects.

Retrieving the truck from behind the hotel, Chip wound his way off the Lynam's Point peninsula and cut across what he thought of as the western part of the "lobster claw" that Mount Desert Island resembled on a map. He passed through Somesville and then crossed the eastern part of the "claw" on Eagle Lake Road. It was early October, and normally he would have been wearing a jacket, but the island was enjoying a glorious Indian summer, the cloudless sky a startling blue. Chip had woken to frost on the fields only a few weeks before, but then the temperature had climbed and the sun had beaten down on Mount Desert, baking the little remaining moisture out of the fields and forests. There hadn't been a good rain since May.

Just outside Bar Harbor proper, Chip turned off Eagle Lake

Road onto Cleftstone Road and then turned between two granite pillars joined by an arch of metalwork with *Jardin d'Eden* worked into its apex. This summer "cottage" had been built by James Furness Senior, who had started a lumber business and made the family fortune through some shrewdly negotiated government contracts during the First War. James Junior, who had rarely set foot in a lumber mill, had expanded that fortune further in the Second.

When James Junior and his wife, Josephine, had inherited Jardin d'Eden in the 1920s, they had set about making it the cultural mecca of Bar Harbor high society. They brought chamber orchestras up from New York for performances for their fellow society luminaries, decorated the rooms with museum-quality works of art, and hosted parties that were described with breathless excitement in the society columns of the Boston and New York newspapers.

At the end of each summer season, after the Furnesses had relocated to their winter home in Palm Beach, George Pritchard, Jardin d'Eden's majordomo, hired a number of local boys and men to help with repairs and maintenance. For the last couple of years, after Lynam's Point Hotel closed for the season, Chip's father had sent him to work part-time at Jardin.

But this year, the Furnesses had extended their stay on Mount Desert and today the house was abuzz with preparation for that evening's hastily arranged party. Gardeners carried baskets of flowers up from the greenhouses and gardens for which Jardin was famous. A delivery truck from Bar Harbor rattled by, headed to the kitchen entrance with crates of wine. A girl was setting up luminaria along the drive —no doubt an alternative to the usual tree-hung Japanese lanterns, dictated by the tinder-dry conditions. Beyond the veranda, Chip could catch a glimpse of the links at the Kebo Valley Golf Club and, beyond that, the town of Bar Harbor. In the other direction rose the thickly forested slopes of Great Hill.

Chip parked the truck behind the greenhouses with the other workers' vehicles and went to find Pritchard.

He found him in the kitchen talking to Millie, one of the maids, who was polishing glassware with an old linen napkin.

"Check them all," Pritchard was saying. "Last time, there was lipstick on one of the glasses and Mrs. Furness was none too pleased."

"There's no lipstick on a glass on my watch," said Millie. "Must have been someone else in charge of the glassware for that party."

"Well, let's just make sure it doesn't happen tonight," said Pritchard.

"She just said it won't," said Chip.

Pritchard turned to Chip. "And what do you want, Lynam?"

George Pritchard was a local man made good. He had ingratiated himself with Mrs. Furness by towing her Packard out of a ditch after her chauffeur lost control on a slick patch of road. When Mrs. Furness heard his only slightly embellished story that he had served as a driver for high-ranking brass during the war, she immediately fired the chauffeur and replaced him with Pritchard, and since then Pritchard had risen quickly through the ranks of the Furness household. He had taken to his new high society life, and lost no opportunity to remind the locals of the importance of his position. They made fun of him behind his back, but each regretted that he had not been the one to have happened upon Mrs. Furness in the ditch.

"Dad told me you asked me to come by to help," said Chip.

"Oh, right."

Millie rolled her eyes at Pritchard's back and gave Chip a friendly smile, then returned to polishing.

Pritchard gestured with the clipboard he was holding.

"Come with me." He left the kitchen and strode down the wide gallery that ran through the middle of the house toward the front door. "The Furnesses are having a party—last-minute thing, guest of honor just showed up yesterday. Ship from Italy, and train and car from New York. You'd think he could have given them a little more warning."

"They're having a party for a foreigner?"

"Well, it probably won't be much of a party for him since he doesn't speak much English, but he brought a painting that Mr. Furness bought. Mr. Furness is pretty pleased with it." Pritchard looked at the clipboard. "Mrs. Furness wants fires laid in all the public rooms in case it gets chilly this evening."

"Not likely to get chilly with this weather."

"She says she wants fires and she's the boss. Go on then."

Chip turned toward the back of the house.

"And mind you make them so they're not smoky!"

Chip waved an acknowledgement.

Chip had made up fires in the other first-floor rooms, with the last one to lay in the library. The door had been closed and Chip had postponed, thinking Mr. Furness must be in there and that he would wait until the room was empty, but then he had seen Mr. Furness outside talking to Pritchard. Perhaps the door had been closed accidentally. He knocked tentatively on the door and, getting no answer, opened it and entered with his basket of wood.

A young man—in fact, just about Chip's age—stood at the window in an almost military stance, his arms held at his sides, his fingers curled. He had exotically dark hair and olive skin. A slight softening of his hard edges would have made him handsome, but his lean frame was a little too angular, his features a little too sharp.

Two wing chairs that were normally drawn up to the elaborately tiled fireplace had been moved in front of a large window framing a glorious view of Frenchman Bay. The chairs flanked a small table on which rested three champagne glasses. On the table, facing away from Chip, was a painting on an easel.

"Sì?"

"I just came to lay the fire." Chip gestured to his basket.

"Sì." The dark-haired boy clasped his hands behind his back. "Faccia pure." He waved imperiously toward the fireplace.

Chip crossed to the fireplace, knelt, and began arranging the kindling.

After a moment, the boy said, "Aspetterò in veranda," and walked stiffly to the door and disappeared into the hall.

Chip finished laying the fire and then crossed to the easel to see what was on it.

It was a painting of a young woman—dark hair loose around her shoulders, dark eyes meeting his. Her dress was plain but rich-looking, probably silk, puffed crimson sleeves slashed to release a spill of white fabric, the only decoration a pendant of gold, garnet, and pearls. Behind her, in muted colors but intricately wrought detail, was a landscape of rolling golden hills and columnar trees and, at the end of a winding road, a distant castle. Her expression was weary and vulnerable, hinting at a life that hadn't lived up to the luxurious promise of the bucolic setting.

In a moment, Chip was transported back almost a dozen years, to the day he had seen his mother framed in the hotel kitchen window. The Maine pines had stood in for those manicured European trees, the hotel boathouse for the Mediterranean castle. Her dark hair had been down, her dark eyes turned toward him. And that look of almost-hidden sadness was the same.

Chip lowered himself onto one of the chairs and stared, entranced. He leaned forward, expecting the realism to fragment into dots of color, but even inches from the canvas, the painting held the same fidelity. He sank back into the chair.

In the years since his mother had disappeared, Chip had schooled himself not to think of her, since to do so was only a source of misery. He had quickly learned not to ask his father questions about her, and had eventually learned not to ask questions even of himself. The pain of her absence was like a finger snatched away, in a moment of inattention, by a spinning blade. The initial numb shock of seeing a hand so deformed was quickly overwhelmed by a bright dagger of pain and then replaced by the dull throb that in the end resolved itself into the leaden acceptance of the loss. He had adjusted his expectations of what life could offer in the face of that loss.

But the lady in the painting was a balm to the pain. He almost felt as if he could reach out and take the delicate hand with the fine, slender fingers in his. The furrow in his brow smoothed, and his mouth relaxed into a smile.

Chip was not quite so lost in the painting that he missed the tread of light steps in the hallway. He leapt to his feet a moment before the door opened and Millie entered, a small tray tucked under her arm. She let out a little yelp when she saw him standing behind the easel.

"Chip Lynam, what are you doing in here?"

"Laying a fire."

"And admiring the new painting, looks like." She crossed the room and stood beside Chip, the sleeve of her black dress brushing his arm. "Pretty, ain't it?"

He nodded. "Yes. She looks like ..."

Millie looked at him expectantly. When he didn't continue, she prompted, "Like what?"

Chip blushed. "Oh, I don't know. Like a princess, I guess."

Millie raised her eyebrows at Chip, then turned back to the painting. "The man who sold it to the Furnesses sent his son all the way from Italy to deliver it. Good-looking boy. That's what the party's for, to show it off." She moved to the table and put the empty champagne glasses on her tray. "Seems like they've got enough paintings already, but I guess folk like that don't think in terms of 'enough.'"

"They just got it?"

"Yup, showed up yesterday, the carpenter's coming this afternoon to hang it."

Chip felt what he could only describe as a twinge of jealousy. "They don't need a carpenter, I could do that for them."

Millie raised her eyebrows archly. "If you're Mr. and Mrs. Furness and a nail needs driven, you're sure to want the nail-driving expert to do it."

"Who's it by, do you know?"

Millie shook her head. "Some Italian artist. Now if you're done mooning over it, you'd best push off before Mr. Pritchard finds you lollygagging."

22

G arrick and Ellen sat in the lounge, Ellen morosely paging through her notepad and Garrick sitting with his fingers interlaced, seemingly relaxed but in fact attentive to any sound from the veranda. He had maneuvered Ellen into the chair facing away from the window, which proved to be fortuitous when he saw Ann's faint form crossing the lawn and then saw her captured in the sudden illumination of the boathouse light.

Ellen turned to look, but not before Ann disappeared behind the boathouse. "Wonder what that was," she said.

"Rodent," said Garrick.

"It would have to be a mighty big rodent to set off the motion detector," said Ellen skeptically.

"Perhaps a raccoon," he said gamely.

"Isn't a raccoon a rodent?"

"No. It belongs to the Carnivora order."

"Sounds like a kind of monk."

Garrick raised his eyebrows.

Ellen tossed the pad to the floor. "He's not coming tonight."

"One never knows. We shouldn't give up so easily."

"Give up easily? We've been sitting here for almost an hour!"

"I'm well aware," said Garrick testily.

Ellen stood and walked to the window. "Carnivora, eh?"

Garrick stood up. "Let's put the kettle on."

Ellen turned from the window. "I thought you wanted to wait for him?"

"Yes, but not here. Maybe he's feeling we're being too demanding. Spirits don't like to feel constrained by human schedules," he said, improvising. "We'll have hot drinks and then come back and see if anything has changed."

"I've got to stop drinking tea in the middle of the night," she grumbled.

"Try hot water. It's cleansing."

Ellen snorted.

"Ellen."

"Oh, all right." She headed for the kitchen. "Maybe there's some herbal tea. You should try herbal tea. It at least has some taste to it."

"It's like drinking an unpleasant potpourri," he said.

When they were settled in the kitchen with their beverages of choice, Ellen said, "This is just like the olden days, Garrick. I had such a crush on you. You were so handsome and dashing."

"You were just a child."

"I was seventeen. Old enough to have money of my own to hire you."

"Money you inherited from your father."

She stirred another spoonful of sugar into her tea. "It made Loring crazy that I used the money that way. But I thought that if you could help us communicate with Daddy, he would give us some tips for running the hotel."

"From what I understand, your father was probably not the best source for business advice, even if we had been able to contact him."

"Why weren't we able to connect with him, do you think?"

"From what you have told me, your father sounds like a man a bit disconnected, even when he was alive."

"Yes, Daddy was sort of a dreamer. But I wish we could talk directly with him and not have to get all our information secondhand through Loring."

Garrick shifted on the stool. "Ellen, is it possible that Loring doesn't know the location of the lady—that he's just pretending to have the information to be difficult?"

Ellen shook her head. "No, Daddy told Loring everything. I wish he had told me. Maybe he thought I was too young." She shrugged, but the pain of not having been included was evident in her downcast eyes. "Loring told me some of the stories after Daddy died, but not this one. Not where the lady is."

"How about your mother?" Garrick had been avoiding suggesting this on the off chance that the lady in question and Ellen's father had had an illicit relationship, but he decided that, even as odd a family as the Lynams were, a father would be unlikely to share stories about his paramour with his son.

"Have you sensed Mother?" asked Ellen, surprised.

"No, but I haven't tried to contact her, you always asked me to contact Loring."

"I wish I had known her, even a little bit. Poor Daddy. He always had the women in his life disappearing. His mother ... his wife." She sighed. "In any case, Mother didn't know where the lady was. At least that's what Loring told me."

Garrick tried another tack. "Have you tried other means of locating this lady? Perhaps a private investigator. Or," he scowled, "the internet."

"No, Garrick, I need you to find out from Loring, it's the only way."

"Very well."

Ellen sipped her tea silently for a few minutes and then burst out, "Loring certainly took the quitter's way out!"

"Loring was always an unhappy man."

"Did you know he killed himself when he was exactly the same age as Daddy was when he died?"

Garrick did in fact know this, but made a noncommittal grunt.

"And he must have known I'd be the one to find him!" She gripped the hot mug of tea. "It took me forever to find a knife to cut him down." Her voice began to quaver.

"Yes," said Garrick tightly. "That was unworthy even of Loring."

"Daddy fought to beat the cancer as long as he could, but Loring never fought for anything! Just fought with the people around him. The people who loved him." Ellen removed a tissue from one of the bulging pockets of her bulky cardigan and blew her nose.

"Don't be melodramatic," said Garrick gently.

Ellen replaced the tissue in her pocket. "Garrick, this hotel is the only tie to my family—to my heritage—that I have left. I don't know what I'll do if I lose it."

"I am hopeful that we still might obtain the information you need to avoid that eventuality," said Garrick.

23

Ann had hoped that she would become more attuned to Loring as he talked—that she would be able to pick up more of what he was communicating—but she found the opposite happened. At first, she could catch snatches of words or phrases, but after a while there were periods when she couldn't hear anything. She could, however, still sense his ghostly presence at her side, and could often perceive his face, or at least his eyes, fading into and out of view. She strained to hear any syllable, and when that didn't work she tried abstracting her attention in the hopes of, if not picking up words, at least picking up the overall sense of what he was saying. Neither approach was effective. There were times when his visual presence was stronger, when Ann sensed he was more animated by the story he was telling her, but this was not accompanied by a coinciding improvement in her ability to understand what he was saying. Soon, she lost the ability to discern even the occasional word and could sense that he was continuing to talk based only on a sort of modulated buzz coming from the place where she sensed he stood.

Eventually, even the buzz stopped. She could see those gray

eyes, faintly luminescent in the darkness, looking at her expectantly.

"Loring, I'm sorry, I didn't understand very much of that."

The gray eyes registered disappointment.

"But 'the lady'—it's not a person. It's a painting—is that right?"

The eyes brightened and the spirit said something unintelligible.

"I'm sorry, I still can't—"

You ... tomorrow. Then the voice faded back to a buzz.

"You want me to come back tomorrow?"

Yes ... light.

"Yes, a light would be a good idea, I'll bring a flashlight—"

... daylight ...

"You want me to come tomorrow during daylight?"

Ann sensed rather than heard his affirmative response.

"Why?" she asked, with little expectation that she would understand his answer.

... show ...

"You'll show me the painting? That would be very helpful. Is it inside the hotel?"

The spirit responded but Ann couldn't understand what he was saying.

"I'll assume it's inside the hotel, or at least nearby. Any particular time?" she asked.

Anytime, she heard with surprising clarity.

Ann pulled back the sleeve of her parka and pressed the button to illuminate the face of her watch. She was surprised that so much time had passed. "I need to leave now, but I'll be back tomorrow. I'll wait for you near the front door of the hotel."

The spirit raised his hand to his forehead, a virtual tip of the hat, and then he was gone—a subtle change in the space he had occupied—and Ann felt herself to be very much alone.

To avoid setting off the light again, she clambered over the railing at the far side of the boathouse, picked her way over the rocks that bordered the water until she reached the lawn, and then scuttled along the edge of the lawn back toward the road and the designated meeting place.

24

Garrick stood in the chill gloom of the lounge, buttoning up his long black coat as Ellen ran her fingers fretfully through her hair. "I can't believe he didn't show up at all. Garrick, we're getting nowhere. We're going to lose the hotel, we only have two more days now."

Garrick put his hands in his pockets and looked toward the windows where, in the daylight, he would have seen the expanse of lawn and the vestiges of the croquet court for which the hotel had formerly been famous. "You really think this lady can help you save the hotel?"

"Yes, I do."

"And you are not willing to employ other methods to find her?"

"No."

He sighed. "Perhaps Loring wants to push his revelation of the lady's location as close to the deadline as he can. I will bring all my resources to bear to attempt to convince him to cooperate." Ellen followed him to the front door, where he removed the flashlight from his pocket and, with a nod of farewell, let himself out. He heard the click of the key in the lock as he descended the steps and made his way to his car, his flashlight illuminating an oval of leaf-strewn gravel.

After he had gotten beyond the drive in front of the hotel, he lowered the front windows despite the cold, in case Ann called out to him from a hiding place along the road. He scowled. They should have established a clearer landmark for their rendezvous. He began growing concerned that he had passed the point where he had dropped her off and was contemplating whether he could back up or turn around without the benefit of headlights when he jumped at a voice from just outside the car.

"Garrick!"

Garrick stomped on the brake, his heart banging against his ribs. As Ann circled to the passenger side, Garrick massaged his neck to one side of his prominent Adam's apple.

Ann got in and eased the door shut. "What are you doing?"

"Nothing of interest." He eased off the brake and the car glided forward.

"Guess what I found out!"

"Not now, wait until we get back," said Garrick.

"Can we turn on the heat, I'm freezing," she said, rolling up her window.

"Very well," said Garrick, not taking his eyes off the road.

Ann pushed the heater up to high. After a minute she asked, "Can you roll up your window?"

"Very well," said Garrick. He coasted the car to a stop, pressed the button to raise the window, and then resumed his stately progress down the road.

They wended their way back off the peninsula, and then up Indian Point Road and across Oak Hill Road to Somesville in silence.

∼

GARRICK PULLED the car up to a detached single-car garage behind the house and turned to Ann, the back porch light throwing the already severe lines of his face into sharp relief.

"Well?"

"The Lady isn't a who, she's a what," said Ann.

There was a long silence. Finally Ann sighed. "It's a painting."

"A painting?"

"Yes."

Another silence.

"That's it. The Lady isn't a person, it's a painting. That's all I got."

"All you got or all he told you?"

"All I got. There was a lot more but I couldn't pick it up. But I'm supposed to go back tomorrow and he'll tell me more."

"Really? That's very promising," said Garrick with unaccustomed enthusiasm. "When?"

"He said it didn't matter."

"Very good," said Garrick, rubbing his hands together. "Perhaps during the day. How long were you there tonight before he appeared to you?"

"I saw him pretty much as soon as I got to the hotel."

"Better and better. And if he is going to show you where the painting is—" He looked sharply at Ann. "Did he say he was going to show you the painting's location, or describe it to you?"

Ann thought back to her conversation. "Definitely 'show.'"

"And his visible presence—it is more perceptible to you than his verbal communications?"

"Yes. The visible part is sort of hazy as well, but if he leads me to where it is I feel pretty certain I can follow him."

"Excellent. If we can devise a way to keep Ellen away from the hotel for a few hours tomorrow, that should be sufficient.

Your driver can drop you off at the beginning of the road after she's away."

"Okay. Garrick, can we go inside? It's still freezing out here."

"Yes, yes." Garrick killed the engine. They got out of the car and Garrick opened the back door to a kitchen that looked like it had been untouched by upgrades for half a century. Ann got a glimpse of a Sputnik-era refrigerator—the word "icebox" popped into her head—and an old wooden table and rush-seat chair before Garrick gestured her impatiently on to the hallway where he hung his coat on one of the pegs on the wall.

"Is your driver picking you up?"

"Oh. Yes." Ann pulled out her cellphone and sent a text to Scott, then followed Garrick into his office, where he was lighting the fire. Ann sat in one of the leather chairs and wished he would offer her at least a mug of hot water.

Garrick sat behind the desk. "It is promising that Loring is willing to share this information with you, but disappointing that you can't comprehend what he's saying." His earlier relative good cheer seemed to have dissipated a bit.

"Maybe I'll be able to understand him better if I spend more time with him."

"Unlikely. Or at least unlikely in the time we have." Garrick tapped his fingers together. Finally he said, "It is not ideal, but perhaps if Loring is aware that I know that 'The Lady' is a painting, this game he has been playing will become less entertaining to him."

"Maybe telling Ellen that it's a painting would be helpful to her—maybe she doesn't realize that."

"Possibly. However, I believe it would be preferable to provide her with the information she ultimately desires—the location of 'The Lady'—rather than providing her with possibly unhelpful partial information. She seems a bit overwrought about the entire situation."

"You could try going during the day to talk with Loring. He didn't seem to have a preference for nighttime when I talked with him. I could go with you."

"No, too great a risk of Ellen seeing us together." Garrick stood up. "I will visit the hotel alone tomorrow during the day and speak with Loring. If he is still unwilling to give me the information, even once he is aware that I know The Lady is a painting, then we will arrange for you to meet with him again."

There was a knock at the front door and Garrick walked to the window and pulled aside the curtain. "Ah, it appears that your driver has arrived. Very prompt. Not local?"

"No, not local." Ann gathered up her knapsack and followed Garrick to the hallway. "So did Loring appear to you at all tonight?"

"Of course not, it sounds as if he was with you most of the time, correct?"

"Yes, I just thought he might have appeared in two places at once."

Garrick snorted. "My dear, you need to do a bit more studying if you wish to be a professional in this field."

ELLEN TRACKED the lights of Garrick's car down the road. She saw him stop—was he going to come back to tell her something? —then the car resumed its progress and eventually the lights disappeared among the pines. When the night was once again Maine-woods dark, Ellen retrieved her purse from the office, looped a long knitted scarf around her neck, and went to her Jeep. She could have waited until the morning, but there didn't seem to be any reason—she wasn't going to be able to sleep, and it was already breakfast time where she was calling.

She drove to Bass Harbor—it was hard to find a payphone

these days—and dialed the numbers she had been given and told to memorize. In a moment a low, cultured voice with a European accent answered.

"*Pronto*?"

"It's me. We just had another sensing. We're making progress."

"Have you found La Signora?"

"No, not yet, but I'm sure we're very close."

"Time is running short."

Ellen fidgeted with the metal cord of the phone. "I know. But I have a good feeling about it. Garrick is very good at what he does."

"You know what you must do. And you know the consequences if you do not do it. I will await further updates." And the line went dead.

Ellen hung up the phone, the receiver rattling against the cradle. She smoothed her hair back and took a deep, steadying breath. Garrick would find the lady, he had never failed her before. And if the hotel survived, if she had a chance to bring it back to its former glory, it would all be worth it. And she was sure Garrick would be there to help her with that, as well.

25

1947

O n Friday, October 17th, a fire started in a cranberry bog about seven miles northwest of Bar Harbor. The water in the bog had burned off under months of unrelenting sun and the marsh grass and shrubs left behind were scorched to a tinder dryness. A hundred acres burned before it was contained.

A northwest wind carried a pall of smoke over Great Hill to Jardin d'Eden. As the air thickened, Mrs. Furness's asthmatic cough echoed from her bedroom through the upstairs hallway of Jardin. When the staff closed the windows against the smoke, the still air caused even the unafflicted to gasp. Mr. Furness decided it was time for them to relocate to their winter residence.

As Chip went up the drive to Jardin on Saturday morning, the Furnesses' Packard Custom Super was going down, the chauffeur whom Pritchard had hired to replace himself in the driver's seat, Mr. and Mrs. Furness in the back. The Packard was followed by another car carrying Mr. Furness's secretary and

Mrs. Furness's personal maid; a pile of luggage was strapped to the back.

"Where are they going?" asked Chip when he found Pritchard preparing for the regular round of repairs and maintenance.

"Airport. Mr. Furness chartered a plane. They're going to the Palm Beach house."

"But what about the fire? Don't they want to stay here to keep an eye on things?"

"That's what they pay me to do, Lynam," Pritchard growled. "Plus, the fire's small, just smoky. The boys will keep it in check."

As Chip worked at Jardin d'Eden through the weekend, adjusting sliding doors that had become balky over the summer and repairing a broken window in the greenhouse, he periodically heard the three blasts of the fire whistle. If Pritchard wasn't around, Chip would go outside to see if the direction of the wind or smoke had changed.

Passing the closed door of the library one day, he had a sudden alarm as he thought of soot settling on the painting—on The Lady, as he had come to think of her. He tapped lightly on the door and, getting no answer, tried to turn the doorknob, but the door was locked. His concern escalated slightly. Was someone keeping an eye on the painting? He went to find Millie —she would have a key.

She was in the butler's pantry in her usual black dress, but without the white cap and apron required when Mrs. Furness was in residence. There was a sparkling pile of silverware to her left and an even more sparkling set carefully lined up on her right. She was working her polishing cloth vigorously over a demitasse spoon.

"Hiya, Millie," said Chip from the doorway.

"Hiya, Chip, what's up?"

"Is the window in the library closed?"

"I should think so. Why?"

"Just thinking that if someone left it open, the smoke wouldn't be any good for that new painting of Mr. Furness's."

"Ah, right. You do fancy that painting, don't you? I'm sure Mr. Pritchard would make sure the windows are closed."

Chip reluctantly started to turn away, then turned back.

"But can we check to make sure? You don't even have to go, I'll just borrow the key for a minute."

"Oh no you don't, I'm not handing a key I'm charged with over to anyone." Millie put down the polishing cloth and drew a large ring of keys from her dress pocket. "Let's go see so you'll stop fretting and get back to your real work."

When they got to the library, Millie knocked then, after waiting a moment, unlocked the door and peeked in. "All closed up safe and sound."

Chip put his hand out to keep the door open. "Can I just take a quick look?"

Millie shook her head in wry amusement, then glanced up and down the hall. "You are a strange one, Chip Lynam. Okay, but make it quick."

Chip slipped past her into the room. The drapes were drawn across the window and the room was dark so he flipped on the light, illuminating the crystal chandelier.

The painting had been hung over a giltwood console on which Mrs. Furness's collection of antique glass paperweights was displayed. Chip crossed to the painting. It had been hung so that The Lady's eyes were even with his own, and the proportions were life-size; Chip had an almost dizzying sense of looking through a window and seeing not the smoke-laden view of Cleftstone Road, but instead the serene eyes of this beautiful young woman with the clear air of an Italian summer day behind her. He gazed back at her, shifting slightly back and forth to enjoy that sensation of her eyes following his. He leaned forward, marveling over the detail: each strand of her dark hair, the delicate arch of her eyebrow. He leaned forward a bit more, resting a hand on the console, lightly brushing one of the paper-weights, which rocked on its base.

"For heaven's sake, be careful!" gasped Millie from the door-way. "That's enough—you come out now, Chip."

"One minute, Millie ..."

He heard a little huff of exasperation and then Millie clicked off the light. "Now, Chip. You've checked that the window's closed, you've seen your favorite girl, now let's go."

Chip stepped reluctantly back and, with one last look—the painting still dimly illuminated by the light from the open door —followed Millie out of the room.

26

The next day, unable to think of a viable excuse to get Ellen away from the hotel, Garrick decided to drive out to the hotel and merely explain to her that with time running short they needed to try a different approach, such as allowing him to speak privately with Loring. However, as he drove down Indian Point Road he passed Ellen in her Jeep going the other direction. She appeared to be rummaging around in something on the passenger seat, probably her purse—why would a driver ever take his or her eyes off the road?—and didn't see him. He whistled a few bars of Poulenc's *Sonata for Flute and Piano*.

Garrick pulled the Cadillac up to the steps leading to the veranda—he had no wish to appear to be trying to avoid detection should Ellen return while he was still there. He walked to the west end of the hotel, where the entrance to the now-defunct kitchen was and, lifting a flower pot containing the crackly remains of an unidentifiable plant, revealed the key whose hiding place a seventeen-year-old Ellen Lynam had shown him so many years ago.

Returning to the veranda, he unlocked the door and stepped

into the lobby. He had found that one of the keys to his success in interacting with the dead was to know how a particular spirit preferred to be summoned. If you wished to summon a shy person, it did no good to be strident. If you wished to summon an aristocrat, it did no good to address them as if they were a member of the hoi polloi. If you wanted to speak with the spirit of a common man, you called to him in a common way.

"Loring, it's Garrick. I'm in the lobby." He heard the empty echo of an uninhabited building, punctuated by the ticking of a clock from the office.

He waited less than a minute before Loring appeared in the doorway leading to the lounge.

"Not on your usual midnight schedule today?" said Loring.

"We have done our best to accommodate your evident preference for nocturnal interactions but, as you know, time is running short and I needed to find a way to accelerate our discussion."

"Accelerate, eh?" Loring leaned against the doorframe. "I'm all ears."

"I know that 'The Lady' is a painting."

Loring regarded Garrick expressionlessly for a few moments, then said, "Did Ellen tell you that?"

"I don't feel compelled to share the source of my information." If Loring was going to pretend he hadn't spoken with Ann, Garrick didn't feel like arguing with him. "Knowing that The Lady is an object rather than a person brings a somewhat different perspective to the question. When I assumed that 'the lady' was a person, I wondered why Ellen didn't engage some alternate means of obtaining the information she is looking for. However, now knowing that The Lady is a painting, then I must assume you have sequestered it in a location of which only you are aware."

Loring turned back to the lounge and crossed to the

windows overlooking the remains of the croquet court and water beyond. Garrick followed him, standing for a moment in the doorway then crossing the room to sit in his regular chair, which was still standing in the middle of the room from the previous night. He folded his hands and waited.

Finally Loring said, still looking out the window, "I'm going to tell you something, but I'd recommend you don't just regurgitate it all verbatim to my sister."

"How charmingly put."

Loring glanced back at Garrick and then back out the window. "It's not a person, but it might as well have been, the way Dad acted. It was one of those paintings where the eyes seem to follow you. And it had this little smile, like it was going to share a secret with you."

"It was a painting that belonged to your father?"

Loring turned from the window, crossed the room, and sat down in his regular place. He studied Garrick appraisingly. Finally he said, "It was a gift." He crossed his legs. "He was seventeen when he got it. You remember how it is when you're seventeen—some obsession is practically required, right? But most seventeen-year-olds get obsessed with an actual girl—" He gave Garrick a small, unfriendly smile. "Well, maybe not you but, trust me, that's how it is for most seventeen-year-olds. But Dad got obsessed with The Lady." Loring stretched his legs out and leaned back, gazing at the ceiling. "In fact, he was so obsessed with it, he didn't want anyone else to see it. He hid it away. When he was alone, he would just sit there and look at it. It was like he was hypnotized."

"How do you know this if he kept it such a secret?"

"When he found out he was dying from the cancer, he told me. He'd invite me to join him. Father-son bonding, I guess. Thought I'd be as smitten with it as he was. Told me the story about it so many times I thought I'd scream. Happened I was seventeen at the time, but I was one of these seventeen-year-olds who would have been more interested in actual girls ... if I'd had time for that sort of thing."

"Did Ellen participate in these discussions with your father?"

"No. She was seven when Dad died, he thought she was too young to keep a secret. But he wrote her a letter about the painting—described it in all its poetic glory—and gave it to the lawyer to give to her when she turned seventeen, same time she got her inheritance. What there was of it, at least. Dad put a lot of store in the importance of seventeen," he added bitterly.

"Did the letter include mention of where he had hidden the painting?"

"No."

"One would think he would have wanted her to know where it was."

"Guess he thought I'd show her. That the two of us would sit around admiring it and thanking Dad for leaving us such a fabulous gift."

Garrick crossed his legs. "It's difficult to understand what incentive you would now have for keeping that location a secret."

"I have my reasons."

"She says she needs it to save the hotel."

"Oh, I don't think it would save the hotel," said Loring, examining his nails.

"You don't want her to have it?"

Loring sat forward suddenly. "I didn't want any of us to have it," he said savagely. "That thing sucked Dad's energy and attention as if he'd had a mistress. Ellen never had a mother—Mom died giving birth to her—and for all I know she would have latched on to 'The Lady' like a gosling imprinting on a goose and spent all her time mooning over it. I was hoping there would be at least one person in the family who could help me try to keep this miserable place afloat."

"So what will you do now?"

Loring sat back again and looked at Garrick for a few moments. Finally he said, "I have no reason to want to help her find that painting. And if I were to give anyone a message to convey to my sister, it certainly wouldn't be you. Letting her piss away her money on your 'consulting services,'" he said contemptuously.

Garrick raised his eyebrows. "I find it hard to believe you still doubt my abilities since you're conversing with me."

"It's not your abilities I doubt, Garrick—it's your scruples. You let a young girl squander her money on ideas even you never believed would work. Ghost tours. Séances." Loring snorted. "Ridiculous."

"I wasn't in a position to turn away business, Loring. That's a situation with which you are certainly familiar."

Loring sat forward again. "I know you're in a position to turn away business now, Garrick. Don't come back. I have no reason to tell either of you anything." He pushed himself to his feet, crossed the lounge, and disappeared into the lobby.

27

1947

On Monday, October 20th, Chip drove home from Jardin d'Eden through a haze of smoke from the fires that continued to spring up in the tinder-dry slash that had been left behind from logging and brush cutting. He passed trucks filled with young men on their way to help fight the fires. He felt guilty, heading toward the fire-free western "claw" while men and boys his own age were working to protect the timber and parkland that provided their livelihood and the homes those livelihoods enabled. But his father had been very clear that Chip was to come directly home after his day at Jardin.

That evening, as he finished a bowl of the soup his father had heated up from a can, he broke the silence that was the usual accompaniment to their meals. "I think I'll sign up to help fight the fires tomorrow. They've got quite a job to do, they can probably use all the help they can get."

"That isn't a job, it's volunteer. Those boys are never going to get paid for that work."

"It's only a couple of days, I can make up the time and the money at Jardin."

"You've got a commitment to Jardin, you go there like you told them you would."

"You wouldn't complain about me volunteering if the fire was coming toward the hotel," Chip muttered.

"What did you say?" demanded his father.

"Nothing."

His father took a deep breath. "If you think—"

"I'll do like you say. I'll go to Jardin." Part of Chip was sorry to miss out on the excitement of the fire lines, but he realized that the place he really wanted to be was near The Lady. The forests and homes seemed to have plenty of people who were fighting to protect them, but who was fighting to protect her? Certainly not Pritchard. If his father thought the money he'd earn at Jardin was the most important thing—well, that was as good an excuse as any to stay near The Lady.

The next day, on his drive to Jardin, Chip saw fresh smoke roiling up from the land to the north of Eagle Lake Road, and the fire whistle blew as Chip pulled the truck into its usual spot. He jogged to the veranda and looked out toward Bar Harbor, but the air was hazy with smoke carried by a strengthening wind from the fire, the view of which was blocked by the bulk of Great Hill.

"Lynam!" he heard a voice call behind him—George Pritchard with his ever-present clipboard. "What are you doing here? Shouldn't you be out helping with the fires? I hear they're going to be calling in reinforcements from Dow Field."

"Dad told me to come here. Don't you need me?"

"They need you more there. If the fire reaches Cleftstone, there's not much that one extra pair of hands here will accomplish."

"But what about ... the artwork?" Chip had been about to say

"The Lady," but didn't want to endure the teasing that would result should Pritchard find out about his obsession.

"Mr. Furness says to keep the house locked up and to wet the roof if the fire gets close—he says that the art's more likely to be damaged by moving it than by keeping it here."

Only if it were moved by uncaring hands, thought Chip. He needed an excuse to stay at Jardin in case the circumstances—or Mr. Furness's instructions—changed. "I have some things to finish up, maybe I'll just stay long enough to do that."

Pritchard shrugged. "Suit yourself, just don't be telling your dad that I was the one who kept you around here."

Chip didn't bother saying that keeping him working at Jardin was evidently exactly what his father wanted.

Chip worked distractedly at the greenhouse window repair —which was proving to be trickier than he had expected—his concentration broken by the repeated sounding of the fire horn and the increasing thickness of the air. He found an excuse to walk by the library, trying the door although he knew it would be locked. He overheard Pritchard telling one of the other men that the women were home packing things up in case of evacuation. He wished Millie was at Jardin so that he could sweet talk the key to the library away from her, although he suspected that Millie might not be susceptible to his sweet talk any more, if she ever had been.

At five-thirty, the electricity went out and Pritchard insisted that he leave. "If you don't want to help out with the fires, at least go home and help your father."

Chip set out in the truck. When he cleared the trees at the bottom of Cleftstone Road, he could see a huge funnel-shaped cloud, purple and yellow like a bruise in the sky, roiling overhead.

The roads were crowded with vehicles. Family sedans loaded down with possessions headed away from the fire, Army trucks full of men and firefighting equipment and some cars that appeared to be carrying sightseers headed toward it. He started toward Eagle Lake Road until he encountered a barricade—the fire had jumped the road and was now burning in Acadia Park. He finally made his way back to Lynam's Point via Eden Street to Hulls Cove, Salsbury Cove, and Town Hill.

That night, his father told Chip to stay and keep an eye on the hotel and then headed out in a truck with some fellow business owners from the western side of the island. They had heard reports of a black sedan filled with foreigners—perhaps the men responsible for setting the fire. When his father returned to the hotel, the "foreigners" having eluded the men, he reported that the fire had burned across McFarland Mountain and Brewer Mountain. The next peak would be Great Hill.

28

Breakfast at the inn was, surprisingly, Mexican-themed, and Ann found that she didn't have much stomach for the salsa omelet that she normally would have enjoyed. She was waiting to hear from Garrick about the outcome of his meeting with Loring and felt draggy and at loose ends. By late morning, Scott had decided a picnic would cheer her up.

They were in the sitting room of the inn, still sipping coffee from breakfast. Ann leaned to look out the window. "It doesn't seem much like picnic weather."

"We can have the picnic here. We can get all that nice picnic type of food—bread, cheese, fruit. Wine," he added for Ann's benefit.

At that moment Nan appeared in the doorway with the coffee carafe. "Can I top you off?" she asked.

"Not for me, thank you," said Scott. "Annie?"

Ann shook her head. "Thanks."

"We had a question for you," said Scott. "We're thinking of having an indoor picnic if you wouldn't mind us using the dining room."

"Not at all," said Nan. "You're the only ones here, please feel free to spread out. You could even have your picnic in here by the fire. It's so raw out."

"Where's the best place to get picnic supplies?" asked Scott.

"Well, the fanciest place is Finn's Market—it's right down the street, but," she added, lowering her voice, "it's pricey. The Food Mart is only about a mile away and much less expensive—it's where all the locals go. I'd recommend going there for the fruit and wine, and going to Finn's for the bread and cheese."

After they finished their coffee and Scott sent an email update to Mike, including a postscript from Ann, they headed out for the Food Mart. Ann pulled on her cap as protection against the nip in the morning air.

The Food Mart actually had quite an extensive selection of wine. "Wine in the grocery store—that's so civilized," said Scott, accustomed to Pennsylvania's restrictive regulation of alcohol. "You pick out some nice wine and I'll get the fruit," he said, and headed off to the produce section.

Ann's eyes roved idly over the racks of bottles, registering labels but not names: frogs, deer, rabbits. She usually got red but perhaps she should get white—that might go best with picnic food. She glanced down the aisle, looking for Chardonnay.

There stood Ellen Lynam, only about ten feet away and absorbed in the label of a can of coffee on the other side of the aisle.

Ann was faced with the same dilemma she had been when Ellen had come out the front door of the hotel the day before— whether to try to scuttle away or whether to greet her. She glanced the other way down the aisle—she was closer to Ellen than she was to escape. With her back still toward Ellen, she drew her sunglasses out from where she had hooked them into the neck of her sweater, slipped them on, and then turned, intending to reassess the situation. Instead, Ellen stood right in front of her.

"Yikes!" yelped Ann.

"Oh, sorry to startle you, Miss Near—I didn't mean to sneak up!"

"Oh, no problem!" Ann wondered if it looked odd that she was wearing sunglasses in the dim light from the store's fluorescent bulbs.

"I see you're slumming a bit. Most of the tourists go to Finn's, but I like the Food Mart, prices are much better, and easier than driving all the way to the mainland to go to one of the big chain stores. Laying in some supplies?"

"Yes!" She had to dial it back, working undercover seemed to bring out her overenthusiastic side. "Yes, we're going to have a picnic lunch at the inn where we're staying."

"You're here with your fiancé?" Ellen glanced up and down the aisle. "That's so romantic!"

"Yes, my fiancé!" said Ann. "He's somewhere around here ... looking for something. Maybe I should go find him. Heaven only knows what he might pick up if he's unsupervised."

"Me unsupervised?" said Scott, appearing at her side with a bunch of grapes and a box of clementines.

"Hello!" said Ellen brightly.

"Hello!" said Scott.

Ann linked her arm into Scott's. "Honey, this is the woman I told you about. At the hotel I went to look at. For our reception. Ellen, this is my fiancé, Scott."

"Yes, her fiancé!" said Scott gamely.

"She even remembered my name, called me 'Miss Near'!" Ann turned to Ellen. "Although please call me Kay."

"I wish I could remember names," said Scott, who never forgot a name. "So you work at a hotel in the area?"

"Yes, I own Lynam's Point Hotel," said Ellen. "A beautiful place for a reception. For the wedding, too, if you're not looking for a church. I wish you could see it in season."

"The wedding—why not!"

Ellen turned her attention to Scott, clearly the more enthusiastic participant in the wedding planning. "How many people do you think you'll have?"

"Oh, lots!" Ann nudged him slightly with her elbow. "Well, not too many."

"We've had receptions with anywhere from a dozen to two hundred. With a tent, of course."

"A tent, honey!" he said, turning to Ann. "That sounds nice!"

"Yes, dear," said Ann.

"Without the tent, we'd recommend no more than about fifty, in case the weather is bad and people have to stay inside."

"Well, fifty would be a very nice number also." He leaned over and kissed Ann on the cheek. "Whatever you think is best, sweetheart."

"It's not until July, we have lots of time to think about it," said Ann, starting to nudge Scott down the aisle. "Nice running into you, Ellen."

Ellen beamed at them. "Hope to hear from you," she called after them.

After they paid for their purchases and got back to the car, Ann said, "Sorry about that."

"Sorry for what? That was fun! What are we doing? Why are we getting married in Maine?"

"I'm helping Garrick with something and that was my cover story—that I was looking at places for a wedding reception. I didn't expect to run into her again. I wonder what Garrick will think. It's supposed to be a big secret."

"Curiouser and curiouser," said Scott, starting up the car.

29

Having returned the hotel key to its hiding place and driven sedately back to Somesville, Garrick sat in his office letting his mug of hot water grow cold. He had hoped that, once confronted with Garrick's knowledge of the true nature of The Lady, Loring would acquiesce and reveal its location. What possible incentive could the man have to keep such knowledge a secret?

And why should Loring be willing to share information with Ann that he was not willing to share with Garrick? He did seem to harp excessively on the topic of women, perhaps Ann's gender was to her benefit. If only she were more skilled in understanding whatever information Loring was attempting to communicate.

Garrick drummed his fingers on the desk, then opened his desk drawer and removed a black leather address book and opened it to the K tab. After additional drumming, he picked up the handset of the rotary phone on his desk. He dialed a number and after a few rings the call was answered.

"Ann Kinnear Consulting," said a male voice.

Garrick hung up the phone. "Drat." Didn't everyone these days give out their personal cellphone numbers?

He was standing to go to the kitchen and refresh his water when the phone rang. He looked at it suspiciously for a moment, then picked it up. "Yes."

There was a pause on the line, then, "Masser?"

"With whom am I speaking?" said Garrick, fully aware of the identity of the caller.

"This is Mike Kinnear. Why did you call me?"

"I did not call you," said Garrick haughtily.

"Of course you did. I just had a call come in from this number," said Mike.

Double drat. "I was not calling you, I was calling your sister."

"Don't you have her cellphone number?"

"Evidently not." There followed a long pause. "It would, however, be helpful to me to have that number."

"Are you asking me to give you her cellphone number?"

"It would be helpful."

Garrick heard a sigh on the other end of the line. "Let me check with her and I'll call you back."

"Very good. I will give you my number."

"Obviously I already have your number."

Triple drat. "Of course. I will await your call." Garrick hung up the phone and sat down again, his eyebrows drawn together in an ominous V.

A few minutes later, the phone rang again. Garrick picked it up. "Yes."

"She said it's okay to give you her number. Got a pen and paper?"

"I have no need for a pen and paper."

"Well bully for you," said Mike, and read off the number.

"I shall call her now."

"Don't mention it," Mike said, and hung up.

Garrick replaced the handset on the phone and sat staring ahead for a moment, then took his fountain pen from the drawer and jotted the number in his address book. Picking up the phone again, he dialed the number and waited somewhat apprehensively. He was relieved when a female voice answered, "Hello?"

"This is Garrick."

"Hi, Garrick! You'll never guess who we just ran into."

"Ellen Lynam."

"How did you guess?"

"With whom else would you have an encounter on this island that would be of interest to me?"

"That's true. Anyhow, we ran into her in the grocery store."

"You and your driver?"

"Yes, me and my driver."

"Did she recognize you?"

"Yes, she stopped to talk to me. I told her Scott—uh, the driver—was my fiancé."

"Hmph," said Garrick.

"So, did you go out to the hotel and see Loring?"

"Yes, he was most unhelpful."

"So you still need me to try to find out the location of the painting from him?"

"As you say," said Garrick grumpily. "We need to find an excuse to get her away from the hotel so you can follow Loring's directions to the painting unobstructed. She has evidently run her errands for the day, and we can't count on her being away from the hotel for very long, or on her going out again later."

"Hey, I know—she thinks Scott is my fiancé and he played along with it. Maybe he can call her and say he wants to discuss that some more."

"Without the prospective bride in attendance?" said Garrick skeptically.

"Well, Scott acted much more interested in the whole wedding-and-reception thing than I did—he could just tell her that he is in charge of arrangements and that I had other things to do this afternoon."

"And why would he want to have this meeting somewhere other than the hotel?"

"Hmmm." They were both silent for a few moments, then Ann said, "I know, Scott acted very excited about the idea of having a tent. He could tell her he wants to visit someone who rents out tents and wants her there with him to discuss ideas."

"Is this a realistic scenario?"

"I don't know, I've never arranged a wedding, but it seems plausible. Doesn't it?"

"I'm sure I wouldn't know," said Garrick. "And you say your driver isn't from around here? If he's from the area, she might recognize him."

"That's right, he drove me up from Pennsylvania. He's 'from away.' Not from Mount De-ZERT," she added.

"How very colloquial of you. However, if you yourself were not 'from away,' you would know that the locals refer to the island as 'MDI.'"

"Oh," said Ann, somewhat deflated.

"In any case, I believe we should proceed as you suggest, if you think it's a good idea." Ann started to interject that she didn't necessarily think it was a good idea, just the best she could come up with on the spur of the moment, but Garrick continued. "You would be able to arrange this yourself?"

"Sure," said Ann uncertainly. "Let me talk with Scott."

"The less he knows about the actual circumstances, the better," cautioned Garrick.

30

1947

On Wednesday, October 22nd, the Lynam's Point Hotel's gardener, his neighbor, and their families, who had been evacuated from their homes north of Eagle Lake, arrived at the hotel. After a brief discussion between the gardener and Chip's father, they unloaded their luggage into several of the guest rooms and the possessions they had brought with them onto the veranda. Then the men in the group said that they were going to head back to the eastern side of the island to help fight the fires.

When they had gone to the shed to get shovels, Chip said, "Dad, can I go?"

His father, who was rearranging things on the veranda, didn't look up. "No, I need you here."

"But it sounds like they need all the help they can get—"

"I said no. Probably every person on that side of the island is running around like chickens with their heads cut off, making things difficult for the professional firefighters. Plus, what if the fire comes this way? You need to stay here."

Chip thought it unlikely that the fire would jump Somes Sound, but he knew better than to argue further.

He spent the morning getting the evacuees settled in. Then the women—much to his father's consternation, Chip guessed —decided that food and drink should be provided for the men fighting the fire, so they commandeered the hotel truck, along with Chip as a driver, and made a run to Southwest Harbor for supplies. Back at the hotel, they assembled several dozen sandwiches, fried up a pile of doughnuts, and brewed gallons of coffee with which they filled the hotel's coffee urns. Chip secured the urns, the bags of food, and a box of coffee mugs in the back of the truck. His father climbed into the driver's seat, muttering about "do-gooders."

"Dad, I'll go," said Chip.

"I already told you I need you to stay here."

"Okay," said Chip agreeably. "When more people start showing up, I'll get them settled in."

His father narrowed his eyes at Chip suspiciously. Finally, with a sigh, he said, "I guess I'd better stay." He climbed stiffly out of the truck and Chip was struck by how old he looked.

Chip climbed in, his father standing next to the car, his face pinched with discontent.

"Best fuel up in Somesville. Go to Fernald's, they'll fill it on credit."

"Okay, Dad." Chip started up the truck.

"Don't you spend a lot of time over there—and don't you drive into anywhere where the fire's burning. There'll be plenty of men just standing around guarding where the fire has already come through or keeping an eye on fires that have been put out—you can give the sandwiches to them. The men busy fighting an active fire won't be able to take time out for a meal."

"Okay, Dad." Chip pulled away.

"And keep a count of the mugs, make sure you bring them all back!" his father called after him.

Chip waved out the window to him.

He wound his way back to the eastern "claw," going north to Town Hill and then east, following a convoy of Army trucks coming in from the mainland.

When he entered the burn area, the devastation was like a punch to the gut. In some places, the fire had left the jagged stumps of tree trunks stabbing up through a blanket of gray ash—in other places, not even stumps remained. In the distance, black smoke boiled up, so thick that if Chip didn't know better he might have thought that the earth had belched up a new mountain overnight.

He found a group of men in a burned-over field, swatting out flare-ups. A few had Indian tanks holding a few gallons of water strapped to their backs, but most were armed with nothing more than shovels and water-soaked brooms. There were more men than equipment, so the extra men rotated out to Chip's truck for food and coffee.

"Is it going to Great Hill?" Chip asked a boy about his age.

"I hear they stopped it at Duck Brook," said the boy, "but now it's burning north and south." He pointed to a billow of smoke to the east. "That's Youngs Mountain." He pointed further to the south. "And that's the fields west of Eagle Lake. If they can hold it there, Bar Harbor should be okay, but Hulls Cove might get it. That's where I'm from."

Chip scuffed his toe in the dirt. "Sorry to hear that."

"Hasn't gotten there yet," said the boy stoutly. "Maybe the wind'll turn. Maybe it'll rain."

They both turned their eyes to the still smoke-laden but cloudless sky.

"Or maybe not," said the boy.

When the sandwiches were gone, the urns empty, and the

coffee mugs accounted for—one having broken when a tired firefighter fumbled it—Chip started back to Lynam's Point, then pulled to the side of the road. His father didn't really need him at the hotel—all those evacuees could take care of themselves. Heck, he probably wouldn't even be missed. But he could help at Jardin d'Eden. He turned the truck around.

He took the northerly route he had taken the previous day, through Salsbury Cove and Hulls Cove, coming into Bar Harbor via Eden Street, which was lined with the "cottages" of the Furnesses' fellow millionaires. Most of them only summered on the island, and would now be gone to wherever they spent their winters. He wondered what they were thinking right now, opening their newspapers in Palm Beach or Charleston or Havana or, if the lines were up, maybe taking a phone call from their own Pritchards about the situation on Mount Desert. Would they be frantic as the flames closed in on their castles or would they, as his father sometimes suggested, be relieved to be rid of the responsibility?

When he got to Jardin, he found half a dozen men, ladders propped on the sides of the house, wetting down the wooden shingles of the roof.

"Lynam! Over here!" Pritchard had discarded his clipboard and was wrestling with a length of hose, trying to give the man on the ladder some extra reach. Chip ran over and helped haul the hose.

Pritchard stepped back and brushed dirt from his hands. "You give these guys a hand. Mrs. Furness called, she wants a fur coat sent down to Palm Beach."

"She needs a fur coat in Florida?" asked one of the men, hauling on the hose.

"What I want to know is why she thought she needed a fur coat here in the summer," said one of the others.

"Just because we're baking now doesn't mean it doesn't sometimes get cold in the summer," retorted Pritchard.

"The telephone's still working?" asked Chip.

"So far. I'll pack up the coat and then you can take it down to the Express Office."

"The Express Office is still open?"

"Jeez, Lynam, you sound like an old lady," muttered Pritchard as he hurried inside.

As soon as the door closed behind Pritchard, one of the other men—a young man named Sean who had been glancing nervously at the smoke drifting over Great Hill—dropped the hose.

"I'm going—I got a baby at home and a wife who's expecting another and I'm not going to hang around here hosing down the Furnesses' roof hoping my own roof isn't going up in flames with my family under it!"

"I'm with you there," said one of the other men, Mel. "My uncle's got a couple of boats in Northeast that he wants to get out on the water and I'm going down there to give him a hand."

"It's not going to get to Northeast," scoffed the third man.

"I ain't waiting to find out," retorted Mel.

"I wouldn't want to be out on the water with the wind like this," ventured Chip.

Mel shrugged. "We might get banged around a little but it's better than just sitting by waiting for the fire to get it." He turned to Sean. "Can you give me a lift out that direction?"

"Sure thing." Sean scanned the rest of the group. "Sorry about this, fellas, but we've done what we can here—I recommend you let Pritchard worry about Jardin and you go home to look after your own."

The two of them jogged off toward the greenhouses and in a minute their truck passed the group and disappeared down the drive.

The remaining men looked at each other uncomfortably, then one of the older ones shrugged. "I ain't got no family and I live in a boarding house—if the fire gets it, no skin off my teeth. We're getting paid for this, right?"

They took turns climbing the ladder and hosing down the roof, waiting like children around a broken vase for the parent to show up. Eventually, Pritchard emerged with a box. He scanned the group.

"Where are Sean and Mel?"

"Left to take care of their own," said the older man mildly.

Pritchard shook his head, his lips tight. "Well, we got most of the roof wetted, we can keep it wet with a smaller crew. Lynam, bring your truck around."

Pritchard handed the box over to Chip with all the usual cautions, then Chip drove into Bar Harbor, which was crowded with Army vehicles, soldiers, and firefighters, official and unofficial. Most of the stores were closed, but people wandered through the streets, anxious-looking but not panicked. Chip dropped the box off at the Express Office on Cottage Street, which was doing a brisk business as people tried to get their valuables off the island. As he was leaving, he saw another of the seasonal Jardin d'Eden workers—Millie's older brother, Eliot—trapped in the snarl of traffic, the back of his truck loaded with furniture. Eliot noticed him and waved him over.

"Chip, right? Hey, can you see what the holdup is?"

Chip backed a few steps away from the truck so he could see down the street. "Something going on near the green, looks like it opens up after that."

Eliot nodded toward the Express Office. "Wish I could just pay to have my valuables flown away," he said, drumming his fingers on the wheel. "I'm taking mine up to the airport but they're not going any further, I hear they're letting people store furniture and such on the field."

Chip was struck by a sudden inspiration. "Hey, do you know where Lynam's Point is, on Lynam Narrows? My dad has a hotel there, you could store your things there."

"A bit further of a drive, though."

"Better than having your valuables all jumbled up with other folks' stuff at the air field, right?"

Eliot scratched his chin. "You're sure your dad wouldn't mind?"

Chip was fairly sure his dad *would* mind, but it would be a way of getting a message to him without having to talk to him. "It'll be no problem. Can you just let him know I'm helping out with things at Jardin and will be home as soon as I can?"

"Sure. Lynam's Point, off Indian Point Road, right?"

Chip nodded and stepped back as the traffic began inching forward.

"Thanks," said Eliot, waving from the truck. Over the line of traffic, beyond the town, Chip could see flames at the tops of several mountains on the other side of Eagle Lake.

Chip drove back to Jardin where, of the remaining crew of three, two were raking pine needles and dry ground cover away from the foundation and one was consulting with Pritchard about the removal of a large pine tree growing close to the house.

"Let me call Mr. Furness," said Pritchard. He disappeared into the house, only to emerge a minute later. "Line's dead." He ran his fingers through his hair. "Okay, let's take her down. Let's move the trucks down the drive first in case the tree blocks it."

The rest of the daylight was occupied by the felling of the tree, which did, as Pritchard had anticipated, come down across the top of the drive. As they were cleaning up the branches as a precursor to cutting the truck into moveable chunks, another of the men—whose elderly parents lived on the eastern shore of Somes Sound—slipped away.

When darkness fell, Pritchard sent Chip in to warm up some soup and brew some coffee. On his way to the kitchen, Chip stopped by the library and, glancing up and down the hall, tried the door. Locked.

Chip found some cans of chowder in the pantry and dumped them into a pot. While the soup warmed, he slid open some of the drawers, wondering if Millie carried the ring of keys with her or hid them somewhere at the house. He would feel better if he could just take a quick look into the library to make sure The Lady was okay. He found only drawer after drawer of immaculately arranged silverware and carefully folded and pressed table linen.

The night was warm and the air still. After they finished their meal, they settled down on the veranda, some with backs propped against the wall of the house, some lying on their sides, using their arms as pillows. They listened to the fire whistle sound periodically and tried not to think about what the fire might be doing out there in the darkness.

31

The next day at noon, Scott stood by the Audi in the parking lot of Mainely Tents in Ellsworth, awaiting Ellen Lynam's arrival. When he saw her Jeep pull into the parking lot, he hit Send on a pre-entered text: *she's here*. He waved as Ellen pulled into the space next to the Audi and, when the car stopped, opened her door for her.

"Thank you so much for meeting me on such short notice. Kay and I only have a short time in Maine and we want to get as much planning for the wedding done as possible."

Ellen grunted slightly as she exited the Jeep. "It's no problem. But you do realize that I'm not sure what our schedule is for July ...?"

"Oh yes, but I'm very hopeful we will be able to work something out. Kay was so complimentary about your hotel and the surroundings. She said the view is quite spectacular."

"Yes. It might be helpful if you see the setting first and then discuss a tent ..."

"She gave me quite a detailed description. She just loves it, much more so than any other place we've looked at!"

"Where else have you looked?" asked Ellen.

"Oh, all places near Philadelphia where we live," he said, reeling off some of the places he and Mike had talked about as wedding or reception locations. "But Kay likes your hotel best. I'm sure that if you're booked in July, we would be willing to change the wedding date as needed to accommodate." Scott ushered Ellen toward the Mainely Tents office, opening the door to the jangle of a bell.

In the office, a short, squat man with a military crewcut and enormous walrus mustache stood behind the counter. "Ellen, this is Donald. Donald, this is Ellen Lynam of the Lynam's Point Hotel." Scott had spent some time chatting with Donald before Ellen's arrival and was now familiar with, among other aspects of Donald's life, the difficulty of subsidizing a child's medical-school tuition on a tent-rental owner's earnings.

"Yes, we've worked together before," said Ellen. "How are you doing, Don?"

"Pretty good, Ellen, you?"

"Can't complain."

"Sorry to hear about Loring. That's tough," said Donald uncomfortably.

"Yes. Well." There was an awkward silence, then Ellen turned to Scott. "Will Kay be joining us?"

"No, here's the thing." He leaned forward conspiratorially and Ellen and Donald leaned forward as well. "It's a surprise for her! Kay has always wanted an outdoor wedding in a big tent. But until recently, that was out of the question based on our budget. But unbeknownst to her, a distant relative of mine passed away and left me quite a bit of money. I'm going to make sure she has the wedding she's always dreamed of, and on our wedding day I'll reveal our good fortune!" He leaned back and smiled expansively at them.

"That will be quite a wedding present," said Donald, eyebrows raised.

"Yes, that certainly sounds very nice," said Ellen wistfully.

"So I'd like to take a look at the various tents that might be available for different numbers of people and how each one might be set up on the hotel grounds. And any options for the tents—for example, do they all come with flaps that can be put down if the weather gets bad? And if the weather does get bad, will the tent be safe? What types of tests are run to ensure they're stable? And who have you worked with on tent decorations, because I imagine the tent setup and decorating have to be closely coordinated. What other services might I need to coordinate with the tent setup? I'm sure Ellen would like to know how long after the event it will be before the tent's taken down. And is there any possibility of damage to the lawn? Are there different colors to choose from? And what is the tent made of?" Scott thought that should hold them for quite a while. Just for good measure, he added, "And how is the tent made? You'd need something like a giant sewing machine, wouldn't you?"

Donald, whose possible objections to sitting around with a potential client discussing tent minutia had been circumvented by a $50 contribution to the college fund, went in back to get them some stools and put on a pot of coffee.

32

When Ann got Scott's text, she turned to Garrick and said, "Okay, she's at the tent place."

Garrick, who had been reading a small, ancient-looking book in what Ann guessed was German, slipped the book into an inside pocket of his coat and started the engine. After checking carefully in both directions, he coasted out of a side road off Indian Point Road that lay in the opposite direction Ellen would have taken to get to Ellsworth and turned onto Lynam's Landing Road. This time, he took Ann right to the front steps of the hotel. He turned off the car and got out.

"I'll show you where the key is, then you can return it there when you're done."

Ann followed Garrick toward the west side of the building. "Why don't you just stay? It sounds like you can understand Loring better than I can."

"I think he's demonstrated that he's unlikely to make an appearance were I to stay." He pointed to a flowerpot. "It's under that."

Ann picked up the pot and retrieved the key.

"I will come back in an hour. I'll meet you at the front door.

If you're not there, I'll assume you need more time and will
come back again after another half hour. Your driver will send
you a text message when Ellen leaves Ellsworth?"

"Yes."

"It should take her half an hour to get from Ellsworth to the
hotel, so we shouldn't wait any longer than twenty minutes after
you've heard from him before we leave, even if your assignment
isn't complete."

"We should have a back-up plan in case he can't get
reception."

"I beg your pardon?"

"If he can't get cellphone reception to send me a text." Ann
pulled out her phone. "For that matter, what if I can't get reception to get a text? It's pretty spotty around here."

"Good heavens. What good are the things if they don't
work reliably?" muttered Garrick. "I will watch the road so I'll
see if she comes back. If you hear her car, just let yourself out
of the hotel on the water side. You'll have to leave that door
unlocked, but she'll just chalk that up to her own absent-
mindedness. Heaven knows she's a bit distracted by the stress
of the situation. And circle back to the road through the
woods, not along the shore—the tidal flats are like
quicksand."

"Okay." Ann followed Garrick back to the veranda and
climbed the steps. She inserted the key and, with the squeak of
old metal on old metal, unlocked the door. She turned back to
Garrick. "I'm about to break and enter."

"That sounds very melodramatic. It's for the client's own
good."

"And for the lucrative fee."

"Yes. That too, of course. Lock the door behind you in case
you don't hear her car and you're still in the hotel when she
returns. That way she won't sense that anything's amiss and you

can hide in the hotel until an opportunity to escape presents itself."

Ann hesitated. "Garrick, I'm starting to feel kind of funny about this."

"Nonsense. In the worst case, she will discover you and wonder why the overenthusiastic bride-to-be is scouting the hotel while her betrothed is selecting a marquee."

"Maybe she'll just think I'm an intruder and shoot me before she recognizes me."

"Don't be silly. Ellen Lynam doesn't carry a gun."

"Maybe she'll call the cops."

"Well, yes," Garrick admitted, "that would be the worst case. But highly unlikely." Considering that assessment to have closed the discussion, he returned to the Cadillac, started the engine, and drove slowly around the drive and down the road. When Ann lost sight of him in the pine trees, she opened the door and stepped into the lobby, locking the door behind her.

"Loring?" she called.

The only sound was the ticking of a clock from somewhere behind the bare reception desk. She waited a minute, then called again.

"Loring, are you here?" She had started to move toward the center of the lobby when she heard his voice.

Yes ... here.

The voice came from the shadows of the lobby, opposite the windows, and Ann could perceive a faint flicker of grayish light, the same color as his eyes, marking his presence. The flicker moved toward her, then became more difficult to perceive as it entered the brighter part of the room. However, she could still track his progress by the irregularity in the path of the dust motes illuminated by the sunlight.

When he reached where she stood, he began to speak. As before, his eyes were his clearest aspect and, also as before, she could catch only snatches of his words. She heard "fire" several times—had The Lady been lost in a fire? But Loring had said he was going to show it to her. And then "safe"—that seemed promising. When it became clear to her that she was not going to be able to understand any more, she interrupted him.

"Loring, I'm sorry, I still can't understand you very well, but I can see you. Can you take me to The Lady?"

Yes. He turned from her and moved across the lobby. *Upstairs.*

She followed him into the relative darkness of the stairwell, where the light resolved itself into the suggestion of a human form.

They climbed to the second floor. The hallway was littered with off-season detritus: paintings leaned against the walls; extension cords, unattached to any electrical device, snaked across the floors; and halfway down the hall, an enormous pile of old bed pillows tumbled out of a closet. An open door to one of the rooms displayed a sparkling view across the Narrows through uncurtained windows. On the stripped bed lay a pastel drawing of two children, a broken fragment of its ornate oval frame lying on the glass like the unearthed bone of a dinosaur.

Ann followed him on to the third floor and finally to the fourth. Here, the low ceiling and more utilitarian woodwork suggested that it was likely the staff quarters. On the right, a basically outfitted but modern bathroom opened directly onto the hallway, and across the hall, with a stunning water view out of its low windows, was what Ann surmised was Ellen's room. A single bed, built in under the sloping ceiling, was rounded by blankets and quilts. On the bedside table was a glass of water and copies of *The Little Prince* and *Jonathan Livingston Seagull.* A blue dresser with a corner of its top knocked off, likely a cast-off from one of the guest rooms, held a lamp, its shade slightly askew.

Ann turned and began to ask, "In here?" but the spirit had continued down the hallway and she just caught the flicker disappear into the last room on the left.

She followed it into a small room, misshapen by the low ceiling and by a chimney that jutted into the room. There were no windows and the only illumination filtered in from the hallway. A mid-century-style hanging light sat on top of an old desk, the hole it had left in the ceiling revealing a rafter and the darkness of the attic beyond. Built-in shelves held accordion files, likely old hotel records. Miscellaneous supplies—mops and brooms, a metal bed frame, gallon containers of Pine-Sol—took up the rest of the space. The floor was a linoleum "rug"—a hideous multicolored center bordered by a sedate Greek key pattern. At least it would be difficult to discern footprints in the dust, Ann thought. If Ellen Lynam took advantage of her trip to the mainland to visit one of those big chain stores and pick up some supplies, she wouldn't wonder who had been visiting the storage room in her absence. Ann was starting to think like the trespasser she was.

Ann heard, *Behind there.* A faint wave of light indicated a stack of paper towels.

Ann moved several bales of rolls, revealing a worn wall of wainscoting.

There. Hook ... into the hole.

Ann scanned the wall. "I don't see what you mean ..."

... floor.

Ann knelt down and saw what looked like a small mouse hole. "Is this what I'm looking for?" she asked dubiously.

... pull up.

Ann inserted her finger into the hole and pulled up; a section of wainscoting about three feet wide rose up from the floor. It must have had a counterweight attached to it, because it rose effortlessly with only a slight squeak. Behind it was a plywood panel.

Left ... swing open ...

Ann found a barely noticeable gap on the left of the panel, hooked her finger in, and swung it open. On it hung the painting.

"Wow," said Ann after a moment.

Thought you'd be surprised, said the spirit with a smile in his voice.

33

_1947_

On the morning of Thursday, October 23rd, after a restless night on the porch and a breakfast of stale toast and coffee, Pritchard sent one of the men into town to get the news and to check at the Express Office for any telegrams from Mr. Furness. The man returned with a copy of the _Bar Harbor Times_—the headline read "Entire Island Menaced By Fire," but the word was that Hulls Cove was in the greatest danger. Trying unsuccessfully to hide his relief at this news, Pritchard nevertheless set the men back to soaking the roof and went inside to pack another box of Mrs. Furness's treasures.

Chip followed him into the house, watching enviously as Pritchard unlocked the door to the dining room, just across the grand center hall from the library. A stack of boxes was piled next to the dining room table, a pile of newspapers on top.

"Don't you think the paintings should be taken away?" Chip asked.

"It's not up to me to decide. Mr. Furness said the artwork stays where it is."

"But that was before, he can't know how bad things are now. I think that—"

Pritchard wheeled on him and Chip could see the accumulated stress of the last days etched on his face. "It's not up to either of us to *think*, Lynam," Pritchard said with barely contained fury. "It's up to me to discharge Mr. and Mrs. Furness's instructions. And those instructions are to pack up Mrs. Furness's valuables and get them to the Express Office. Now get outside and help the men."

Pritchard began pulling china out of a massive mahogany breakfront and wrapping the pieces in newspaper.

"I could help. Wrap things, I mean. I'd be careful."

Pritchard didn't look up from his job. "We'd just get in each other's way."

"I could work in another room. The library. Mrs. Furness has that collection of glass paperweights in there. I imagine they're valuable, and they'd be pretty easy to pack up."

Pritchard ran his fingers through his hair, which was now standing straight up and grimed with soot. Finally he said, "Fine." He placed the plate he had just wrapped in the box and then crossed to the library, sorting through his keys. "Get a box and paper."

Chip snatched up the supplies and followed Pritchard. Pritchard unlocked the door, flipped on the light, and pointed to the collection of paperweights on the table underneath The Lady.

"Just those things, nothing else without checking with me first." He stood next to the table as Chip arranged the packing materials, and Chip realized he was counting the paperweights. "And please God don't break anything." Pritchard turned on his heel and stalked out of the room.

Chip carefully lifted the first glass paperweight from the table and wrapped the newspaper around it, glancing around the room. Now he was here, but what could he do? Hulls Cove might be threatened now, but the wind had been whipping around from all directions—if it moved to the northwest again, Great Hill could be the fire's next victim. Could he convince Pritchard to let him drive the painting to safety—to the mainland, or even to Lynam's Point? But Pritchard had gotten his orders and he was going to keep operating under those orders until he got new ones. Chip walked to the desk and picked up the receiver, but the line was still dead. He packed more and more slowly, hoping that a little extra time would reveal an option he hadn't considered before, but when he packed the last paperweight he was as much at a loss as he had been when he'd started. Casting a glance back at The Lady, he picked up the box and carried it to the hall, closing the door to the library behind him.

Pritchard was just closing up his own box and glanced up. "Anything broken?"

"Nope, all safe and sound."

"Okay, let's get them in the truck and you can take them into town." He hoisted up his own box.

Chip followed Pritchard down the hall to the front door, where they loaded the boxes onto a hand truck they were using to get things to the trucks parked on the other side of the downed tree.

"Do you think the phone at the Express Office might still be working?" asked Chip.

Pritchard grunted as he lifted a box. "Might be. Why?"

"I was thinking I could call Mr. Furness, let him know what the situation is, see if he had any new instructions."

A whole host of emotions crossed Pritchard's face—irritation that he hadn't thought to do that himself, conceit that he should be the one to call Mr. Furness, and relief that his employer might have updated instructions for him based on knowledge of the developing situation. He stood with his hands on his hips, looking toward the smoke drifting over Great Hill.

Finally he said, "Couldn't hurt. You tell him you're calling for me, that I stayed to look after the house." He patted his pockets, retrieved a scrap of paper and pencil stub, and jotted a number on it. "There's the number for the Palm Beach house. They'll help you make the call at the Exchange Office."

Chip got in the truck and rolled down the drive to Cleftstone Road, then turned onto Steepways, his heart a little lighter now that he was taking some concrete steps to ensure the safety of The Lady. He noticed that the wind was picking up, but the leaves and ash were swirling so that he couldn't tell from which direction it was blowing.

When Chip got into Bar Harbor, traffic was almost at a standstill. In one car, the driver gripped the steering wheel and stared grimly forward as if he could will the cars in front of him to move. In the passenger seat, a young woman held a baby-blanket-blue bundle to her shoulder and glanced nervously behind them at the angry sky over Great Hill. Another car pulled to the side and two middle-aged women emerged and, arms linked, hurried away in the direction of the athletic field, leaving everything but their purses behind.

He parked the truck and was crossing the street to the Express Office when he heard the seven blasts of the fire horn that signaled the evacuation of Bar Harbor. A dance of ash whirled around him as he turned.

The fire had reached Great Hill. And The Lady would burn even before the flames reached Bar Harbor.

Chip rushed back to the truck and clambered in. He negoti-ated the first few blocks in an agony of frustration, his progress continually interrupted by panicked pedestrians who were more concerned with the danger of the fire than with the hazards posed by the equally distracted drivers. Drivers added the blare of their car horns to the cacophony of the evacuation signal. Once he was out of the center of town, though, he was able to pick up speed.

Chip negotiated Eden Street and squeezed his truck through a gap in the opposing line of traffic and shot up Steepways. He reached the intersection with Cleftstone Road just in time to see a truck pulling out at an equally brisk pace. Pritchard and the two other men who had been left at Jardin were squashed into the cab. Chip instinctively honked his horn to get their attention, but its bleat was drowned by the shrieking of the wind and a crescendoing roar from beyond the hill. Pritchard was obviously intent on putting distance between his truck and Great Hill and, not seeing Chip, disappeared down the road leading toward Eagle Lake.

Chip slammed the truck into gear and sped up Cleftstone. When he turned into the drive to Jardin d'Eden, he saw what Pritchard and the other men were fleeing.

The sky over Great Hill glowed red behind Jardin. A tendril of smoke twisted from one of the trees silhouetted against the crimson sky, then, like a giant match being struck, the entire tree burst into flames. The fire leapt to the next tree and began to work its way down the trunk toward the tinder-dry carpet of pine needles and leaves that blanketed the ground right up to the house, except for the narrow strip that the men had cleared. The sight brought Chip to an awe-struck standstill, but in the next instant he recovered himself and hit the gas. With a squeal of tires, the truck shot forward.

At the top of the drive, the giant pine that the men had felled earlier blocked his way, the ropes they had used to direct its fall away from the house twisting like tentacles across the ground. The idea that taking down this one tree would make a difference to the fate of the house now seemed laughable, like believing that withholding a morsel of food would weaken a wild beast and keep it from attacking.

Chip skidded the truck to a halt, jumped out, vaulted the tree, and ran up the steps to the front entrance. He twisted the large brass knob, expecting his momentum to carry him into the grand central hallway, but his shoulder cracked painfully into the door—he hadn't counted on the door being locked.

The window—he could get to The Lady through the window. The library was on the first floor but, due to the slope of the hill, it was far from the ground. Could he get a ladder out of the groundskeeper's shed in time? But luck was with him—the ladder that the men had used to attach the ropes to the tree was lying in the driveway. Chip hoisted it up and, despite a protest from his shoulder, hauled it around to the side of the house. The ladder was far too long for his purposes and he staggered under its weight while branches from the decorative shrubs lining the walkway snagged its trailing end. Although the house now partially blocked his view of the flames, Chip could hear over the howling of the wind the explosive bangs as the trees torched. Ash drifted down on him, but he didn't have a spare arm to cover his nose and mouth.

He counted off windows, hoping he was calculating correctly, and swung the ladder up next to what he believed to be the library window. It crashed through a window on the second story, a few shards of glass raining down on him. It was a little too far from the window. Sensing each second ticking by, he jerked on the ladder to reposition it but it was jammed into the second floor window. No matter—it was close enough.

He grabbed one of the smooth, round cobbles that marked the edge of a now-dormant flower garden and scrambled up the ladder. Drapes blocked his view into the room, but the material looked like those in the library. He heaved the stone through one of the panes of the casement window, and, leaning over, reached through the broken glass, flipped the latch, and pulled open the window.

The ladder was further from the window than it had looked from the ground, and the metal window frame looked flimsier than he remembered it. He thought briefly of checking to see if any other outside doors might be unlocked, but if Pritchard had locked one door he no doubt would have locked them all. A swirl of ash danced around the corner of the house; Chip didn't have much time.

He leaned out and was counting himself lucky that the ladder was jammed in the second floor window when his movements unjammed it and he felt it shift in the opposite direction. He lunged, getting his upper torso through the window before the ladder toppled away from him, leaving his legs dangling. His feet scrabbled on the shingles, but there was no purchase and he felt his weight pulling him out the window. Bracing his elbows on either side of the window frame and trusting to the workmanship of the craftsmen—the best of the best—who had been brought in to build this millionaire's "cottage," he levered himself upward and forward, through the drapes and into the room.

The drapes and the rod came crashing down on him as he hit the floor. He thrashed his way out of the yards of fabric, gasping with a mounting panic, but then he was free and—thank God—in the library.

And there she was, her dark eyes on Chip—abandoned by the people who should have taken care of her. The Lady.

34

A fter the spirit revealed the location of the painting to Ann, there followed a period when he was obviously trying to tell her its story, but her ability to understand him seemed to decrease in inverse proportion to his enthusiasm. Eventually all she could perceive was a bright but amorphous light that had lost all semblance of human form.

At last, her frustration with her inability to understand him trumped her sympathy for this spirit who so obviously wanted some connection with a living person.

"I'm sorry, Loring, I still can't understand what you're saying. Why don't you tell Garrick? He'll be able to understand, and he can tell me." The light dimmed somewhat, but again took on a somewhat more human form.

She wasn't sure Garrick would, in fact, tell her—he seemed pretty hung up about the theoretical confidentiality of the engagement—but, as far as she could tell, Loring had taken a liking to her and perhaps this would be an incentive for him to be more forthcoming with Garrick.

Taking one last look at the painting in the dim light from the hallway, she closed up the panel and pulled down the wainscoting, then replaced the bale of paper towels in front of it. "Maybe once the hotel is safe, I can come back and spend more time—I do want to hear your story. And the story about the painting."

The light brightened a bit. She felt like she should give it an encouraging pat but, since that seemed impractical, she gave a little wave and sensed a tendril of grayish light returning the gesture. She made her way downstairs, locking the door and replacing the key under the flowerpot.

She glanced at her watch. Garrick wasn't due back to pick her up for some time, and Ann didn't fancy hanging out at the hotel waiting for him to arrive. There had been no text from Scott, so it was likely that Ellen was still with him. She decided to walk back along the road—she figured if she heard a vehicle coming, she could hide in the woods.

As she walked, she realized that although the canopy of pine boughs overhead was dense, there wasn't much undergrowth to hide behind. Well, she thought, in the unlikely event that Ellen came back unannounced, she could fall back on the excuse of being a (rather obsessive) prospective bride taking one more look at her favorite wedding venue.

She got back to Indian Point Road without seeing anyone— Ellen Lynam or otherwise. She turned right toward where Garrick was waiting and he must have seen her because she heard the engine start and then the car glided out from behind the pines. He stopped and she got in.

"Did he show it to you?"

"Yup, he—"

"Do we need anything else at the hotel?"

"No, he—"

"Wait, not while I'm driving." Garrick turned around in the intersection and then drove off to the south, concentrating resolutely on the road. In a mile or so they pulled off onto another road, which ended a short while later in a parking lot and boat

208

launch. Garrick pulled into a parking space and turned off the engine. He turned to her expectantly.

"It's on the fourth floor, last room on the left."

"The storage room?"

"Yes."

Garrick looked out past the boat launch to the water beyond. "That's where Loring hung himself."

"You didn't tell me he killed himself!"

"It didn't seem germane."

"Well, it would have been nice to know. I would have been more, I don't know, respectful."

"I'm sure you were admirably respectful, although I hardly think—" He stopped and cleared his throat. "Where was it in the room?"

She described the location and operation of the secret compartment. "It's a portrait. Finely done—and it looks old."

"Interesting," said Garrick, sounding only moderately interested.

"Maybe if having the painting helps Ellen save the hotel, I could go back later and try to communicate with Loring again, even if I have to keep pretending I'm Bride-zilla. It seems like he still has some things he wants to talk about."

"It won't be necessary at that point."

"Yes, but I feel bad for him. He seems like a nice enough guy. I don't know why you have such problems with him."

"Perhaps your gender has enabled you to ingratiate yourself with him."

"I don't think that's the only reason," Ann muttered.

Garrick raised his eyebrows. "What do you mean?"

"Well, you can be a little ..." She considered. "... off-putting."

He raised his eyebrows further. "Off-putting?"

"Not very approachable."

Garrick snorted. "I would in fact prefer not to be in a position to be 'approached' by Loring Lynam—"

"I rest my case."

"Hmph," said Garrick, looking grumpy.

"What will you do now?" Ann asked.

"I'll go back to the hotel tonight at the regular time and take Ellen to the painting."

"Pretending that you've finally convinced Loring to give you the information."

"Of course."

"Clever."

Garrick glanced at her suspiciously. "As you say."

35

Garrick drove back to Somesville via a roundabout route to reduce the possibility of passing Ellen, in case they had missed a message from Scott that she was on her way back from Ellsworth. Ann texted Scott that he didn't have to detain Ellen any longer and soon received his response: *okey doke she just left*. Ann tried a few times to open a discussion with Garrick about the painting, but he shushed her each time—evidently driving and talking were incompatible activities.

When they got back to Somesville, he got out of the car to open the double doors on the garage and pulled the Cadillac in. It was the only garage Ann had ever seen that contained absolutely nothing other than the car.

"Where do you store your stuff?" she asked.

"Such as?"

"I don't know—yard stuff."

"I have no yard stuff."

"How do you take care of your yard?"

"I have people who take care of the yard. Is your chauffeur coming?" He shooed her out of the garage and locked it up.

He opened the back door and stepped into the kitchen and strode toward the hallway leading to the office.

Hoping to get some insight into Garrick's private life, Ann said, "Maybe we can have a cup of tea in the kitchen while we wait for Scott."

Garrick scanned the kitchen with a look of distaste, as if the practically bare counters and table held dirty dishes or unpaid bills.

"I have no tea."

"We could have something else."

"I hardly think so."

"Why not?"

"It's not an appropriate room for receiving visitors." He turned back to the hallway. "We'll wait in the consulting room."

Ann hurried down the hall after him. "Wow, 'consulting room.' You sound like Sherlock Holmes."

"And you sound like your brother," said Garrick warningly, stopping to hang his coat on the peg on the wall.

Ann followed him into the office, dropped her parka onto one of the leather wing chairs, and sat in the other. Garrick went to the fireplace, struck a match, and lit the already-laid fire.

"We should celebrate," said Ann.

Garrick sat behind the desk. "What do you suggest?"

"We could have a drink."

"I don't have any tea."

"We could have an alcoholic drink," she said, curious as to what response this would elicit from Garrick.

Garrick pulled his watch out of his pocket, looked at it pointedly, and then looked at Ann with an eyebrow raised.

"Hey, I found The Lady, I think that deserves a celebration."

Garrick contemplated her for a moment, then rose and left the office. Ann wondered if he had found the suggestion so offensive that he had left in a huff but in a moment he was back, carrying a small tray holding a bottle and two small but intricately cut crystal glasses. He unstoppered the bottle and poured a few thimbles-full of a dark ruby liquid into each of the glasses and handed one to Ann. She stood to take it.

He raised his glass. "To a successful engagement."

Ann blushed, pleased by what was, for Garrick, effusive praise. She raised her glass. "Cheers."

They sipped their drinks.

"Port?" she asked.

"Yes." Garrick sat at his desk, putting the glass to one side. Ann picked up the bottle from the desk.

"Dow's?"

"Very well received, but not yet at its peak."

"Garrick, are you a wine connoisseur?"

"Certainly not," he said severely.

Ann held up her empty glass. "May I?" Garrick waved toward the bottle. She poured a few more thimbles-full of port into her glass and sat down again in the wing chair.

Ann sipped her drink contemplatively. "The painting looked old, although the light wasn't good. I wonder where it came from."

"I'm afraid that, even were I able to ascertain that, I would be unable to share that information with you."

"Yeah, I know. Highly confidential and all."

"As you say."

"When do you think we'll be able to get back to the Biden Firth issue?" she asked.

"If it is in fact a 'Biden Firth' issue."

"Do you see anything now?"

Garrick stood and took a quick circuit around Ann's chair. He sat back down behind the desk. "No."

"Maybe it's gone."

"Perhaps. It would still be beneficial for me to see you in the evening. Perhaps tomorrow, assuming I can conclude the engagement with Ellen Lynam tonight."

They lapsed into silence, Garrick gazing at the fire, Ann wondering if it would be bad form to refill her tiny glass. She was saved from having to decide by a knock on the front door.

She stood and set her glass on Garrick's desk. "That's probably Scott."

Garrick moved the glass to the tray and then followed her into the hall. As she reached for the doorknob he said, "Check who it is first."

There was a peephole in the door and she stood on her tiptoes, but it was several inches too high for her.

"Allow me," said Garrick, and put his eye to the door. "Yes, it's your chauffeur." He swung the door open but rather than ushering Ann out, as she expected, he stood aside to let Scott in.

"Good evening," said Garrick to Scott.

"Good evening," said Scott cheerfully. "I've brought back that book you loaned me," he said, holding it out. "The author certainly has a number of interesting case studies to support his position."

Garrick took the book. "Yes, it was considered to be quite groundbreaking at the time."

"Seems he didn't believe in spirits so much as believed in an explanation for why some people saw them."

"Yes, paranormal experience explained as a reaction to normal physical or medical conditions."

"Not what you and Miss Kinnear experience."

"Certainly not," said Garrick. "Would you be interested in another book? One presenting a different perspective?"

"Of course!" said Scott.

Scott and Ann followed Garrick into the waiting room across from his office. He replaced the small book on the stand and then, after considering a moment, pulled another book from one of the shelves.

"You may find this one of interest," he said, handing the book to Scott.

Scott opened the book carefully. "*An Essay Towards a Theory of Apparitions*," he read.

"It contains an interesting chapter on 'A lawyer's argument for the existence of witchcraft,'" said Garrick. "It presents a similar position to the first book, but with some diverting case studies. You may skip over the sections written in Latin."

"What about me?" said Ann.

"What about you?" asked Garrick.

"Are you going to loan me a book?"

"Are you interested in borrowing a book?"

"Well, not really, but it would be nice to be asked," Ann grumbled.

"Feel free to alert me when you develop an interest," said Garrick pointedly, and showed them to the door.

Ann and Scott walked to the car, Scott glancing back to admire the house. He followed her to the passenger side and opened the door for her.

"My, how chivalrous of you," she said.

"He's looking out the window at us, and I *am* supposed to be your chauffeur," said Scott with a little bow.

"I think he likes you," said Ann when Scott got in the car.

"Who wouldn't?"

"No, I mean I think he *likes* you. Scott, is Garrick gay?"

"Not unless my gaydar is on the fritz," said Scott blithely.

"Boy, if Mike thinks he doesn't like Garrick now, just think how he'll be when he hears Garrick has designs on his boyfriend."

36

W hen they got to the inn, Ann went up to her room. The nausea that used to accompany sensings now struck her only occasionally, but the experience did tire her. She intended to lie down for only a few minutes, but when she opened her eyes to a tapping on the door, full darkness had fallen.

"Annie?" she heard Scott call softly.

She scrubbed her face with her hand and glanced at the clock on the bedside table: 9:00. "Come in."

Scott opened the door, silhouetted in the light from the hallway. "Are you feeling okay, sweetie?"

"Yes, I was just tired."

Scott came in and sat on the bed beside her. "I didn't want to wake you up for dinner so I got you a lobster roll. It's in the fridge. Mace says there's somebody she knows who's playing at that jazz club in Bar Harbor—want to go after you have something to eat?"

"Gee, tempting as that sounds ..." said Ann with a smile. Scott knew she found jazz annoying.

"Is it okay if I go?"

"Of course." Ann nudged Scott with her knee and he stood to let her swing her legs off the bed. "I'll just hang out here and do some reading. Thanks for getting me dinner."

"Sure thing. You're going to have the place to yourself—Nan is away but Mace thought since you and I are the only guests it would be okay for her to go out as long as we left you with provisions. There's Chardonnay in the fridge."

"Lobster and wine—what more could I possibly need?"

"If it weren't for the jazz, I'd stay in myself—it's getting really cold out." He examined her appraisingly. "You sure you're okay?"

"Yup. Have a good time."

He bent over and gave her a kiss on top of the head. "You don't know what you're missing!"

"I think I do know what I'm missing," she said pointedly.

IN AN EFFORT TO snap herself out of her post-nap grogginess, Ann took a hot shower. She pulled on fresh jeans, a long-sleeved white t-shirt, and a dark red sweater. Going down to the inn's kitchen, she took the lobster roll and a glass of wine to the dining room and settled down with her iPad. Based on the style of the painting and the clothes worn by its subject, she did some searches on "renaissance portrait," then refined that to "italian renaissance portrait" and further to "italian renaissance portrait lady." She was rewarded with dozens of images similar to the one she had seen in the secret compartment—formal portrayals of richly clad women against pastoral backgrounds, sometimes cradling a small dog or a lamb or, in one case, a unicorn, which was much smaller than she would have expected.

She scanned idly through the images, enlarging the ones that looked in style most like the painting she had seen. But most of them lacked the finesse of the portrait of "The Lady"—

the fine brushwork, the subtle shading of the background, the detail of the material of the dress. She had at first assumed that it was a well-done reproduction, but perhaps it wasn't impossible for a family with enough money to own a hotel to have enough money to purchase an original. She had dipped her toe into the commercial art world with her own paintings, but she had no experience with fine art dealing. On the one hand, what Garrick had said about the Lynam family's bad financial luck made it seem unlikely that they would own an old master. On the other hand, the sale of the painting would evidently provide the funds needed to save the hotel, so its value must be significant.

Well, she would try to get more information from Garrick once he had seen the painting—she didn't doubt that in his well-stocked library in Somesville were some books on Renaissance portraiture.

She flipped the cover of her iPad closed and, having finished her lobster roll, took the plate to the kitchen and refilled her glass. She went to the sitting room and scanned the shelves, locating, to her surprise, a dog-eared copy of a Nero Wolfe mystery—Rex Stout had been a favorite of her mother's. She saw that a fire had been laid and she lit the kindling and was rewarded with the pleasing crackle and pop as the wood caught. She settled herself into one of the overstuffed chairs. Much nicer than the unpredictable warblings of small-town Maine jazz, she thought.

But the painting in the secret compartment kept intruding on her thoughts, and eventually she flipped the book closed on the adventures of Nero and Archie and returned to her iPad in the dining room.

She experimented for some time with various searches, for a while getting drawn into pages describing the loss and retrieval of artworks stolen by the Nazis before and during World War II.

Could Ellen's father, or possibly grandfather, have fought in the war and smuggled a masterwork home with them? She tried entering "italian renaissance portrait lynam" but none of the entries contained "lynam." She tried "italian renaissance portrait maine" and one of the results caught her eye.

It was an article about the Golden Age of Bar Harbor and the summer "cottages" that the fabulously rich—the Vanderbilts, the Pulitzers, the McCormicks—built there. She scrolled through images of summer homes the size and opulence of extravagant city halls. In one, two women in Victorian garb sat down to an al fresco tea at an enormous mahogany table that must have been transported with backbreaking effort from the dining room. In the background were gardens that would have required an army of caretakers to maintain.

It had all come to an end in 1947, when fire swept across the eastern side of the island, burning many of those estates to the ground. She happened upon a series of before-and-after photos —mansions reduced to nothing but their chimneys and the pillars that had flanked their entrances.

One article included a photograph of a man and woman standing in an elegantly decorated mid-century room. The caption read:

> Jardin d'Eden, the summer home of Mr. and Mrs. James
> Furness, was one of the casualties of the fire. The cottage, first
> thought to be out of danger until a shift of the wind drove the
> flames toward Bar Harbor, burned to the ground along with
> Mr. Furness's priceless art collection, including this recent
> acquisition ...

Ann zoomed in on the painting. The reproduction of the photograph was poor and the original had likely been grainy to start with, but she felt the thud of recognition—this was the painting in the secret compartment. Garrick wasn't on his way to resolve a sibling dispute over a father's inheritance. He was going to reveal the location of a priceless masterwork to a desperate woman who might do anything to save her family's legacy.

37

1947

Even with the fire roaring at the crest of Great Hill and the evacuation sirens wailing from Bar Harbor—even with the glass of the window gone where he had crashed into the room, the drapes puddled at his feet—a still-ness presided in the library of Jardin d'Eden. Chip kicked the drapes away.

He crossed the room to The Lady and her eyes followed him. Those eyes were quiet and sad—her life had been difficult and people cruel, he could tell. But he wasn't a child anymore, and he could protect her.

What would be the best way to get her away? The painting was a little more than three feet tall and a little less than three feet wide, surrounded by a carved, gilded wooden frame. He thought briefly of trying to remove the painting from the frame, but he was afraid that he might damage her in the process. Furthermore, although the frame would make the painting more awkward to carry, it would provide some protection. He wished he knew what had become of the crate he was sure the painting had been shipped in, but he didn't have time to go looking for it. He needed to wrap her in something—he needed a large cloth.

He crossed to the door to the hallway. Despite the fact that he remembered carrying the boxes of Mrs. Furness's china and paperweights out to the truck without Pritchard relocking the library door, he still heaved a sigh of relief when it opened. But his relief was cut short when he looked across the hall through the open doors of the dining room and the large arched windows beyond. Flames were creeping down the hillside like soldiers crossing no man's land on elbows and knees. The air was thickening with the advance guard of the smoke.

Chip crossed the hallway to the dining room. He expected to have to search through the stack of linen tablecloths in the breakfront, but there was a tablecloth on the table. He snatched the corner and gave it a yank, sending a large brass candelabra and a pair of Oriental-looking porcelain dog statues crashing to the floor. Returning to the library, he lay the tablecloth on the floor, then lifted The Lady carefully off the wall.

"It's going to be okay," he murmured, trying to convince himself as much as his helpless charge.

He lowered The Lady onto the cloth and folded it around her. His hands shook, but he tried not to rush—it would be no good to come this far to rescue her and then have himself rather than the fire be the one to damage her. Once she was bundled into her cocoon of cloth, he would have liked to have found twine to tie up the package, but the stillness of the library was now being overtaken by the sounds of alarms and destruction coming from beyond the broken window. He tucked the corners of the tablecloth into the bundle to hold it in place.

He gathered up the awkward package and headed down the hallway to the front door.

When he opened the door, the heat hit him like a physical

blow—he could feel his exposed skin shrinking from the onslaught. The creeping vanguard of flames he had seen from the dining room had turned into an all-out assault, fire rolling from tree to tree like a crashing wave. Now the howling wind was carrying not just ash but burning cinders that pricked his skin.

He ran down the drive, The Lady turned away from the flames, keeping his body between her and the scorching heat. He managed to scramble over the downed tree without putting her down. When he got to the truck, he eased her into the passenger side, then skittered around to the driver's side. His heart was hammering and his lungs ached to take deep gulps of air, but he forced himself to breathe shallowly, every breath singeing his throat. The truck started on the first try, as if it were as anxious to escape Jardin as Chip was. He got the truck turned around in a frenzied series of back-and-forths. He hit the gas, but then almost immediately slammed on the brakes.

The fire had progressed down the hill more quickly here than directly above the house. Partway down the drive, fire burned on both sides, flames licking up the trunks, the tops of the trees torching. He saw movement and realized that small animals—a rabbit and several squirrels—were making their escape from the flames down the drive.

The fire-born wind was shrieking. Chip heard a crack and saw a tree fall, its top brushing the border of the drive. He hit the gas and shot past the burning tree just as he heard another crack and crash, accompanied by the fingernails-on-a-chalkboard screech of a branch on the truck's back window.

At the bottom of the drive he turned to look back at Jardin. Flames were licking at the eaves and smoke boiled off the roof. Red-hot cinders spun out of the woods and a carefully manicured bush next to the front door burst into flame. He turned back to the road and accelerated, and narrowly missed a deer that shot out of the woods just yards ahead of the flames and bounded down Great Hill.

When Chip reached the bottom of the drive, the smoke and flames forced him back to Eden Street and into Bar Harbor. He made his way back into Bar Harbor on Mount Desert Street and then turned right onto Main Street. At the fork south of the village, most traffic turned left to follow Schooner Head Road along the shore, but Chip took the right fork onto Otter Creek Road, hoping the faster progress enabled by fewer cars would compensate for the fact that its more westerly route would take him nearer to the fire.

Abetted by the smoke that his headlights barely cut through, late afternoon turned to a livid dusk as the slow caravan made its way through Otter Creek and Seal Harbor, past Asticou and up Sound Drive. When they reached the top of Somes Sound, most of the cars turned right to make the dash across Mount Desert Narrows via the only bridge to the mainland, but Chip turned left, passing through Somesville and then cutting across the western "claw" on Pretty Marsh Road.

It was dark by the time he reached the turnoff to Lynam's Point, although the sky to the east glowed orange, like a ghastly sunset in some backward version of the world. The howling wind had died down to a light westerly breeze, so the air held only a hint of the tang of the fire.

Chip wended his way around the peninsula toward the hotel. Now that he had, at least for the moment, escaped the fire, the subject of his anxiety switched to the reception that would greet him when he reached home. Had his father gotten Chip's message from Eliot? Perhaps Eliot had decided to take his belongings to the airport on the mainland after all. His father had never hit him, but then Chip had never committed a transgression of this magnitude—disappearing with the truck for so long when it was no doubt badly needed at the hotel.

He decided that his father hitting him would not be so bad. He was taller than his father now, and broader—he could track the weight his father had lost in the last few years by the markings on the notches of his leather belt. He realized that he was not so concerned about any physical damage his father might inflict on him—or about the humiliation of the tongue-lashing he likely faced—but what about The Lady? What if his father found her before Chip had a chance to hide her?

Chip had just reached the stone pillars that marked the edge of the Lynam property and was considering turning around to find a hiding place for the painting outside the hotel grounds when his headlights picked out a shape moving into the road. It was his father.

He had to keep his father away from the truck until he had gotten The Lady out. Chip jumped out of the truck and walked quickly toward where his father stood, ready to accept his punishment as long as he could keep The Lady safe.

In the glare of the headlights, Chip could see that his father was even more pale than usual, his posture more stooped. There was something wild in his eyes.

Chip stopped in front of him. "I'm sorry, Dad, I had to help at Jardin."

His father's mouth worked and at last he choked out, "You ... where ... I thought ..." and then burst into tears.

His father covered his face with his hands, his shoulders shaking, as Chip stood before him, mouth agape. Long moments passed, punctuated only by the sobs his father was trying to hold back. Finally, his father made some jerky motion with his hands that Chip thought was intended to shoo him back to the truck, then he turned away and began a stumbling walk back toward the hotel.

Chip stood rooted to the ground until his father's figure had faded into the darkness, then he turned and made his way slowly back to the truck. He climbed in, feeling like an old man himself. He rested his hand on the bulky package beside him.

"I think he ..." But he didn't know what to say.

W<small>HEN</small> C<small>HIP GOT</small> to the hotel, having parked the truck as far from the house as he felt he could without arousing suspicion, he found their small band of evacuees, increased by a few since he had left, in the kitchen making pies. This past summer had been the first since the war that sugar wasn't rationed, and there had been a frenzy of pie-baking, as if the island's bakers were making up for lost time.

They said his father had gone out for a walk a few hours ago, but they were sure he would be back soon.

Eventually, the group drifted onto the veranda and Chip seized the opportunity to carry The Lady up to his room, the same room he had occupied as a child. He had little immediate fear that he would be displaced—unless there was a huge influx of evacuees, they could house any additions in the guest rooms without having to resort to using the family quarters on the top floor. He slipped The Lady under his bed, hidden behind that same board that had protected Timothy until his father had moved the bed. He didn't like the unceremoniousness of her position, but he knew it would be only temporary—he knew where he was going to hide her.

He didn't see his father until the next morning, in the second floor hallway, carrying an armload of sheets. His father wouldn't meet his eyes, and eventually gave him some chores to do which kept him outdoors for the day. Chip stayed close to the hotel, not wanting to invite a repeat of his father's reaction of the night before, and plotted how he would keep The Lady safe.

38

P ushing away her iPad, Ann glanced at her watch—a little after ten. Garrick was likely already at the hotel, but she dialed his office number nonetheless. No answer. If Garrick carried a cellphone, she didn't know the number.

She dialed Scott's cellphone and was eventually greeted by his voicemail: "Hello, this is Scott, please leave a message and I'll get right back to you."

"Scott, it's Ann. I need to get in touch with Garrick right away and I need you to drive me. Can you come back? Call me if you get this message."

She stood and paced into the living room, where she stared into the now-dying fire. Should she call the police? But what if Garrick, rather than being in danger, was complicit with Ellen Lynam—it sounded as if they were friends, or had been at one time. She paced back to the dining room. But if Garrick was in collusion with Ellen, wouldn't it have been risky to involve Ann? On the other hand, if both Garrick and Ellen needed information from Loring, and Loring wouldn't provide it to Garrick and couldn't provide it to Ellen, maybe involving Ann was the only option they had.

She shook her head. She just couldn't see Garrick being involved in a scheme involving stolen artwork—it wouldn't have fit with his sense of propriety.

If she could get to the hotel, where she assumed Garrick and Ellen were, she could come up with some excuse about the wedding—it didn't even have to be a believable excuse, just anything to get Garrick away from Ellen.

She walked to the front window, pushed the curtain open, and looked out into a black night lit only by the almost-full moon. It must have rained earlier, but the temperature had evidently dropped—she saw a car make its slow way down the road, its headlights illuminating the black sheen of ice. She began to turn back to the room when something caught her eye and she returned to the window. Audrey was in the parking lot of the inn. Evidently Mace and Scott had taken Mace's car to the jazz club.

Ann hurried up the stairs to Scott's room and tried the door —unlocked. She went to an armoire and opened it. Scott's extra pants and shirts were hung inside, a pair of hiking boots arranged neatly on the floor. She patted the pockets of the pants guiltily, listening for the jingle of keys. Nothing. Closing the armoire, she scanned the dresser tops and the bedside table—it only held the book of Mt. Desert trivia and the book Garrick had loaned Scott. Why would he have taken the keys if he wasn't driving? She looked through the drawers of the dresser and even peeked inside the toiletry bag in the bathroom—still nothing. With a rising sense of panic, she started back downstairs to put in another call to Scott, then paused and retraced her steps to his room. She went to the bedside table and flipped open the Mt. Desert book. Scott's keyring was marking his place—a photo that the caption identified as Great Hill looking toward Bar

Harbor, a stripe of red autumn foliage running from the hill to the town.

She returned to her room and replaced the shoes she was wearing with her hiking boots and pulled on her parka, stuffing her gloves and cap into her knapsack. Back downstairs she tried Garrick's and Scott's phones again—still no answer. She sent a text to Scott—"Pls call me"—and paced the downstairs for five minutes waiting for a response.

Finally, stuffing her iPad into the knapsack, she let herself out the front door of the inn and began to make her way to the parking lot. She had to slow her pace when she barely recovered, arms pinwheeling, from a slide on the icy walkway.

She got to the car without mishap, adjusted the seat, and started it up. Then she turned it off.

What trouble might she get into if she drove to the hotel? She tried to push her concern for Garrick to the back of her mind and open her senses to her environment. Was there any indication of Biden Firth, or any other spirit, in the car with her? She couldn't sense anything other than her own agitation. She was suddenly angry—Garrick couldn't even tell if what was surrounding her was a spirit at all. Maybe all the caution about having Scott drive her was a farce; maybe she wasn't suffering from anything more serious than clumsiness. She was sick and goddamned tired of being afraid of a ghost that might not even exist.

She started the car again and, taking a deep breath, backed it out of its parking space and began her slow drive to Lynam's Point Hotel.

In the daylight, she might have been able to find the hotel on her own, but the darkness distorted the distances and hid road signs. After a few minutes, she pulled to the side of the road to plug the hotel name into the GPS on her phone. She hardly needed to pull over—hers was the only car on the road.

Finally, she saw Lynam's Point Road and carefully made the turn. During the drive she had been able to submerge her concern for Garrick with a single-minded focus on her driving, but now, feeling her goal to be near and with the sense of urgency to reach Garrick returning, she sped up a bit, forgetting the hard left turn that the road took to follow the south portion of the peninsula.

She realized her error as she saw the turn approach and was correcting when a stabbing pain shot from her right hand up her arm. She reflexively jerked her arm back just as a spasm clamped her hand onto the steering wheel and the front of the car obediently veered to the right while the car as a whole continued its trajectory across the intersection, slamming sideways into the embankment at the T in the road.

39

G arrick sat in the lounge with Ellen, in their accustomed seats. Ellen looked at him intently, the pencil gripped in her hand, the tip, pressed onto the notepad, creating a little spray of graphite on the paper. Garrick barely contained his impulse to reach over and snatch the implement out of her hand.

Loring was later than usual and Garrick thought that perhaps he was elsewhere looking for Ann—based on Ann's reports, it sounded like Loring was quite smitten with her. He decided he had waited long enough.

"He's here," he said, tracking his gaze from the lounge entrance to the empty chair. Inconveniently, at that moment Loring did, in fact, appear at the door of the lounge. Garrick sighed. Why must anything related to the Lynams always be more annoying than necessary?

"Tell him this is it, we've run out of time," said Ellen raggedly.

"Yes, Ellen, I know," said Garrick, making a shushing motion, trying not to let his gaze flicker from Loring's usual chair back to the actual Loring, who was still standing in the doorway. Ellen put the pencil crossways in her mouth and bit down on it.

"Hey, Garrick, you've got your circuits a little crossed—I'm over here," said Loring.

Garrick knit his brows and glared at the empty chair.

"Everything okay there, Garrick?" asked Loring, propping his shoulder on the doorframe.

Garrick made the shushing motion again, this time at Loring.

"I didn't say anything," said Ellen angrily around the pencil.

Garrick turned to Ellen. "He's ready to tell you where the lady is."

Ellen snatched the pencil out of her mouth. "Really?"

"Yes, really."

Loring raised his eyebrows. "I can't wait to hear this."

"Follow me," said Garrick. He stood and Ellen did as well, dropping the pad and pencil on the chair. Loring unpropped himself from the door and stepped aside as Garrick strode past him through the door into the lobby.

They both followed him across the lobby. Garrick removed the flashlight from his coat pocket and started up the stairs.

"Garrick, what are you doing?" said Loring, his voice tight.

Garrick kept climbing. He could hear Ellen's heavy tread behind him and could sense Loring's presence behind him as well.

"Garrick, wait a minute." A note of panic began to sneak into Loring's voice.

They climbed to the fourth floor. Ellen was starting to puff.

"Garrick, you don't want to do this," said Loring.

Garrick stopped at the top of the stairs to let Ellen catch up. Loring squeezed past Ellen and she absently waved at the air he had just passed through, as one might wave away a barely perceived cloud of gnats. Loring dashed up the stairs past

Garrick and then turned as if to block the way, but Garrick figuratively brushed him aside, encountering the chilly pocket of air where Loring's torso was.

"What are you doing?" puffed Ellen.

"Cobwebs. Follow me."

Garrick strode down the hall to the last door on the left, Loring following.

"How did you find it? Don't show her, it's not a good idea—"

"I have my sources," said Garrick.

"I'm sure you do," said Ellen, close behind him.

Garrick swung the door open and stepped into the small storage room.

He gestured to the stack of paper towels. "Behind there." He stood back to make room for Ellen. He found that clients preferred to unearth their discovered treasures themselves.

Loring was in the room too, his lips pressed in a tight line, glancing anxiously between Ellen and Garrick.

Ellen hesitated. "You want me to move the paper towels?"

"Yes, it's behind there."

Ellen shifted the bundles and looked back at him questioningly.

He shone the flashlight along the baseboard. "He says there's a hole, it will look like a mouse hole ..."

"There!" said Ellen, falling to her knees and pointing to a small opening.

"Hook your finger in there and pull up."

Loring let out a groan. Ellen did as she was told and the panel rose. Startled, she fell over backward, but the panel's counterweight held it in place. "I've looked in this room a million times before! I thought it might be here because ... you know ..."—her eyes turned toward the rafter exposed in the hole in the ceiling where the light had hung. "But I never found *that*!" She looked back at Garrick. "Now what?"

"He says there is another hole on the left," said Garrick, playing the flashlight along the left edge. "He says use that to swing it open."

Ellen ran her finger along the edge until she found the irregularity, then pulled the panel open.

"That's it!" she cried. "Garrick, you found it!"

Garrick trained his flashlight on the painting. "Good heavens," he said, his eyebrows climbing.

40

Ann regained consciousness to a pounding in her head so violent she could barely open her eyes despite the darkness. She put her hand to her head and her fingers came away wet. She wiped them on her parka. She groped around the ceiling of the car for a light, but none of the protuberances she stabbed at resulted in illumination. She tried opening the driver's-side door but it thumped into an obstruction, leaving a gap of only an inch or two.

She felt for her knapsack on the passenger seat but the seat was empty, although the air on her ungloved hand was cold— even colder than the already-cold air of the Maine night. Her groping eventually located the knapsack on the floor of the passenger side. She hauled it into her lap, which sent a protest of pain stabbing at her temple. She sat back while a wave of nausea passed. She fumbled her cellphone out of an outer pocket of the knapsack, painstakingly located the flashlight app, and flicked it on.

To her left, the driver's-side window was a bizarre mosaic. On the inside was a smear of blood, startlingly red in the light.

On the outside, broken twigs and orange leaves were plastered to the glass. She swept the light to the right.

There, sitting in the passenger seat, was Biden Firth.

She let out a scream, pressing herself back against the driver's-side door. Her phone fell to the floor, the flashlight app casting an eerie LED glow into the car's interior.

Biden's visible presence was completely different from any other spirit she had sensed. When she perceived spirits as more than just lights or scents—when she sensed them in a more life-like physical form—they usually presented an amorphous body, a somewhat clearer head, and clearly defined eyes. Biden's body, on the other hand, was suggested only by a somewhat opaque area. His features were undifferentiated and distorted, like a robber wearing a stocking mask. His eyes were two darker spots within that mask. But what was completely clear were his hands: two almost disembodied appendages, apparently resting on his knees. The left hand rose, moving toward her, and she screamed again.

She grabbed the driver's-door handle and banged her shoulder against it, but the car was tight up against the embankment. She turned back toward Biden, anchoring herself with her hands on the steering wheel, and Biden grabbed her right hand. Her third scream was as much from pain as from fear as the familiar jolt ran up her arm. She snatched her hand back. A blackness opened in the space where Biden's mouth must be and that taunting laugh that had plagued her at her cabin filled the car.

Turning away from him again, she fumbled at the side of the seat, searching for the seat-back release. She hit the lever almost by accident and flopped back.

She tried to kick herself into the backseat, but something was holding her down. She began to thrash until she realized that her seatbelt was still fastened. Her right hand was still painfully cramped from Biden's touch so she stabbed at the seat-belt release with her left, one of Biden's hands floating through the air toward it, the laughter now enveloping her like a noxious miasma. Just as Biden's hand reached hers, one of her stabs released the seatbelt and she scrambled into the backseat. Turning to lunge toward the back passenger door, she saw Biden once again in the seat next to her.

"Stop it!" she gasped.

Again the laugh enveloped her.

Was she trapped in the car with an insane spirit? Was she destined to scramble from front to back to front until ... what? Would he disappear when the sun rose? She should know these things. She looked around frantically—the banging in her head made it hard to think.

The sunroof. It would at least be harder for him to block her.

She hauled herself into the front seat again. Biden again materialized in the passenger seat. The engine was still running and she pressed and held the button to open the sunroof. She saw the spectral hand again reach for her own, but this time the pain was less and she was able to keep her hand on the button, her fingers curling into claws as the cramp intensified through the seemingly interminable seconds until the sunroof opened. Then she grabbed her knapsack and threw it out of the car and hauled herself up behind it.

She slid down the front window and scrambled off the hood, sprawling on the ground and jarring another protest from her head. She turned to face her tormentor.

In the moonlight, the car looked almost disturbingly normal —the engine purred, the headlights illuminated a swirl of fog. In the darkness, the only sign of something wrong was the slight angle at which it sat, the driver's side tipped slightly down into the ditch next to the road. She snatched up the knapsack. As she did, she thought she caught a glimpse of two disembodied hands outside the car and moving toward her, like some sort of grasping creatures from the deep.

It was so hard to think with her head pounding and those hands reaching for her. A thought floated out of the confusion—Garrick. He would know what to do. She had been on her way to find him, so she needed to follow the road. But no—there was a shorter way. Along the tidal flats. Maybe it would be harder for Biden to follow her there.

41

Garrick squatted next to Ellen and examined the painting. The Lady looked serenely but sadly out at them.

"It's Daddy's Lady! Has she been here the whole time?"

"I don't know how long it's been here. Where did your father get this?" asked Garrick sharply.

"He found it. I almost feel like I know her ..."

"Where did he 'find' it?"

Ellen scrambled to her feet but Garrick stayed down, his eyes sweeping appraisingly over the painting. By one of the Old Masters, certainly—perhaps Bronzino or even Raphael.

"It doesn't matter where he found it. She's going to save the hotel."

"How?"

"I'm going to sell her."

Garrick turned, his knees protesting, to see Ellen standing over him, a squat and oddly flimsy-looking gun pointed at him. He tried to rise, but his knees rebelled and he fell over backward, thumping into the wall inches from the painting itself. He dropped the flashlight, which rolled on the linoleum, casting crazy shadows on the walls until it came to rest near Ellen's feet.

"Be careful, Garrick!" Ellen gasped, stepping toward the painting as if to check for damage and then leaping back to stay out of Garrick's long reach. The object still trained on Garrick, she bent and retrieved the flashlight and shone it in Garrick's face.

"What is that thing?" he said, glowering at her.

"It's a Taser."

His already pale face went a shade paler. His heart began a painful hammering in his chest and his hand went automatically to his neck, massaging next to his Adam's apple. "And what do you intend to do with it?"

She lowered herself onto a box of Pine-Sol. "I'm sorry, Garrick. I need to be able to sell the painting and I need to make sure no one knows. What are you doing?"

"Carotid massage. It quiets my heart."

"Yes, your heart problems. Even as a young man you had a weak heart."

"It's not weak, it's balky," he snapped. "You can't sell that painting—it's obviously stolen. It's Italian Renaissance."

"I have a buyer. He doesn't mind where it came from."

"You'll go to jail."

"Only if I get caught, and I'm not going to get caught. It's all thought out." Ellen nodded her head toward the Taser. "It will be less painful than a gun. And less ... messy." She paused. If she was waiting for Garrick to reply, she was disappointed. "It doesn't mean you'll be gone, Garrick—I'm sure that your spirit will continue. And if anyone can enjoy the benefits of both worlds, it's you. I hope that we will be able to communicate ... afterwards. Maybe you can give me a message from Daddy."

"You are planning on Tasering me to death," said Garrick,

enunciating each word with fuming precision, "and then you're hoping that you and I will continue to have friendly chats?"

"Well ... yes. I hope so." Her voice sounded uncertain, but the hand holding the Taser never wavered, the red dot of its laser centered on Garrick's chest. "We've always had a special relationship, haven't we, Garrick?" Again she got no reply. "Plus, I think that in many ways you are already more of the spirit world than the material world."

"Don't be ridiculous, I'm a living being and if you kill me neither one of us knows what will happen to my spirit."

"You can stay here with me. You can be part of the hotel becoming what it used to be." Her voice was becoming dreamy.

"Ellen, I hardly think—" said Garrick, beginning to lever himself up from the floor.

Ellen pulled the trigger.

There was a popping noise accompanied by a little spray of confetti and then Garrick was on the floor, his back arched, two small darts embedded in his torso—one in his chest and one in his stomach. Ellen pulled the trigger several times and current continued to flow.

"Jesus, Ellen, stop it!" cried Loring.

Garrick writhed, a jagged groan escaping his lips. After half a minute of this largely silent but horrible tableau, the clicking from the cartridge ended and Garrick puddled to the floor. Ellen ejected the cartridge and drew another one from her cardigan pocket. The only sound was the labored whistle of Garrick's breath.

Ellen pushed a strand of hair back from her face. "Garrick?" she said tentatively.

"Ellen," Garrick croaked, "I'm not the only one who knows the painting's here."

"Don't be silly, you told me you wouldn't involve anyone else. You're making that up."

"I involved a fellow senser to get the information from Loring," he wheezed out, each word an effort. He turned to Loring, who was standing in the doorway, his fists balled at his sides. "Loring, warn the person you spoke to about what Ellen's planning to do."

"I don't know what you're talking about," said Loring, his voice tight with anger.

"Who is Loring supposed to warn? Is he here with us?" asked Ellen. She looked wildly around the room. "Loring, did Daddy hide it here? And then you killed yourself in the same room? I still can't believe you did that to me—making me find you!" She turned back to Garrick. "I don't believe you. I don't believe you would have involved someone else after promising me you wouldn't."

"You seemed so," Garrick glared at the Taser, "desperate." He turned to Loring again. "The person you spoke to will come back at some point—maybe with the police if I disappear."

"Garrick, I really don't know what you're talking about," said Loring. "I didn't tell anyone where the painting was."

"Well, someone did, and the person who has the information will come looking for me. And that person will be in danger unless warned of what's happening."

"Stop talking to him!" cried Ellen, and she pulled the trigger again.

Again Garrick's body arched, and this time he couldn't hold back a cry.

"God, Garrick, I'm sorry," she quavered. "With your heart how it is, I thought it would be faster."

"Ellen, please, Ellen, stop it," groaned Loring. "Can't you hear me at all?"

For another half minute the current flowed, and then Garrick's body collapsed back on the floor.

Ellen ejected the second cartridge and loaded a third. The

room was silent except for the tiny ticking of Garrick's pocket watch. After a minute, she whispered, "Garrick, are you still there?"

There was no answer. Another minute passed. Finally, Ellen set the flashlight on the ground pointed at Garrick's face and glanced around the room, the Taser still trained on his torso. She picked up a broom and, gingerly grasping the end, slid it across the floor into Garrick's arm. The arm moved slightly, no more animate than a boat rocked by a wave. She withdrew the broom and watched him again for a minute. She then slid the broom across the floor again, toward his face. She thought his eyes were closed, but she couldn't be sure—they were hidden by a strand of hair. She hoped they were closed. She pushed the broom into his face and then, not eliciting any response, withdrew it again.

Just to be on the safe side, she Tased him again.

Then, she loaded her last cartridge.

42

Ann backtracked the short distance to the causeway that carried the road over the tidal flats. She couldn't see those disembodied hands any more, but she strained her ears for any indication that Biden was following her. She wasn't even sure if a spirit would necessarily make noise. She should know these things.

When she reached the causeway, she looked north up the tidal area and could see the rectangular mass of the hotel over the tree tops. She struggled over the guardrail and then fell to her knees on the other side, the effort reawakening the clanging in her head. She put her hand to her temple and felt the stickiness of drying blood, but also felt the drip of fresh blood down her neck. She should have someone take a look at that.

911! She almost laughed at her foolishness—all she had to do was call 911 and they would come and help her. She reached into the outer pocket of the knapsack, her groping becoming increasingly frantic as she searched. Then she remembered: seeing Biden, dropping the phone on the floor of the car. She shook her head, which proved to be a bad idea.

Okay, if she couldn't call for help, she would go get help.

With frequent glances over her guardrail bastion in the direction of the abandoned Audi, she located her cap and a packet of tissues in her knapsack. Pulling the tissues out of their plastic sleeve, she pressed them to her head, then pulled the cap over her makeshift bandage. This seemed like progress. She felt a bit more optimistic about ... whatever it was she was supposed to do.

She would think about it later. She zipped her knapsack closed, slung it awkwardly onto her back, and struggled to her feet, using the guardrail for leverage. She closed her eyes for a moment, dizzy and unaccountably breathless, and when she opened them there were two ghostly hands resting on the guardrail next to hers.

She snatched her hands back, stifling a scream—she had screamed enough for a lifetime already—and took a step backward. Her feet tangled in the long grass and she fell, twisting so she could at least see where she was falling. Her ankle sent out a strident protest. She scrambled to her feet and half limped, half fell down the rest of the slope to the muddy flats, that jeering laughter floating behind her.

She looked toward the end of the peninsula and thought she saw a faint light—but whether it was from a lamp in the hotel or from the stars that were now dancing before her eyes, she couldn't tell.

43

E llen stepped into the hall and flipped on the light, then returned to the storage room and, putting the flashlight in her cardigan pocket, moved cautiously toward Garrick. She bent, the Taser pointed now at his head, and grasped the collar of his heavy black coat. She leaned back and Garrick's body slid slightly on the linoleum. She repositioned herself and leaned back again and gained another few inches.

Inch by inch she got him to the door, but the hallway was carpeted in a nubby fabric and she couldn't move him on it with one hand. Putting the Taser in her pocket, she grabbed the collar of his coat with both hands and pulled, but his arms flopped upwards and she could see that she was just going to pull his coat off with this approach. Instead, she moved to his feet and, grabbing the heels of his boots—unfortunately very heavy but fortunately tightly laced up—rotated him and then started to drag him down the hallway toward the elevator. The three Taser cartridges still attached to Garrick's body trailed at the ends of their wires. His coat peeled off his arms as she dragged him down the hall.

By the time they reached the elevator, she was gasping for

breath. She went back to the stairs and descended to the first floor, grabbing for the railing when she stumbled—it wouldn't do for her to break an ankle now. In the lobby, she slid the wooden door and the metal grate of the elevator open, entered, closed the door and grate behind her, and moved the brass lever, which sent the elevator trundling upward.

On the fourth floor, she was relieved to see no sign of movement from Garrick. Grasping his feet again, she wrestled him into the small elevator. She jammed his legs into one corner and pushed his head in with her foot then, pulling the doors shut, returned the elevator to the first floor. She dragged Garrick onto the wooden floor of the lobby, then she re-entered the elevator and sent it up to the second floor.

She took the stairs back to the first floor slowly—her breathing was ragged and her legs were rubbery. When she reached the lobby, she went to the window next to the elevator and from behind the curtain pulled a metal rod—pointed at one end and with a metal loop at the other. She inserted the pointed end into a small hole in the elevator door and poked around for a moment, then the door slid open, revealing the empty elevator shaft. Cables hung like guts from the darkness above. Below, in a space several feet deep, was a huge spring—questionable protection in case the cables failed.

Ellen turned Garrick's body so that his feet were toward the elevator shaft and then lowered herself the several feet onto the floor of the shaft. She had chosen this hiding place thinking it would be a relatively easy place to hide the body—assuming she was able to incapacitate him in the hotel—and that, since the column that had been added to the hotel to house the elevator shaft was uninsulated and the weather cold, she would have some time to decide how to dispose of his body before the smell might attract an off-season visitor's attention.

But this was more work than she had anticipated. She

should have gotten him to walk to the first floor before Tasering him. Plus, once she decided how to dispose of the body, she would have to find a way to get it back out of the bottom of the shaft—she hadn't considered that. But she could take her time hooking up a winch of some sort. She was good at that kind of thing, just like her father and brother had been.

A new thought struck her. Would his spirit remain with her if she moved his body elsewhere? She had counted on the location of Garrick's death bonding him to the hotel, just as the location of Loring's death—as it turned out, the very room where he had hidden the painting—had seemingly held him here. Lacking any other instructions from Loring himself, she had scattered his ashes in various locations on the property; maybe that had strengthened the bond. Perhaps she could bury Garrick's body in the Lynam pine woods. Perhaps his spirit would advise her on the best approach.

Grabbing Garrick's ankles one last time, she hauled him toward the shaft. She tried to be careful, but when the weight of his lower body overbalanced the weight of his upper and he tumbled to the floor, his head cracked with a sickening thud on the side of the shaft. Ellen winced.

"I'm sorry, Garrick," she murmured.

Taking the flashlight out of her pocket, she turned it on and put it on the floor of the lobby to provide some illumination. She pushed and pulled until she had him arranged as flat as possible on the floor of the shaft—she had no wish for part of him to get crushed when she brought the elevator back to the first floor—and then hoisted herself out onto the lobby floor. In the process, she knocked her glasses off and, taking a step toward where she thought they were, she felt her foot connect with something that went skittering across the floor. She sighed. It didn't matter—she could find her way around the hotel in the dark. She'd look for the glasses tomorrow.

Picking up the flashlight and returning the metal rod to its place behind the curtain, she climbed slowly back to the fourth floor and retrieved Garrick's coat. Then, trudging back to the first floor, she tossed it as carefully as she could over his body. She didn't think she could do another climb in and out of the shaft.

She grasped the door of the elevator, ready to pull it shut, when she thought she heard a faint sound. She switched on the flashlight again and shone it on the heap on the shaft floor.

"Garrick?"

She heard the croaking beginning of a word, a pained cough, and then his voice, reed thin. "Ellen, for God's sake ..."

Sighing, she aimed the Taser one last time.

44

Ann's head didn't hurt as much now, but she was cold—the night chill was seeping into her bones. Her shoulders began a violent shaking. And she was getting sleepy. She wasn't sure what she was doing out in the middle of the night, in the middle of nowhere, but she felt it was important that she keep going, although she couldn't remember what her destination was. How long had she been stumbling along ... an hour? a minute? She thought she should be watching out for hands, but that didn't make any sense.

She had been picking her way along a series of rounded rocks, but in the light of the moon she could now see that between the rocks and the water was a narrow strip of beach—it would be much easier to walk there. She crawled carefully across the rock and stepped onto the flat and her foot disappeared up to her ankle.

She tried to step back onto the rock, sending a protest up from her twisted ankle, but momentum carried her forward and her other foot came down onto the flat just ahead of the first and disappeared into the muck. And then, amid the jumbled confusion of her thoughts, one popped out with desperate clarity:

Garrick cautioning her to go through the woods if she couldn't follow the road on her way back from Lynam's Point Hotel—"the tidal flats will be like quicksand."

Claustrophobia clamped down on her and panic bubbled up —a faint voice of reason whispered for her not to fight, not to thrash. She took a hitching breath and pulled up tentatively on one foot but the only result was that her other foot slipped another inch deeper. Even her increasingly violent shivering felt as if it was shaking her further down into the mud.

Trying to keep her feet as still as possible, she twisted to look behind her. She was just a few feet from the rocks. She stretched her arm out, but they might as well have been a mile away. Turning forward again, she looked across the flats. The skim of water across the mud reflected the moon, the tops of the trees on the opposite bank created a lacy pattern against the star-speckled sky beyond. It looked so peaceful. She might disappear into the mud and no one would ever find her body. She had a sudden vision of two hands pushing her head under, water and sand filling her nose and her lungs. A whimper escaped her.

Trying to steady her breathing, she reached slowly down into the mud and began working the laces of her hiking boots loose, her breath catching at each new pull of the mud. When she got them both untied, she wriggled her feet to loosen them, with the result that she sank a bit further and mud began to fill her boots. Still moving like someone defusing a bomb, she worked her knapsack off her back and then, twisting, placed it gently onto the mud behind her. Then she removed her parka, the wind cutting like knives through her sweater.

In one awkward, flailing movement, she pulled one foot out of a boot and, twisting, lunged onto the knapsack. As it began to sink, she tossed her parka onto the last stretch of mud separating her from the rocks and, pushing off from the knapsack, pulled her other foot free, and stepped onto the parka just as her knapsack disappeared beneath the mud. A last, sticky scramble brought her onto solid ground.

She lay on the rock gasping. The pain in her head and her ankle, which had been pushed to the back of her mind by fear, came rushing to the fore again, clamoring for attention. She put her head down on her arm.

She would lie here, just for a minute—like Dorothy in the poppy field. If she could rest, maybe things would make more sense. Maybe she would remember why she was here and where she was going.

The shaking in her shoulders was starting to affect her torso —her back muscles were cramping against the cold—but her mind floated peacefully, pleasantly even. Then she heard a voice, close beside her and insistent.

"Hey, wake up!"

She dragged her face up. Her vision seemed to have clouded, but she could see clearly enough the man standing over her—a man who had shown her a painting but now seemed more vital. Clearly, though, a spirit.

"What?" she asked blearily.

"Don't fall asleep. You need to come with me. What's your name?"

"Ann. We've already met."

"I don't think so."

His name bubbled up from the depths of her sluggish brain. "You're Loring. You showed me the painting."

The man looked blank for a moment and then smiled thinly. "Ah, now I see. Yes, I'm Loring but I think you spoke with my father. Ann, you need to come with me, Garrick needs you."

"Garrick?"

"Yes—please, come with me right away, it's not far." He backed away from her, beckoning. "And you look like you could use some help, too. You can call for help from the hotel."

Ann dragged herself to her feet. "I have to warn Garrick."

"I think it's too late for a warning," he said grimly, "but you might still be able to help him." He turned away and began climbing the hill that led away from the tidal flats. "This way, it's safer."

Ann hauled herself up the shallow incline, sometimes putting her hands to the ground for balance, her head and ankle throbbing. Loring stopped periodically until she caught up, then walked quickly ahead. "Hurry!"

At some point she was no longer climbing and could sense, rather than the openness of the tidal flats, the enclosed space of the pine forest. Loring was ahead of her, urging her on, clearer than she had ever seen a spirit.

At last the pine woods were behind her and she realized she was on the edge of the hotel lawn. The shadow of a person moved in the lobby. She looked around for her guide.

The bang to her head must have been worse than she had originally thought because now she was seeing double—two figures, side by side, lean and muscular, with wavy brown hair and light gray eyes. One faint, one vivid. But then she saw that they weren't identical but just very similar—a family resemblance. Father and son—the Loring who was her guide to the painting and the Loring who was her guide to the hotel—frozen by death at the same age.

The faint figure moved toward her, obviously concerned, and the vivid one reached out a hand to stop him.

"Dad, leave her be, she needs to get to the hotel."

The faint one said something Ann couldn't quite make out.

"Something bad has happened, but we can't help, only she can," the clearer Loring said. He turned to Ann. "Be careful of Ellen, she has a Taser. Stay as far away from her as you can. But in case she does come after you, there's a wooden box with croquet mallets in it on the veranda, get one of those—it's better than nothing. Go on now."

Tasers? Croquet mallets? None of this made any sense, except that Garrick was at the hotel. Ann turned from the two figures and limped across the lawn, the wind slicing through her clothing as if she were naked. After what seemed like an interminable trek, she reached the veranda. She hauled herself up the steps using the handrail, but tripped on the last step and landed with a thump.

She heard a woman's voice from the lobby call tentatively, "Loring?" Then, a moment later, in a more tremulous voice, "Garrick?"

Garrick must be in the hotel, just like Loring had said. She crossed the veranda. She had a vague memory of being told to get something from the veranda, but she didn't need it anymore now that she had found Garrick. She fumbled open the door to the lobby and stepped in, just outside of the pool of light shed by the one illuminated lamp. A woman was standing near the elevator. Ann knew her but couldn't remember her name.

"Who are you?" asked the woman sharply.

Forgetting why she was wearing the cap, Ann pulled it off to be polite. Her hair, loosened from its customary ponytail, fell around her shoulders, dark with drying blood. Her red sweater had torn during one of her falls and a tuft of white t-shirt poked through. She was weary and battered and she wanted nothing more than to sink into one of the chintz armchairs. She stepped toward the chairs and into the light.

The woman by the elevator shrieked. "You?!"

This was not the reception Ann had expected. She took another step forward. The woman stepped back.

"What are you doing down here?" the woman asked, her voice high and quavering, peering at Ann with a nearsighted squint.

"I was looking for you." Ann remembered now—the woman's name was Ellen, and it had been important for Ann to find her as well as Garrick.

"No, I was looking for you! You belong to me now!"

Ann didn't know what to make of this. The feeling of relief she had felt upon reaching the hotel was slipping away. "It took me a long time to get here," she said plaintively.

"But you've been here all along. Loring kept you from me."

"No, Loring helped me get here." Ann decided to stop trying to make sense of what Ellen said. "I'm going to sit down," she said and started for a chair when the person she had really been looking for all along appeared behind Ellen. "Garrick!" cried Ann with relief, then put her hand to her head as the room began to spin.

Ellen spun with a shriek and looked crazily around her. "Where is he?"

"He's right behind you," said Ann. She started to lower herself into the chair but halted at Garrick's voice.

"Don't sit down!"

Ann stumbled back to her feet. "Why not?"

"Who are you talking to?" cried Ellen, fumbling in her pocket.

"Oh for God's sake," muttered Garrick, and Ann followed his gaze to where a barely discernible Biden Firth stood just inside the front doorway.

Ann let out a stifled scream.

Ellen whirled toward the door. "What? Who's there?

"It's Biden! Garrick, he's been hurting me!" Ann limped behind the chair, putting it between her and Biden.

Garrick strode toward the figure in the doorway. "I have no time to deal with a pathetic imbecile like you," he said furiously. "Your presence here is most unwelcome. In fact, your presence anywhere is most unwelcome. As far as I can tell, you were pathetic in life and you are worse than pathetic in death. Now leave us, we have no time for you."

Ann would have thought that it would be difficult to describe a spirit as blanching, but that is exactly what happened to Biden in the face of Garrick's verbal onslaught. Garrick whirled and strode back to the elevator, blocking Ann's view of Biden for a moment. When Garrick passed, the doorway was empty.

"Come here. But watch Ellen," said Garrick, motioning Ann toward the elevator.

Ann circled to the elevator while Ellen began backing toward the stairs.

Garrick motioned to a window next to the elevator. "Behind that curtain—there's a metal device. Get it."

"Garrick, what's going on?"

"I'll explain later—do as I say."

Ann pulled the curtain aside and lying on the ledge was a metal rod.

"Pick it up."

Ann picked up the rod. "Garrick, I had such a hard time getting here—"

"Later. Watch out for her," he said, gesturing toward Ellen. "Now, insert the pointed end of that device into that small hole in the elevator door."

Ann did as she was told.

"You need to lift a latch on the other side of the door."

Ann jiggled the metal rod around in the hole.

"No, lift it."

Ann tried to lever the invisible latch on the other side of the door up.

"Hook the rod under the latch and *lift* it."

"I'm trying, Garrick, just calm down."

"It's important, Ann. Please."

There was a note of pleading in Garrick's voice that she had never heard before. Just as she turned to look at him, she felt and heard a click and the elevator door slid aside, revealing not the elevator but the empty shaft. The light from the single lamp barely illuminated the bottom of the shaft, but Ann could make out a crumpled form partially covered with a black coat.

"Garrick?" Ann said tremulously.

"Ann, step aside!" said Garrick sharply and Ann stepped to the right just as Ellen stumbled past her and, arms pinwheeling, toppled into the elevator shaft. Garrick winced as Ellen landed on the crumpled form on the floor. They heard a crack and Ellen shrieked in pain.

Just then, lights from the drive swept the room and Ann and Garrick turned toward the windows. They heard the slam of car doors and steps on the patio and then the door opened and Scott was in the lobby followed by Mace.

"Good heavens, Annie," he said, "what happened to you?"

45

S cott hurried across the lobby to where Ann stood, leaving Mace at the door, mouth agape. At the bottom of the elevator shaft, Ellen was struggling to a sitting position, cradling her arm. Scott peered into the shaft at Ellen and then back at Ann. "What happened?" he asked again. "Are you all right?"

"Ah, excellent," said Garrick, "the chauffeur. Tell him to get the defibrillator. It's in the office."

The pounding in Ann's head had started again. She stumbled back toward the chairs, thinking she might be sick. "Can't you tell him yourself?"

"Ann, I think you know I can't tell him myself," said Garrick at the same time Scott said, "Tell who myself?" and hurried over to help lower Ann into the chair.

Ann looked toward where Garrick was standing by the elevator and Scott followed her gaze. "Don't worry, honey, I'll help her in a minute."

"Scott, do you see him?"

Scott looked back again toward the door where Garrick stood. "See who, sweetie? I think you've hurt your head. You just sit there and I'll call 911." Scott reached into his pocket for his phone.

"Now, Ann. He has to get it now," Garrick said.

Ann fought her way back to her feet. "Scott, there's someone else in the shaft. Get the defibrillator, it's in the ..." Her voice trailed off as Scott hurried from Ann to the open elevator door.

"The office," said Garrick, his voice strained. "Behind the registration desk."

Ellen, huddled in the corner of the shaft, whimpered, "My arm ..."

"We're going to help you, ma'am," said Scott. "Oh my God, you're right, Annie, there's someone else in there!"

"Scott, come with me," said Ann. She limped quickly across the lobby and went around the registration desk to the door to the office. She flipped on the overhead light and steadied herself on the frame of the door, scanning the room. "I don't even know what it looks like!" she yelled.

"In a box on the wall behind the door," Garrick called from the lobby.

Scott eased past Ann and scanned the room. "You don't have to yell, sweetie, I'm right here. They're usually in a box on the wall ..."

"Behind the door," said Ann.

Scott peered behind the door. "Ah yes, here it is." He opened the glass case, and removed a bag about the size of a bulky brief-case. "Did you examine whoever that is? How do you know this is what he needs?"

"He told me. Hurry." Ann started back to the elevator, followed by Scott.

"If he's talking, we shouldn't shock him, it would do more harm than good," he said.

Ann reached the elevator and lowered herself to the floor of the shaft.

Ellen squeezed herself even more tightly into the corner. "You see him, don't you? You're talking to him. See, it doesn't matter whether he's dead or alive, he's still with us!"

Scott also lowered himself into the shaft, which was now quite crowded. Ann tugged at the form on the floor, setting off a wave of dizziness and reigniting the pounding in her head. Scott squeezed by her and eased the body over.

"It's Mr. Masser!"

Ann slumped against the wall of the shaft. "Scott, you need to shock him with that thing."

"Tell him my heart has stopped," said Garrick.

"His heart has stopped," said Ann.

Scott felt for a pulse at the neck. "You're right." He quickly unbuttoned the shirt then pulled up a black t-shirt, revealing a painfully thin torso. He pulled a machine out of the case which he lay on the floor of the shaft and activated with the press of a button. He extracted two white pads that were attached to the machine with wires and, pulling a paper backing from each, attached them to the chest, one on the side of the ribcage and one on the other side of the chest near the collarbone.

An automated female voice intoned, "Stand clear, do not touch the patient." For a few moments the only sound was Ellen's fast, uneven breathing. "Shock advised. Charging. Stand clear."

Scott shuffled back as best he could in the tight space. "Ma'am, can you pull your legs back a little?"

Ellen shifted her legs.

"Press the flashing shock button," the machine said.

"Good heavens," Garrick muttered from the lobby as Scott pressed the button and the body on the floor of the shaft jerked.

"Shock one delivered. It is safe to touch the patient. Begin CPR now," said the machine.

"I don't know how I can in this space," said Scott. He turned toward Ellen. "Ma'am, can you stand? I need more room. Annie, can you help me get her out?" Scott grasped Ellen's uninjured arm and tried to pull her to her feet.

Ellen let out a squawk. "It hurts!"

"Leave her," came a croak from the form on the floor.

"Garrick!" cried Ann and turned toward where he had stood a moment before, but the lobby was empty except for Mace, who was pointing her mobile phone at them.

"Excellent! This is going to get a million views!"

46

Ann and Scott were playing gin rummy on Ann's wheeled hospital table the next morning when Mike burst into the room.

"Sweetie!" cried Scott. He put his cards on the table—face up—and crossed the room to hug Mike. "How did you get here so fast? Did Walt fly you up?"

"Nope—I drove." Mike went to the bed where Ann was propped up on pillows. "How are you?"

"I'm okay, just a little banged up." She glanced at the clock on the wall. "How *did* you get here so fast?"

Mike and Scott sat down side-by-side in the guest chairs. "I did think about calling Walt but I didn't feel like waiting around until he got the plane ready and flew down from the Adirondacks. I figured I could get here almost as fast on my own." He turned to Scott. "Let it never be said that the Prius can't be a high-performance car with a determined driver at the wheel. Only got one speeding ticket. 'It's six hundred miles to Bar Harbor, we got a full tank of gas, half a pack of cigarettes, it's dark ... and we're wearing sunglasses.'"

Ann groaned. "Did you spend the whole drive thinking about delivering that line?"

"I had other things on my mind," Mike said, smiling at her. "You're a lot less out of it than I was afraid you'd be, but you are kind of a mess."

"Concussion, sprained ankle, miscellaneous cuts and bruises," said Scott.

"Largely self-inflicted," said Ann.

"They weren't self-inflicted!" Scott scolded her. He turned to Mike. "Biden Firth was chasing her."

Mike raised his eyebrows at Ann.

"He was in the car with me, he's the one who's been giving me the pain in my hands. He made me lose control. I crashed Audrey," she added sheepishly.

Mike waved his hand. "That's not important. What happened?"

Ann described the slide into the embankment, eliciting a wince from Mike, although whether for herself or for the car, she wasn't sure. With prompting from Scott, she described her confusion after the crash, the shock of seeing Biden in the seat beside her, her escape through the sunroof, Biden's pursuit of her.

"All she could see were his hands," whispered Scott to Mike.

"And I got stuck in the mud flats."

"Wait until you find out how she got out of that! Very clever." Scott smiled at her proudly.

"Then I got to the hotel."

"Just in time to save Mr. Masser."

"Scott saved Garrick. Garrick's client, Ellen Lynam, shot him with a Taser. A lot, evidently."

"Sounds like a client to avoid," said Mike.

"I'm guessing he had a preexisting heart condition," said Scott. "The stress must have sent him into cardiac arrest."

"Scott shocked him back to life with a defibrillator," said Ann.

"Annie told me where it was," said Scott.

"Garrick told me where it was," said Ann.

"That's certainly a handy skill to have," said Scott. "I hope that if I'm ever temporarily dead I can tell someone how to save me."

"By the way," said Ann, turning to Scott. "How did you know where I was?"

"I got your voicemail and your text—a little while after you left them, the club was noisy—and tried calling you but I didn't get any answer. Then when we got back to the inn and the car was gone I got worried. You had been so mysterious about that place where you had me drop you off for your solo hike that I asked Mace to drive me back there. That road only went to one place and Mr. Masser's car was out front."

"How do you know what kind of car Masser has?" asked Mike.

"It was sitting outside the garage one time when I picked Annie up at his house."

Ann laughed. "Scott, you're in the wrong business, you should be a private detective."

"Or possibly a criminal," said Mike fondly.

Scott raised his eyebrows at them. "I have left my criminal past behind me. Anyhow—" he turned to Mike, "Annie found a painting—a Renaissance painting."

"Really?" said Mike.

"Yes!" said Scott. "It was hidden in a secret compartment in a room on the top floor. Annie explained to me where it was and I took the police up there when they arrived. They've taken it to Boston to confirm who it's by and where it came from. Evidently when Mr. Masser's client saw Annie, she thought she was the woman in the painting. Gave her quite a turn."

"That, and the fact that I looked like Wile E. Coyote after a run-in with the Road Runner," said Ann.

A nurse had poked her head in the room and heard Ann's last comment. "I think you guys should let our patient get a little rest. Why don't you take a break and stop back in a couple of hours?"

Mike started to protest, "But I just got here—" but Scott stood and touched his shoulder.

"Come on, Annie needs some rest, I'll fill you in." He leaned over and gave Ann a kiss on the forehead. "You take a nap, sweetie, and we'll go find some nice books for you to pass the time."

Mike stood as well. "Do you think Biden might show up at the hospital? It sounds like he has it in for you."

Ann shrugged. "I can't imagine he could cause me to do much harm here—no cars, no knives, no hot coffee. I think I'll be okay for now."

He contemplated her for a moment until the nurse cleared her throat.

"Okay, okay, I'm going." He leaned down and gave Ann a hug. "We'll think of something," he said, then followed Scott out of the room. Ann just caught, "So how bad is Audrey?" before the door closed behind them.

Ann lay back on the pillows as the nurse checked her pulse. What could Biden Firth make her do? Other than fumbling a hand of cards, she couldn't think of much. But she was still sorry when the nurse turned off the bedside light, drew the curtains, and left her alone in the room to her own—and perhaps Biden Firth's—devices.

47

1947

A few days after the fire had swept down Great Hill, Eliot showed up at Lynam's Point Hotel to retrieve some of the belongings he had stored there.

"There's a suitcase with some of my sister's clothes in it that she asked me to pick up."

"Millie?" Chip asked, leading Eliot to the guest room where his things had been stored.

"Yup."

"What does she need the clothes for?"

"They're the only clothes she has—everything else burned with the house."

Chip stopped, turning back to Eliot. "Her house burned?"

"Our house. Me, Millie, our parents. Mom and Dad are staying with relatives on the mainland. I'm staying with some buddies who are fighting what's left of the fire. Millie's staying at a guest house in Bar Harbor, off Main Street."

Chip shook his head. "I'm really sorry to hear about your house. Where was it?"

"Bar Harbor. Forest Street."

Chip unlocked the door to the room containing Millie and Eliot's family's things. Eliot entered and pulled a leather suitcase out of the pile, then began sorting through the other items, adding a collection of odds and ends to a wooden crate he had brought with him.

Chip lingered in the doorway then said, "I could ask my dad if you and Millie could stay here."

Eliot stopped sorting and looked at Chip. "You think that might be okay?"

As with the furniture, Chip was pretty sure his father wouldn't approve. He shrugged.

"Well, I'm okay where I am," said Eliot, "but the place Millie's staying is awful crowded, I know she'd appreciate getting away from there. Plus, I'll bet she could help out around here. She doesn't like to be at loose ends."

"Yeah, I can imagine she wouldn't," said Chip. "I'll ask my dad."

Chip left Eliot to his sorting and went to find his father.

Chip's father had kept even more to himself than usual since their encounter after Chip's return from the fire. Chip eventually found him in the workshop in the shed, sanding the arm of one of the Adirondack chairs he was building to replace several that even his father had to admit were a bit too worn to use for another season.

"Hey, Dad," said Chip from the doorway.

"Yes?" said his father, not turning around.

"Eliot came to pick up some of his things."

"Good. We're not a depot."

"His family got burned out."

His father stopped sanding for a moment and dropped his head, then resumed his work. "I'm sorry to hear that. Lots of folks in that boat."

"His sister is at a guest house in town, Eliot says it's awful crowded. Maybe she could stay here. He says she wouldn't mind helping out."

His father swapped one piece of sandpaper for another. "You know we don't have money to be paying for help during the off-season."

"I don't think he meant it like that, just that she wouldn't mind helping out in exchange for room and board."

His father sighed. "Who is it?"

"Millie."

His father turned. "Millie Reynolds?"

"Yes."

"About your age, right?"

"Yes."

His father pushed himself upright and went to the workbench. He gazed out the small window toward the water. Finally he said, "Yes. That might be all right."

CHIP HELPED Eliot carry the stuff downstairs and load it into Eliot's truck.

"So you're going to Bar Harbor?" he asked as Eliot climbed into the cab.

"Yup. I'll swing by the place where Millie's staying and bring her back here if she wants to."

"I could go," said Chip. "Save you the drive back."

"Not unless you have a pass, at least on the eastern side of the island." Eliot pulled a card out of his shirt pocket and passed it to Chip. It was a form printed in red ink.

BAR HARBOR FIRE DEPARTMENT FIRE-LINE PASS ... The Bearer Eliot Reynolds *is to be passed through Fire Lines on Mt. Desert Island.*

DAVID A. SLEEPER, CHIEF Bar Harbor Fire Department.
(This Is Not A Pass To or From Mt. Desert Island.)

"Have you been back to town yet?" asked Chip.

"Nope, but I've talked with some fellas who have. They say everything this side of Eden Street and Spring Street burned."

"What about Jardin?'

Eliot shook his head. "I hear it's gone. Not just damaged—gone." Eliot stuck out his hand to Chip. "Much obliged to you and your father. For keeping our things safe, and for offering a room for Millie."

"Hey, can I come with you?" said Chip as Eliot climbed into the truck. "I'd really like to get a look at Jardin. Maybe something's left. Maybe they need some help cleaning up. I'll bet they'd let us both through with your pass."

Eliot rubbed his neck. "I don't know, it just has my name on it ..."

"Worst that happens is they won't let me through," said Chip, "and I'd have to find my own way back to the hotel."

"I don't know why you're so fired up about going to Jardin," said Eliot, "but okay, if you're willing to take the chance."

"Sure!" said Chip. "Just let me tell my dad."

Chip's father was no longer in the workshop and Chip eventually found him in one of the rooms on the second floor, smoothing the wrinkles out of the spread on the freshly made bed.

"I'm going over to Bar Harbor."

"Okay. You steer clear of the fire, it's still burning in places."

"Okay. Did someone else show up?"

"What do you mean?" his father asked.

Chip nodded toward the bed.

"You're going to bring Millie Reynolds back from town, right?" asked his father.

"Well, yeah, if she wants to."

His father made a slight adjustment to one of the pillows on the bed. "Well, you make sure she knows she's welcome."

CHIP HAD HEARD the same reports Eliot had about the fate of Jardin, but wanted to see for himself. It seemed uncharitable to hope for the Furnesses' home to have been destroyed, but if the library had survived, it would be hard to explain a blank space on a wall where a painting—or the remains of a painting—should have been hanging.

Eagle Lake Road had been reopened. There was a checkpoint at the entrance manned by a soldier who was obviously frustrated at being stationed at such a dull location and was mostly interested in finding out what they knew about the fire. He gave the pass a cursory glance and waved them through.

They drove into a scene of destruction. As they turned onto Eagle Lake Road, they saw smoke still rising from some fields, small groups of firefighters posted to guard against flare-ups. As they drove east, they entered the areas that had burned a day or two previously. At one former home site, a man tugged ineffectually at what looked like a bed frame sticking up from the rubble while a woman stood to one side rocking a two- or three-year-old girl who cried inconsolably. In some places, fields were scorched to the ground. In others, a few trees, stripped of their leaves, still stood, their charred branches pointing to the sky like skeletal fingers.

Evidence of the fire's capriciousness was everywhere. A grove of pines on one side of the road had burned to the ground, the stumps still smoldering, while on the other side a picket fence had suffered no worse fate than having its white paint dulled by the smoke. The site where a home had stood was marked only by a gaping basement filled with charred wood, while the mailbox was untouched, its jaunty red flag aloft.

As they approached Bar Harbor, Eliot turned off Eagle Lake Road onto Forest, then pulled to the side of the road. He nodded to a pile of debris.

"That was our house."

It looked like an ash heap on which someone had dumped metal scrap—water pipes, a metal barrel, an iron stove, and, on top, a claw-footed bathtub.

Although Chip was jittery with his desire to get to Jardin, he said, "Want to stop? Look around?"

Eliot shook his head. "Why bother? What could be left in *that*?" He turned the car around.

They continued down Eagle Lake Road past the Kebo Valley Club. The clubhouse was gone and even the Building of the Arts which, in all its Grecian glory, had looked like it could survive any conflagration, had been reduced like its less noble neighbors to rubble. Bar Harbor's elegant Malvern and Belmont Hotels had burned and in their places were precarious stepped towers of brick—the multi-story chimneys and fireplaces that had warmed the guests through Bar Harbor's golden age. The bricks that had formerly constituted the DeGregoire Hotel had tumbled into the road and been pushed aside, likely by a bulldozer.

"God almighty," said Eliot, "it looks like Dresden."

When they reached the center of the village, where the fire hadn't reached, all was eerily quiet. The stores were closed, the houses locked up, the sidewalks empty save for soldiers on the lookout for looters. Some windows had been broken by debris blown about by the gale-force winds. Abandoned fire hose snaked through the streets. A scorched funk hung in the air.

They were about to turn onto the street where Millie's

temporary lodgings were when a soldier stepped in front of the truck. He circled to the driver's window.

"Pass?"

Eliot handed him the pass.

The soldier glanced up at them. "Which one of you is Eliot Reynolds?"

"That's me," said Eliot.

"And what's your business here?"

"Picking up my sister, taking her to more suitable lodgings," said Eliot. "She's staying in a guest house on this street."

"This pass is only for you, Mr. Reynolds," said the soldier. "Who might your passenger be?"

"This is my sister's fiancé, Chip Lynam."

Chip blushed to his hairline and smiled weakly at the soldier.

The soldier looked sharply at him and then nodded and handed the pass back to Eliot. "Move along."

Eliot pulled away, his mouth twisted with the effort of not laughing.

"I can't believe you told him that!" Chip muttered.

Eliot shrugged, still smiling. "Got you through, didn't it?"

They pulled up in front of the guest house, where a group of women—most of them young—were sitting on the porch.

"Eliot!" they heard, and Millie detached herself from the group and ran out to the car. She gave Eliot a hug and then turned to Chip. "Chip Lynam! What are you doing here?"

"We brought you some clothes I had stashed at Chip's dad's hotel over on Lynam Point," said Eliot.

Millie looked into the back of the truck where the suitcase lay. "Well, aren't you the nicest things—thank you!" She began circling the truck to the tailgate.

"But Chip has a proposal for you," said Eliot, wiggling his eyebrows suggestively at Chip. "Tell her, Chip."

Chip tried to glare at Eliot, then turned to Millie. "We thought maybe you'd like to come stay at the hotel." He glanced nervously at the other women on the porch, all of whom were observing the interaction with interest. Millie turned to him, her eyebrows raised.

Chip scuffed the toe of his boot on the pavement. "I'm awful sorry about your house, Millie. We thought you might be more comfortable at the hotel. You wouldn't have to pay, maybe just help out a little around the place. Just until things get worked out with your family." He gave an exaggerated shrug. "Just a thought."

Millie glanced at Eliot, who nodded, then at the group of women on the porch, all of whom quickly turned back to whatever they had been doing before Eliot and Chip showed up.

"Well, I must say I wouldn't mind having somewhere else to stay," she said in an undertone. "This group is a bit catty." She looked closely at Chip. "This is okay with your dad?"

Although he would never have expected it, Chip was able to say with complete sincerity, "Yes, seems like he thinks it's a good idea."

"Okay then," said Millie decisively. "I appreciate it, Chip. Let me run in and grab a couple of things, won't be a minute."

Millie wasn't gone much more than a minute when she reappeared on the porch with her purse and a small satchel. After a quick conversation with one of the older women, she ran down the steps. Ignoring Chip's outstretched hand, she flipped the satchel into the back and jumped in the cab, shifting to the middle of the seat to make room for Chip.

Eliot got in and started the truck. "Chip wants to go see what's what at Jardin. You mind?"

"I don't mind, but I hear it's gone."

"I know," said Chip, "but I'd still like to go."

"It's okay with me," said Millie. "Just so long as we don't drive past our old place." She turned to Eliot. "I've been by once and that was enough. Have you seen it?"

Eliot nodded grimly. "What there is of it to see."

"Can we drive up Eden Street a bit?" asked Millie. "My friend Janey worked at one of the bayside houses and she's wondering if it's still there."

They drove up Eden Street. Although most of the buildings on the bay side of the road had been spared, the only sign of many of the cottages on the Great Hill side were foundation walls and conglomerations of brickwork and a few granite steps and posts bearing inscriptions of the names of the cottages—Far View, Rocklyn, Rock Brook.

Millie sighed disconsolately. "That's enough, let's go to Jardin."

Eliot turned the truck around and headed for Cleftstone Road.

Chip hoped again—with a flush of shame—that the destruction at Jardin had been as complete as it had been along Eden Street.

It had.

Great Hill had been burned clear of vegetation. The fire had leveled everything in its path, burning even the soil to expose the rocks underneath. As they turned into the drive, they bumped over a ridge of metal melted onto the pavement—the remains of the arch of metalwork that had welcomed visitors to Jardin d'Eden. Even the granite pillars had cracked and tumbled in the heat of the fire.

When they reached the top of the drive, the only thing that stood higher than the truck was George Pritchard. He stood near what would have been the front door, his hands in his pockets, his head down. He turned when he heard the truck approaching.

They got out of the truck and went to stand by him. They

looked wordlessly across the foundations that suggested where the grand cottage had once stood. Finally, Pritchard said, "Guess that's that."

"Yup," said Eliot.

"What a waste. What a goddamned waste. Pardon my French," he grumbled toward Mille, who waved away his apology. He kicked at the rubble. "I should have listened to you, Lynam. I should have gotten the artwork somewhere safe."

Chip flushed and shrugged. "You didn't know what was going to happen."

"I should have known. I should have seen it coming. I should have loaded them into the truck and taken them to the mainland. Especially the painting of that lady. Mr. Furness is especially upset about losing that. He said he paid good money for that painting—can't believe it got taken from him by some laborer tossing a cigarette butt out his truck window."

Until that moment, Chip had not been completely certain what he was going to do with The Lady. Until that moment, it might still have been possible for him to say to Pritchard, "I have the painting. I saved it for him," but he didn't. Mr. Furness had never loved The Lady, he had only loved the idea of owning her. He, Chip, was the only one who cared about her—had been willing to risk his safety, even his life—for hers. She was special and precious and he wasn't about to turn her over to someone who didn't love her the way she deserved to be loved.

"It was a nice painting," said Chip, struggling to keep his tone casual.

"Damn right," said Pritchard morosely.

"What now?" asked Eliot. "Are the Furnesses going to rebuild?"

"I doubt it," said Pritchard, looking across the scorched hillside toward the town. "Bar Harbor isn't the place to be like it was back in the day. I'm not talking about the Furnesses, now, but I think some of these summer-colony types might not be too broken up about what the fire did. Taxes, upkeep—the fire saved them having a white elephant on their hands." He bent to pick something out of the rubble and rubbed it with the sleeve of his shirt, bringing a faint shine to the dull surface. "You know what that was?"

Eliot peered at it. "Nope."

"The door knocker. Now it's nothing but a lump of metal. Useless." He tossed it back and looked again toward Bar Harbor. "You know what the future of this town is going to be, don't you?"

The three of them shook their heads.

"Tourists," said Pritchard with contempt.

48

A nn was released after twenty-four hours of observation, but she asked Scott and Mike if the three of them could stay on MDI until Garrick was moved out of the ICU.

Scott and Mike passed the time exploring the island in Scott's Prius, Audrey having been towed to Ellsworth for repairs. They biked and kayaked, went whale watching, and took a glider ride out of the local airport.

Ann, however, spent most of the time in her room back at the inn, reading all of Nan's Nero Wolfe books while huddled under a mound of quilts. Even days after her trek from the wrecked car to the hotel, Ann still felt as if she might never feel truly warm again.

When Ann got the word that Garrick could have visitors, she asked Scott and Mike to drop her off at the hospital. She found him sitting up in bed in black flannel pajamas with beige piping.

"They let you wear your own pajamas?"

"I hardly think it is within the purview of the medical community to dictate what its patients wear."

"How did you get them?"

"I have resources. My robe is in the closet."

"You don't need to get out of bed."

"I'm not going to receive visitors in bed," said Garrick sternly. He pulled on the robe, also black, slipped his feet into a pair of worn leather slippers, and moved stiffly from the bed to the visitor's chair, which left Ann with the bed to sit on.

"I brought some things for you to read," she said. She handed over the reading material Scott and Mike had gotten for her for her hospital stay—*Lost Bar Harbor* and a copy of *Out & About in Downeast Maine* (or, as Scott referred to it, "Down and Out in Maine")—as well as the book Garrick had loaned Scott.

"Most thoughtful of you," said Garrick grudgingly.

"I read the Alderson book," she said, nodding toward the small, gaudily covered book. "I'm trying to learn more about sensing."

"Most admirable, I'm sure," said Garrick.

Ann leaned forward. "Garrick, what happened with Biden at the hotel?"

He raised his eyebrows at her.

"Biden attacked me in the car and followed me to the hotel. He was hurting me and I couldn't get away from him and I couldn't make him stop. And then you made him disappear. Just like that. How did you do it?"

Garrick waved his hand. "I had more pressing issues to deal with at that moment. Over time, one learns to deal with difficult spirits."

"Can I learn?"

"Perhaps."

"Will you teach me?"

Garrick shifted in his chair with a slight wince. "Instruction has never been my area of focus."

"Garrick!" Ann almost wailed. "I'm hurting myself! I'm having horrible dreams! I can't keep on like this, it's making me crazy! You have to help me."

"I'm not withholding information from you intentionally," said Garrick, more gently than she would have expected. "I've always had this ability to communicate with spirits—it didn't develop gradually in me as it seems to be developing in you, it manifested itself full blown. I never had to learn. And I never had a need—or an opportunity—to teach it. I suspect Biden Firth would not manifest himself again in my presence, which makes it more difficult for me to advise you how to deal with him were he to manifest himself again in your presence."

"Is he dangerous?"

"Not to me. But to you? I don't know."

Ann played with the strap on her knapsack. Finally she said, "I guess I'll go home and see what happens."

"Or perhaps stay with your brother for a time. Avoid activities where a sudden pain in your hand might be problematic."

"Like driving."

"Yes, obviously."

They both lapsed into a sulky silence.

Finally, Garrick said, "I suppose your driver will be returning with you?"

"What?"

"Your driver, Mr. Pate. I gathered he was from Pennsylvania."

"Oh, right. Yes, he'll be returning with me."

"But if at some point you ascertain that you are no longer experiencing the difficulties with your hands, perhaps you would no longer have need of his services."

"I suppose so."

"He seems very resourceful," ventured Garrick.

"Oh yes, he's very resourceful," said Ann with a smile.

"Perhaps ..." Garrick paused. "When you can once again drive yourself, perhaps he would consider relocating to Maine," he concluded stiffly.

Ann raised her eyebrows. "You want to hire him?"

"Well, if it would be acceptable to you, of course," said Garrick magnanimously.

Ann suppressed a wider smile. "He's only driving me as a favor. He's Mike's partner."

"Partner? I thought your brother's business was managing your consulting engagements. Do you have need of two business managers?"

"No, not business partner. Boyfriend."

"Ah, I see." Garrick seemed relieved to learn that Ann's driver was not a professional chauffeur and that her business was not so booming as to need a staff of two to manage it. "Well, he seems to be quick thinking. And polite," he added pointedly. "A useful person."

"Oh yes, very useful," said Ann cheerfully. Good humor restored, she said, "I'm sorry you didn't get your fee."

"An unfortunate eventuality."

"Maybe you could still get it."

"I fear not."

"Ellen's going to have some assets from the sale of the hotel. I'm not sure what happens to those if she's in jail, but—"

"There's no fee," Garrick interrupted.

"What?"

Garrick shifted uncomfortably. "I wasn't performing the engagement for a fee."

"But why, then?"

Garrick looked hawkishly at her for a few moments. Finally he said, "I knew her family for many years. She employed me when I first decided to make sensing my profession. She was so young when her father died, and she was so utterly unlike her brother. She was ... someone who needed someone to care for her."

"*You* cared for her," said Ann, half statement, half question.

"Yes," said Garrick. "I cared for her."

49

1950

A fter the fire, when the Furnesses confirmed Pritchard's prediction that they would not rebuild Jardin and the staff was looking for work, Chip's father hired Millie to help at the hotel. Much to Chip's surprise, his father seemed to enjoy having her around and even occasionally smiled at her friendly teasing. To no one's surprise, Millie turned out to be a natural at the hotel business and had soon become the de facto manager of the operation, charming guests as they checked in and hiring the best of the workers from Jardin to supplement the hotel staff. Millie became such an integral part of the hotel, and she and Chip spent so much time together, that eventually their marriage seemed inevitable. Chip knew he was a lucky man when she agreed to marry him.

They had their wedding at the Lynam's Point Hotel on a rainy Saturday in October, after that year's guests had left for the season. That night, after the reception—attended mainly by Millie's family and friends and hotel staff—had ended and his father had gone up to his room on the second floor (he had temporarily ceded the fourth floor to Chip and Millie for their "honeymoon"), Chip took Millie's hand and said, "There's something I want to show you. Upstairs."

Millie laughed teasingly. "Oh, is there, Chip Lynam?"

"Yes," said Chip. They climbed the stairs. On the top floor, Millie turned to go into Chip's room, but with a tug on her hand Chip led her to the end of the hallway, to the last door on the left. He opened the door, switched on the light, and waved her through.

For many years the room had been used for storage, but in '47, shortly after the big fire, Chip's father had given him permission to turn it into an office of sorts. An old desk was pushed up to the outside wall, although the slanting ceiling left barely enough headroom for anyone sitting there. A cast-off lamp from one of the guest rooms hung from the ceiling and provided the only light.

She peeked in, perhaps expecting a surprise, but saw only the usual sparse furnishings. "Okay. Now what?"

Chip pulled out the desk chair for her. After a brief hesitation, she gathered the skirt of her wedding dress around her and sat down. Chip pulled a stool over and sat down next to her and took her hand.

"I have something very important to share with you," said Chip.

Millie nodded, her face a bit scrunched up with puzzlement.

"Do you remember my mother?"

"Your mother? Chip, that was such a long time ago—I think I only met her a couple of times and I was just little, like you."

"But you remember what she looked like, right?"

"Well, yes, in general."

"She was pretty, right?"

"Yes, Chip, very pretty."

Chip didn't think she sounded completely sincere but plowed ahead nonetheless.

"I loved her a lot, but my father made her go away. He treated her like he owned her—like she was an object. And when she left, I couldn't protect her."

"Good heavens, Chip, you were—what—six years old? You couldn't help what was happening between your parents, or what happened to your mother."

"I should have found a way. Then when she died, I missed her so much, and I thought I'd never be able to make it up to her, but then I did find a way."

Exasperation was now mixing with puzzlement on Millie's face. "Well, I can't imagine how, but I'll bite—what did you do?"

"Do you remember that picture the Furnesses had? The one in the library?"

Millie's eyebrows drew together. "The one the Italian man brought?"

"Yes, that one! And it looked so much like my mother—it was like she had come back—"

Millie stood up. "Chip Lynam, it is our wedding night, and I would have thought you would be interested in me, not in thinking about your poor dead mother and certainly not thinking about some creepy painting that burned up years ago!"

"Millie, wait—"

"No, Chip. Some other time I'll listen to this story, but not tonight—not on our wedding night." She pushed the skirts of her wedding dress out the door and walked down the hall where he heard the door to his room—their room—close behind her.

Chip sat staring ahead of him for a minute, then got up and closed and locked the door to the hallway. He knelt by the wall and lifted the section of paneling, which slid smoothly upward. Chip was pleased with his handiwork—he had masked the construction of the hiding place by also installing a set of built-in bookshelves in the small room. He swung open the board on which The Lady hung, then sat down in the desk chair that Millie had vacated.

The Lady looked out at him. Did her small, usually sad smile contain a touch of amusement? He had looked forward to sharing The Lady with Millie—now that they were married, she couldn't very well report him to the authorities, could she? He spent a few minutes hoping that she would change her mind and come back, but eventually he acknowledged that once Millie had made up her mind to a course of action, she was unlikely to change it without good reason. So perhaps The Lady was meant to remain a secret living solely with him. But perhaps not—perhaps someone would happen along someday with whom he could share the experience.

After a last look, he swung the board shut and pulled down the panel and, closing the door to the room behind him, went down the hall to his new bride.

50

G arrick used the key from under the flower pot to open the hotel's front door. The hotel was now the property of the buyer, and its demolition was scheduled for the following week. The lobby was completely empty now, stripped not only of furniture but even of the architectural details that were sellable—the registration desk, the fireplace mantle. Even the brass fittings on the elevator were gone.

Accompanied by the tap of the antique cane he carried, he made his way across the lobby to the lounge. He had replaced the unattractive utilitarian affair provided by the hospital with a striking Malacca cane with an ivory handle. He no longer needed it for support, but kept it because he was secretly pleased with the effect.

The lounge was as bare as the lobby, the bar having been an especially popular find for the dealers. Garrick crossed to the shallow window seat, beyond which lay the million-dollar view of Lynam Narrows. He lowered himself carefully onto the seat.

"Loring?" he called.

A minute passed, and then Loring appeared at the door to the lobby.

"Good afternoon," said Garrick.

"Afternoon," said Loring, his hands in his pockets.

Several seconds passed in silence, then Loring crossed the room to the window and gazed out, his shoulder propped on the window frame.

"So," he said eventually.

Garrick remained silent.

"How's Ellen?" asked Loring.

"She's in Augusta. In Riverview."

"Ah, the criminal nuthouse. No trial?"

"No. She pled guilty by reason of insanity. Ergo," added Garrick coldly, "she was sent to the 'nuthouse.'"

Loring frowned and scuffed the toe of his shoe through the dust growing thick on the floor, leaving a mark that only Garrick could see. "Insane because she believes in ghosts?"

"No. Her lawyer convinced the judge that her belief that my death would not be the end of my existence indicated her inability to distinguish fantasy from reality."

Loring sighed and looked back out the window. "I'm sorry to hear they put her away."

"As am I."

Loring glanced at Garrick. "I would have thought you would be happy after what she did to you."

Garrick turned to look out the window. "Your sister is unbalanced. She misunderstood what she was doing."

"I think you were always a little sweet on her."

"She was a spirited young woman born into a difficult situation."

"Yeah." They both looked out the window for some time, then Loring spoke. "Garrick, I know it's too little too late, but I'm sorry for what happened to you. I never thought you'd actually find the painting. I'd seen the guy buying the hotel come to look at the lot with his architect, heard them talking about their plans, before living people started to fade for me. I figured I could put the two of you off until it was too late, they'd tear down the hotel, and that would be that. It was just icing on the cake that I got to have a little fun at your expense, you were always such a pompous bastard. And I was enjoying having a captive audience—Lord knows I didn't get a chance to tell my story when I was alive."

"Why did you tell Miss Kinnear where the painting was?"

"That wasn't me, that was Dad."

"She was directed to the painting by someone answering to 'Loring'—I thought his name was Chip."

"Chip was his nickname. All the first sons in the Lynam family are named Loring."

"Ah. That would explain why she described the man she encountered as being pleasant."

"Touché, Garrick." A smile flickered across his lips and then faded. "What was Ellen planning on doing with the painting?" he asked.

"She claims she had a buyer."

"Ellen found a buyer for a stolen piece of artwork?" said Loring, his eyebrows rising.

"That's what she says," said Garrick neutrally.

"Jesus, if I had been able to figure out how to find a buyer for it, I would have jumped on it. Maybe I should have told her where it was after all."

After a moment Garrick said, "Why didn't you want Ellen to have the painting?"

Loring sat down on the end of the window seat and stared unseeingly toward the marks on the opposite wall where the bar had been. Finally he said, "That painting ruined Dad's life. It ruined my life. He let life pass him by because he couldn't pull himself away from the painting, and life passed me by because I couldn't figure out how to get rid of it. At first, after Dad died, I didn't want to turn it in because I didn't want everyone to know he was a thief. Then I didn't want to turn it in because I didn't want to get in trouble for not having turned it in." A cynical smile pulled at the corner of his mouth. "But I guess it had me a little under its spell, because I couldn't bring myself to destroy it either."

He stood and turned back to the window. "Then I sort of forgot about it because the hotel was getting deeper and deeper in debt and I was trying to deal with that. And then I found out what we owed in back taxes and at the same time found out that we needed to shore up the foundations or the building would be condemned. I tried to tell Ellen but it was like she thought I was making it up. She was still trying to sell folks wedding packages, for God's sake. And I was drinking pretty heavily at the time, too. One day it just got to be too much. I thought doing it in the room where the painting was hidden was a bit of poetic justice."

"I felt it was unusually cruel, even for you, to hang yourself in a place where your sister was sure to be the one to find you," said Garrick.

Loring began to bristle, then deflated. "Yeah. Not my finest moment, I'll admit." After a moment he continued, subdued. "I'm surprised she didn't look more carefully in that room for the painting, although maybe she wasn't so enthusiastic about going in there after what she found." He shook himself. "Anyhow, when I heard someone wanted to tear down the hotel, I thought that would take care of it." He turned to Garrick. "I gave up on life because that painting took everything from me. But it wasn't too late for her. I figured if she lost the hotel she'd have a few bad months, maybe a bad year, moaning about 'the family legacy.' She'd curse me for giving up on the hotel—Christ, for giving up on myself—and for not letting her have the painting. But then she'd get over it and get on with her life, and she'd have money from selling the hotel. She could do anything—travel, even go to college if she wanted to. People do, even if they're older. She would have been better off for not having this albatross hanging around her neck. And she's not too old to find someone to spend her life with."

"That may be difficult now."

"Yes. Difficult. But not impossible. Maybe she'll find someone at Riverside. Maybe she'll get out someday." Loring ran his hands through his tangled brown hair. "Maybe it is too late for her. But maybe not. I hope not."

They sat again in silence, Garrick turned toward the window, Loring glancing around the room. Finally Garrick broke the silence.

"What will you do now?"

"I'll be here until they tear down the hotel."

"And then?"

"And then I'm done. I thought by checking out I'd leave all this behind—Ellen, the hotel, the painting. But it held me here —I guess I had to wait to see how it all ended. But now they're all gone, or soon will be. Once the hotel goes, then I can too." Loring turned to Garrick and his gray eyes lit up with a smile. "Then I'll be free."

51

A nn stood in the kitchen of her cabin, folding newspaper pages—which had proved surprisingly hard to obtain—around kitchenware that had been staged on the counters. She had decided to keep the nearby painting studio but to rent out the cabin; that would keep her options open. But for the coming winter, at least, she was going to stay with Mike and Scott in West Chester. They had even talked about looking for a bigger place so that she could have more than just a room to herself.

She tucked a snugly wrapped Fiestaware gravy boat into a cardboard box and was reaching for one of the last pieces on the counter—Beau's old water bowl—when she heard from outside the whistle that had meant "come along" to Beau. She sighed and swallowed a lump in her throat. It was good she was getting away from here—this was too hard.

She went to the screen door and looked out onto the unseasonably warm November Adirondack morning. Beau was crossing the cleared area around the cabin, accompanied by the telltale shimmer that signaled the presence of the old woman. But today they were accompanied by ... what was it? A squirrel?

Ann smiled at the thought of Beau escorting a squirrel across the clearing in any other way than right behind it at top speed.

She expected them to cross the yard and disappear into the woods as they usually did, but instead they were coming right toward the cabin. She twisted a page of newsprint in her hands. As they got closer, she recognized the other creature as her neighbor's dachshund who, she had heard, had been killed by a hawk. Beau seemed to be collecting a pack of spirit companions.

Her hand went to the door latch and then hesitated, uncertain. She watched with her breath shallow until they stopped at the bottom of the porch steps, the old woman's eyes piercing, both dogs very clear. She heard the "sit" whistle and Beau sat. The dachshund remained standing, its stubby legs braced.

Ann unlatched the door and slowly pushed it open, expecting her visitors to disappear, but they just looked attentively at her. She stepped onto the porch. For a minute or more nothing happened, and then she heard the "stand" whistle and Beau stood. The dachshund sat. The old woman's eyes disappeared as she turned and gave the "come along" whistle. Beau wagged cheerfully and turned as well, trotting after the diaphanous form of the old woman as she headed back toward the woods. In a few moments they had disappeared into the trees.

The dachshund—a black shorthair with the distinguishing tan markings over its eyes and across its muzzle—had watched their departure and now turned its eyes back to Ann.

"Well, you certainly are ... solid-looking," said Ann. She had always thought that Beau was as present-seeming as he was to her because of their relationship, but perhaps all dogs' ghosts had this characteristic. But then why wasn't she seeing ghostly dogs everywhere? Maybe it was something about the Adirondack gestalt.

She stepped onto the first step, expecting the dog to disappear—either to trot off after its spirit friends or possibly just dematerialize.

The dachshund rose into a beg, a little column of winsomeness.

She descended another step.

The dachshund's tail wiggled hopefully.

She stepped onto the ground in front of the dog with a growing realization and extended her hand slowly. "Good dog."

The dachshund dropped down from its beg and sniffed hopefully at her hand and she felt the tiny breeze of its breath.

Then she did what she knew she never could with Beau— she laid a hand on top of its head.

The dachshund seemed unimpressed, but deigned to let her keep her hand there.

Ann sank onto the bottom step and the dog, obviously considering this an invitation, marched over and propped itself up with its paws on one of her knees. It was very small. She scratched its ears and suddenly felt a knot in her stomach—one that had been there for so long she had ceased to notice its existence—begin to loosen.

"Good dog. Just out for a stroll with my Beau? Do you belong to someone?"

The dachshund was wearing a delicate black collar studded with fake diamonds—rarely had she seen a dog so ill-suited to a walk through the Adirondack woods. She turned the tag so she could read it in the bright morning light. It showed the address of her neighbor and the dog's name: Ursula.

"So, you do belong to someone," she said cheerfully, but suddenly she felt like crying.

She reached out tentatively and lifted the dog up, which it seemed to consider only its due.

"Why don't we give you a snack," the dachshund's ears pricked, "and a drink of water and then we'll get you home."

She stood up with the dog in her arms. She had never held a really small dog. It was a sturdy little thing—probably only about seven pounds, but very muscular. She stroked its sleek black fur, which seemed not to have suffered from its trek through the woods.

She entered the kitchen and put the dog down, then began searching through the jumble on the counter for the tin where she had stored Beau's treats—she had planned to give them to the Federmans for Fizz, their Jack Russell terrier. She located the tin and removed a bone that was about as long as the dachshund's head. "You hit pay dirt today, little guy," she said, turning.

The dog was standing facing the hallway to the sitting room, the fur along its backbone raised in a tiny ridge, its tail held rigid. She followed its gaze.

There, in the dimness of the hallway, stood Biden Firth.

IN AN ALMOST COMIC replay of the horrible scene that had played out with a much larger dog and a living man many months ago, the dachshund shot across the kitchen toward Biden.

"No!" screamed Ann. She lunged to grab the dog, but only caught a clump of fur from the end of its tail as the dachshund continued its dash, accompanied by a bark Beau would have been proud of.

She scrambled up. Biden had moved out of the dim hallway and into the relative brightness of the sitting room, where he had become more difficult to see—except for those hovering hands. But Ann could tell he was backing away from the tiny, noisy force at his feet. The glimpses she could get of his face suggested a panic all out of proportion to the threat any dog that size could pose, even to a living being. He kicked at the dog but it jumped nimbly away, keeping up its furious barking all the while.

Ann moved cautiously toward the sitting room. If she could just grab the dog she could run outside, get to her car, drive to the Federmans. Then she heard Biden.

"Get it away!"

This was unexpected. "What?"

"Get that abomination away from me!" he yelled over the barking.

She stopped in the doorway to the sitting room, the shimmering shape of Biden Firth now having been backed into the far corner by the dog. She stepped into the room.

"Are you telling me you're scared of the dog?"

"Just get it away!"

A small, cruel smile began to play around Ann's lips. She stepped closer. "You've been making me hurt myself."

"You *killed* me, for Christ's sake!"

"And now you're asking me to rescue you from a dachshund?"

"Little piece of shit!" yelled Biden, taking another swipe at the dog with his foot.

Ann reached the dog and bent to pick it up, keeping her eyes on Biden. The dachshund stopped barking but kept its lips peeled back from its tiny teeth. She advanced on Biden.

"I've been suffering your ... pranks for all this time, and all I needed was a seven-pound dog?"

"You're a bitch just like my wife! She got what she deserved and if you hadn't interfered, it would have ended there!" A querulous note was making its way into Biden's voice. The dog's body vibrated with a low growl.

"You've been making me burn myself, stab myself—"

"I didn't do that, you did that to yourself, you dumb bitch."

"You mean me stabbing myself with the knife wasn't you?"

Biden clearly regretted having shared this information. He waved one of those sea creature-like hands. "It wasn't—but it could have been."

"No," said Ann slowly. "I don't think it could have. I think you only have one way of *bothering* me."

"You've cried over what you did to me—I've seen you!" hissed Biden.

"I never gave a damn what I did to you, you bastard! I only cared what I let you do to my dog!"

For a moment even the sound of the dog's growl was silenced. Then Biden said, "You can't protect yourself forever. And even if you do, I'll find a way to make you suffer like you made me suffer."

Ann tucked the dog more securely under her left arm and extended her right out toward Biden.

"What do you think you're doing?" said Biden, his voice rising a notch.

"I'm seeing what the worst is you can do."

She reached her hand out toward one of Biden's and he drew them back, fists clenched.

"You'll be sorry!"

"I don't think so," said Ann calmly, and grabbed his hand.

There wasn't anything to grab, but she saw her hand move through his and felt that stabbing pain of her clamping muscle. This time, she was ready for it. She pressed her lips into a thin line, resisting the urge to pull her hand back, but then the pain was gone—as was Biden himself. She turned and scanned the room and saw him standing in the hallway to the kitchen, his hands held behind his translucent back, like a boy afraid of having his knuckles rapped with a ruler.

Ann shook her hand to loosen the cramp. "It hurts, but not that much. It wasn't the pain so much as the shock of it. And not

knowing what was causing it. But now I know what's causing it
—nothing but a schoolyard bully."

"I don't care. I got my revenge on you."

"You're dead. *Dead*, for Christ's sake! Is the best you can do
for revenge to hang around and make people spill hot coffee on
themselves? Every time you come back, I'm going to make it a
point to tell whoever will listen to me—and that includes Elizabeth's parents and your mother and father, *especially* your father
—that this is the best you can do, this is the grand revenge you
are exacting."

As she spoke, Biden seemed to shrink from her the way he
had shrunk from the dog—folding in on himself, becoming
dimmer with each word.

"If you can't surprise me, you can't scare me. And," she said,
gesturing to the dog still tucked under her arm, "I have an early
warning system. And you don't have any weapon that you can
use against it."

She began to laugh at the absurdity of it all and, as she did,
Biden Firth melted into the sunlight streaming in through the
window, leaving her and her canine defender alone in the cabin.

ANN WENT to look for the dog bone she had dropped, but the
dachshund found it first, dragging it under the dining room
table and working on it for quite some time. The dog's stomach
was noticeably plumper when it emerged from under the table.

"Good heavens, what a little pig you are," said Ann fondly.
"You must need something to wash that down with."

She reached for Beau's water bowl, but then changed her
mind—it seemed disloyal to use his bowl for another dog. She
reached for a Pyrex measuring cup that was staged behind the
water bowl on the counter and, just as she was lifting it free, the

dachshund gave a sharp, imperious bark. Ann's hand jerked and the measuring cup caught the edge of Beau's water bowl.

The water bowl slid to the edge of the counter and had started its tip toward the floor when Ann's hand shot out and grabbed it. In the process she fumbled the measuring cup which dropped to the counter on its side and was rolling toward the edge when she grabbed it with her other hand. The dachshund gave a happy bark.

She placed the measuring cup carefully back on the counter and filled the water bowl with trembling hands. She put the bowl on the floor and the dachshund crossed to it and lapped delicately at the water. Ann glanced down at her hands, expecting an injury of some kind—a cut from a break in the Pyrex she hadn't noticed, a jammed finger—but there was nothing. She bent down and stroked the dog's sleek fur, then crossed to the screen door and looked out to where Beau had disappeared into the woods with his new master.

"Good boy," she whispered.

52

T he old man took a sip of caffè doppio from a fine china cup. A pressed linen napkin muffled any rattles as he replaced it on the saucer. A copy of *Corriere della Sera*, featuring a story about the discovery of a lost masterwork in the state of Maine in the United States, was spread before him, lit in the dark room by a huge chandelier. The chandelier had been a challenge to recover, the buyer difficult to track down and, when located, determined to drive a hard bargain. It had been one of the last pieces the old man had had to recover to return the villa to its former glory. To have had his family home survive the bombings and the invasion, only to be lost when his father had to start selling its contents to save the villa itself—it had been a bitter pill to swallow.

La Signora was one of the last items to reclaim, and it had been by far the trickiest. He was in New York City waiting for his ship to sail after delivering the painting to Signore Furness when he heard of the fire that had consumed Jardin d'Eden. At his father's telegraphed instructions, he returned to Mount Desert Island. The *custode*, Pritchard, stuck to his claim that everything had burned with the house, but he himself spoke to the boy who, according to the pretty young maid, was so taken with the painting. He understood little of what the boy said, but something about his behavior made him suspicious. The local man he hired to make inquiries in town did uncover rumors of odd behavior on the part of the Lynam family. On the other hand, a number of the people to whom his *informatore* spoke suggested that odd behavior was the norm for the Lynams.

He returned to Italy and to his father's bitter disappointment, but he was not convinced the quest was at an end. The years went by, and he followed the life of the Lynam boy as best he could from the other side of the world. He learned that Lynam had married the pretty maid, and he sent her a letter suggesting that information about the painting could prove remunerative to the family, but never heard back from her.

More years passed and he learned that Lynam and the pretty maid had had a daughter, Ellen. The child grew to an adult and eventually he sent off a letter to her—similar to the one he had sent to her mother decades before—with little hope of receiving a response. However, a few weeks later he received a letter that briefly reignited his hope.

Ellen Lynam believed the painting had survived the fire, that her father had rescued it and had hidden it away for all these years. She asked the old man for his email address, but instead he sent her by express mail a phone number and calling card. When she called, he told her what he was willing to pay for the painting. It was not as much as he would have paid had it been for sale through legitimate channels, and, considering she was selling a stolen artwork, he had the leverage to force a lower price. However, it was a considerable amount of money—he was too old to be dickering over a few tens of thousands of euros. Miss Lynam jumped at his offer.

She told him that her father had never revealed the location to her, but he had told her brother, Loring—how could he have missed the fact that there had been a son with the same name? The son had killed himself that very year—again the old man thought his quest was stymied—but Ellen Lynam seemed to think that death might not put the knowledge of the painting's location beyond their reach. He scoffed at first, but then began researching the man she thought could help them—Garrick Masser, they all had such strange names—and he began to believe that perhaps the search was not at an end after all.

Ellen was surprised when he told her everything had to be done with the utmost secrecy—wasn't he just reclaiming a family heirloom? If it had been a family heirloom there would, in fact, have been no need for secrecy on his side, but La Signora was the only one of his family's possessions that had been a recent addition—an acquisition, albeit a somewhat involuntary one, from a Jew in Turin. His father had been infatuated with the painting. It has been among the last of the possessions he had sold—only retaining the villa itself was more important— and although his father had not been able, physically or emotionally, to accompany La Signora to America when he was finally forced to sell her to Signore Furness, he had sent his son as his emissary. His father instructed him to familiarize himself with La Signora's new owners and new situation, hoping to improve the family's chances of reclaiming it when their fortunes improved. If the painting's provenance was ever discovered, the bleeding hearts would no doubt take it from him.

Ellen was surprised but not averse to his insistence on secrecy until he pointed out that, in the end, no one save herself could remain who knew of the painting's recovery. She had initially rejected his insistence that Mr. Masser must die, and he had had to proceed carefully, over many months, to convince her that for a man who could so easily bridge the worlds of the living and the dead, his death would be no more traumatic than a relocation to a new country—a country that spoke one's own language, at that. He sent her those childish books about the boy and the bird, offering up visions of a glorious existence beyond death. And when she began to believe that she would be doing no wrong by killing a man, he sent her the Taser, describing it as a humane way to hurry Mr. Masser to his destination. He didn't add that it was also the only weapon he could imagine a middle-aged woman using on a man of indeterminate fitness that would not leave messy evidence behind.

And now, according to the newspaper, this woman Ann Kinnear had succeeded in reviving Mr. Masser, in pulling him back from that destination that awaits everyone. These Americans were being hailed as heroes in his own country, and La Signora had been taken by those very meddlers he had spent so much time and effort attempting to circumvent, and was on its way back to Turin.

Now his own final destination was nearing and the quest he had spent the greater part of his life pursuing had proven unachievable. And it was only a matter of time before the *polizia* or, worse, the *giornalisti* showed up at the door of the villa, impugning his father's reputation, digging up history that was best left buried.

Perhaps it would be most humane to hurry himself along to his destination as well, and he had no need to take precautions to avoid some messiness. He pushed himself slowly to his feet, his butler leaping forward to pull his chair back for him, and, the tapping of his cane marking his progress toward his library, he drew the key to his gun case from his vest pocket.

THE END

NEXT IN THE ANN KINNEAR SUSPENSE SERIES ...

Book 3: The Falcon and the Owl

A small plane crashes in the Pennsylvania Wilds ... and only Ann Kinnear has the ability to discover the force that brought it down. Will the secret the victims carried die with them, or come back to haunt her?

Ann Kinnear is indulging her love of aviation by working toward her pilot's license at Avondale Airport—and protecting her privacy by discouraging the attentions of a filmmaker intent on documenting her spirit-sensing abilities.

Little does she know that a fiery plane crash in the Pennsylvania Wilds will embroil her in a race to track down a contract on which two rivals are banking their futures. And when airshow pilot Gwen Burridge launches a smear campaign against Ann, she is even more determined to uncover the truth.

Ann travels to the crash site and learns what brought the plane down—but it's only part of the story.

Will Ann land safely, or be the latest victim of a secret someone is willing to kill to keep?

Find out in Book 3 of the Ann Kinnear Suspense Novels, *The Falcon and the Owl*!

'Tis unnatural,
> Even like the deed that's done. On Tuesday last,
> A falcon, towering in her pride of place,
> Was by a mousing owl hawk'd at and kill'd.
> — William Shakespeare, *Macbeth*

Join Matty Dalrymple's occasional email newsletter (mattydalrymple.com > About & Contact) and receive an Ann Kinnear Suspense Short and notifications of book launches and author events!

AFTERWORD

Many of you who live on or have visited Mount Desert Island likely recognize the Claremont Hotel as the inspiration for Lynam's Point Hotel—Lynam's Point borrows the structure and general layout (minus the restaurant wing) of the Claremont, but relocates it from Southwest Harbor on Somes Sound to the more remote Bartlett Narrows (renamed Lynam Narrows) on the renamed and reconfigured Bartletts Landing Road. But I hasten to add that the Claremont suffers from none of the deterioration that afflicts Lynam's Point Hotel—Lynam's Point failed to make the transitions to the twentieth and twenty-first centuries as successfully as the Claremont did. Here's hoping that those in the twenty-second century still get to enjoy the Claremont's gorgeous views and gracious hospitality—without resorting to murder.

The painting of The Lady is a mash-up of *Young Woman with Unicorn* (sans unicorn) by Raphael and *Portrait of Lucrezia Panciatichi* and *Portrait of Eleanor of Toledo and Her Son* by Agnolo di Cosimo, known as Bronzino.

ALSO BY MATTY DALRYMPLE

ABOUT THE AUTHOR

Matty Dalrymple is the author of the Ann Kinnear Suspense Novels *The Sense of Death, The Sense of Reckoning, The Falcon and the Owl* and *A Furnace for Your Foe*; the Ann Kinnear Suspense Shorts, including *Close These Eyes* and *Sea of Troubles*; and the Lizzy Ballard Thrillers *Rock Paper Scissors, Snakes and Ladders*, and *The Iron Ring*. Matty and her husband, Wade Walton, live in Chester County, Pennsylvania, and enjoy vacationing on Mt. Desert Island, Maine, and in Sedona, Arizona, locations that serve as settings for Matty's stories.

Matty is a member of Mystery Writers of America, Sisters in Crime, and the Brandywine Valley Writers Group.

Go to www.mattydalrymple.com > About & Contact for more information and to sign up for Matty's occasional email newsletter.

facebook.com/matty.dalrymple

twitter.com/mattydalrymple

instagram.com/matty.dalrymple

BIBLIOGRAPHY

Butler, Joyce. *Wildfire Loose: The Week Maine Burned*. Camden, Maine: Down East Books, 1987. Print.

Dyer, Deborah M. *Bar Harbor: A Town Almost Lost*. 2008. Print.

H. A. Manning Mt Desert Island City Directory, 1935. ancestry.com.

Hale, Richard Walden, Jr. *The Story of Bar Harbor*. New York: Ives Washburn, Inc., 1949. Print.

Helfrich, G.W., and Gladys O'Neil. *Lost Bar Harbor*. Camden, Maine: Down East Books, 1982. Print.

Mount Desert Island Cultural History Project. "Barberry Ledge," Christine B. Rowell. Mount Desert Island Historical Society. Web. 01 July 2014. http://research.mdihistory.org/BarHarborcottages/BarberryLedge.htm

Vandenbergh, Lydia Bodman, and Earl G. Shuttleworth, Jr. *Opulence to Ashes: Bar Harbor's Gilded Century - 1850-1950*. Camden, Maine: Down East Books, 2009. Print.

Williams, Anson R., Margaret Williams as told to Mary Wilkes Haley, "The Big Fire." Down East Oct. 1962: 14-41. Print.

ACKNOWLEDGMENTS

Many people had a hand in the creation of this story. Special thanks to ...

Sean Cox and Virginia Mellen of the Mount Desert Island Historical Society for their help with researching mid-twentieth-century MDI and specifically the 1947 fire.

Robyn King and Kate Pontbriand of the William Otis Sawtelle Collection and Research Center - National Park Service - Acadia National Park for their help with fire research, especially photos of the park before and after the fire.

Timothy Stanley, Assistant Manager at the Claremont Hotel, for letting me poke around.

David Fried, MD, F.A.C.P. and fellow Dickinson College alum, for his advice on the medical aspects of the story.

Sandra Paoli for the Italian translations.

Paul Richardson of the Bar Harbor Historical Society for his hospitality.

Faithful readers Mary Dalrymple and Lynda Holl for their insightful feedback.

My editor Jen Blood for making sure my craft was seaworthy.

And, as always, special thanks to my partner in crime (plotting) and in life, Wade Walton, for his unflagging support.

Any deviations from historical fact—intentional or unintentional—are solely the responsibility of the author.

Publisher's Note: This is a work of fiction. Names, characters, places, and
incidents are products of the author's imagination. Locales, events, and public
names are sometimes used for atmospheric purposes. Any resemblance to
actual people, living or dead, or to businesses, companies, or institutions is
completely coincidental.

Cover design: Lance Buckley

ISBN-13: 978-0-9862675-1-2 (Paperback edition)

ISBN-13: 978-0-9862675-6-7 (Large print edition)

Made in the USA
Monee, IL
15 July 2023